HER FAITHFUL Protector

ALESSA KELLY

"My body will tirelessly protect her, and my heart will stay faithful to her until its last beat." ~ Jack Redley Kelleher

1

AVA WEST

Los Angeles, California

I TAP my knuckles against the dining table. Bones on glass, the sound echoes through the room. With each rattling movement of my hand, my heart beats in tandem. For the first time since getting engaged to Willem Botha, I want him home.

As I sit here, my gaze is drawn to the expansive window that resembles a banquet hall, offering a glimpse of the night outside. Beyond the glass, the distant garden lights twinkle like stars against the darkness.

I stride close to the window, my breath creating a mist that momentarily blurs and then clears the view. The gate and garage are on the opposite side of the house. From here, it's easy to overlook his arrival. The latest Mercedes in his collection barely makes a sound, even when he revs up the engine.

Though tempted to go to the living room for a better view, I stick to my routine of always being here at this time. Everything must stay the same, or the change I've planned for months will remain as a plan without execution—or worse.

Elmo, my Labrador retriever, follows me closer than usual. The dog is a clown most of the time, but I think he senses the change in me.

"We're all set for tonight, right?"

Elmo lets out a soft woof.

Finally, I catch a glimmer of light and see Willem's car passing behind the giant hedges that separate this side of the garden from the front of the house. I rush to the kitchen to ensure I have everything I'll need tonight—a surprise he'll never see coming. His footsteps advance, and I swiftly return to the dining room, wiping down the table.

Willem steps in, knowing where to find me. He's still wearing his suit, with his hair neatly styled and tie perfectly straight, just as he did when he left this morning.

"Hey." I greet him with a kiss. I remain as constant as a lake on a breezeless morning, careful not to arouse his suspicion. The way I talk, the way I breathe, the way I look at him. "You had dinner? I made some *potjiekos*. I can warm it up if you like." His Dutch-Afrikaans grandfather used to cook the stew, which has now become one of his go-to meals.

"I'm gonna head straight to bed," he rasps as he rounds my waist, his palms squeezing my ass.

Every part of my being resists, but for now, I respond to him like a dutiful fiancée, as I've always done. I smile and sigh as he rubs his crotch against mine.

"I'll bring your tea in a minute," I whisper.

He loosens his grip, though still pinching and patting every inch of me that his hands pass. "Did you see the article I sent you?"

"Yeah. They're nice."

"The hair and makeup on that model look amazing, don't they?" he says proudly, staring as if imagining me in the bridal attire he's been wishing for. After a few moments, he heads upstairs.

Willem always has his tea before bed. I've never been into chamomile, but I didn't used to mind it. Now, the scent always reminds me of his foulness and control. But that wretched man will soon realize that this is the last time I'll ever serve him anything.

As I carry his tea to the bedroom, I can hear the sound of water from the shower, signaling Willem's nightly routine. I take off my T-shirt and jeans, then slip into a night camisole. My eyes fixate on my forearm, where a vivid bruise encircles it, a reminder of our heated argument over the wedding invitation just yesterday. I was in court, and the trial went overtime. I failed to respond to his call about the color of the cards, igniting his disdain for being ignored.

Willem steps out of the bathroom. "Fuck..." he sighs, his eyes scanning my lingerie-clad figure.

"Your tea is ready," I murmur seductively.

Just as the bottom of the mug clinks against the bedside table, he pulls me to him with force, then shoves me in the opposite direction, making us both roll onto the bed. Despite his impatience and controlling nature when it comes to tasks and errands, I have learned that if I comply with his desires in bed, I will remain unharmed. But this time, I will obey with a hidden agenda.

Willem pins me down, his lips exploring the depths of my cleavage as he removes his boxers. The mixed scent of stale meat and pungent sweat sickens me. It's his. Something that comes hand in hand with the chamomile.

"Fuck, I can't wait to marry you," he grunts as he looms over me. "Invitations are on the way. Our friends and families will be thrilled. You know, they kept saying it was time."

Anger knocks behind my chest. He must've ordered the

cards, even before discussing it with me yesterday, for them to be sent out so quickly. And, when he refers to 'our' friends and families, they are really his. I will have to beg and argue just to have my best friend invited. And as for my family, it consists only of my parents, who always do whatever Willem says. They treat him like their savior or even a god.

I despise my parents for that, but I can't blame them entirely. Willem did help our family when my father's business collapsed. Ironically, we needed the money to save me. That's how I've managed to endure Willem for this long.

Then, we found out I was pregnant, and during the later stages of the pregnancy, I spent most of my time in bed. Willem came to my rescue once again—the rescue that made me cry like a princess locked in a tower. But at least I survived and gave birth to a healthy baby.

Despite Willem making decisions about the invitations and wedding I never wanted, I hide my anger behind a smile.

Willem continues grunting, futilely trying to arouse himself. A cry from the adjacent room startles him, prompting him to yell, "For fuck's sake!" He releases me with a harsh push, my head bouncing against the pillow. "Shut him up, or I will!"

I hurry out of bed, explaining, "That's what babies do. Cry. He's only seven months old."

"You'd better make him a man. I don't want a wimpy heir."

Oh, my son will be strong. I'll ensure he forgets who his father is, and I will never, ever let him become Willem.

Time passes, and Quinton continues to cry in my arms. Something is off. Or rather, something very right is unfolding. By now, Willem should've been at the doorway shouting at me, and I would've been fighting to keep him away from Quinton.

Finally, my baby falls asleep, and I rush back to Willem. I

almost forget to breathe. My fiancé has finished the entire mug of tea and is sleeping like a helpless child.

Who's wimpy now?

But there's no time to celebrate. I hurry to Quinton's room, grab his diaper bag, and place him in a cradle. Everything else is waiting for me in another car, hidden in a remote corner of a distant town. Right now, all I need to do is escape from this prison.

I stand frozen in front of Willem's bedroom door, hearing my own heartbeat. Quinton stirs awake, his cries on the verge of escaping as if sensing his father's presence. I pull the door handle, letting it latch, closing the view to the most despicable room in the house. Then I whisper in Quinton's ear, "It's okay, baby. We're going to be fine."

Elmo the dog follows me with unsteady steps, his eyes fixed on me. Despite the wide-open car door, he fails to jump in. Instead, he whimpers and scratches at my shoes. I ignore the dog for now as I secure Quinton in his car seat. The pup tries one more time to climb up by himself, stretching his short legs in vain.

I chuckle. "Easy, Elm. I won't leave you behind."

With Quinton buckled up, I scoop Elmo's butt, pushing him up so he can come aboard. I then let the two cuties sit side by side. That dog is quite comical, but he has taken his role as a protector seriously ever since my baby was born.

The garage door glides open as I press the remote. The metallic hum is swallowed by the rumble of the engine. The vibrations and noise make Quinton burst into tears. "Oh, come on now, Quinton. Please help Mommy."

I'm driving my own car, a five-year-old SUV that lacks the refined purr of Willem's Mercedes. At the same time, Quinton's all-out bawling resonates in the air, heightening my fear of being discovered.

I step out to comfort Quinton, realizing he has lost his favorite toy, a giraffe teether that had traveled all the way from Hawaii. I run my fingers along the back of the seat and locate the familiar texture. His rosy cheeks crease into a wide smile when I present it to him.

Just like everything else in Willem's mansion, the garage is fitted with high-tech gadgets. The motion sensors detect my presence, and the path ahead illuminates, casting a soft glow on the ground. Adrenaline courses through my veins as the car rolls along the driveway. Every foot feels like an eternity.

A rush of cold sweat blankets me as the twin cast iron gates swing open. The heaviness of the gates, now idle and defeated, affirms that I am truly escaping.

Darkness surrounds me, the only visible lights coming from the streetlamps. The Beverly Hills neighborhood remains undisturbed as if bidding me farewell in silence or perhaps not caring at all.

As I approach the city limits of Los Angeles, I dial my best friend's number. "Morgie, I'm on my way," I say, my voice filled with both relief and excitement.

"Ava? Please tell me you're not joking."

"No. I'm not. I've left L.A., and I have Quinton with me. I'm heading north."

Morgan's exuberant cheer echoes through the phone. "Well done, you!"

"I did it, Morgie. I'll see you in Helena tomorrow."

"You'd better be on time, or my honeymoon will be history!" she warns.

A wave of joy lifts me, thinking about her. She's had her fair share of turmoil, but now she's safe in the arms of her forever love. "I'll be there, Mrs. Hunt."

With a contented smile, I steal a glance at Quinton

through the rearview mirror. He's still chewing on the giraffe teether, occasionally babbling as if conversing with Elmo.

"We'll see Aunty Morgie soon."

Morgan Hunt, my best friend since childhood, would do anything for me. But if circumstances allowed, I would've surprised a certain man in Hawaii, taking a chance on love. However, things have changed since our initial connection in Bozeman. He's a thirty-three-year-old Marine in his prime, hot as sin yet gentle like a dove. Women would throw themselves at him. I'm sure he wouldn't want to be involved with a single mother on the run.

I glance once more at Quinton.

Yet—that man cared about my son. The giraffe teether Quinton chews on was a gift from him, even though we lost touch after our brief encounter. It warms me that he knew about Quinton and made an effort to let me know he hadn't forgotten me.

"You like that, huh? Maybe one day, you'll meet him," I say to Quinton. "His name is Jack. Can you say 'Jack'?"

"Mo!"

"Not Elmo. Jack."

"Mo!" He swings the teether over Elmo with a tight grip, like a wizard working his wand to turn the dog into something else. He's a strong boy, and he holds nothing else harder than that silicone giraffe.

The only contact my baby had with Lieutenant Jack Kelleher was when he was still in my belly. I got to know Jack through Morgan, and that stormy night in Bozeman will forever remain etched in my mind like a painting. And it's not because I'm a courtroom artist with a supposed photographic memory.

Being a California native, my experience of Montana was eye-opening. Jack, the embodiment of Hightower, offered me his jacket to protect me from the elements. It draped over me like an overcoat, providing me with a comforting warmth. I'm sure even Quinton appreciated it.

But above all, I will always remember Jack's greeting. His firm smile matched his commanding physique, yet his gaze held a blend of curiosity, tenderness, and longing—as if he had never encountered anyone quite like me before. His sincerity has left a permanent dent in my heart. Perhaps Jack has also made a lasting impact on my baby.

Quinton continues babbling, trying to wake Elmo up.

"Come on, baby, leave Elmo alone."

"Mo!"

"Jack is a Marine. Do you know what a Marine does?" I try to distract him with what Jack had told me about military life. As if my baby would understand.

Headlights approach from the opposite direction. It shouldn't bother me, but my unease grows as the car passes by and promptly makes a U-turn. "No, no, no!"

It could be my nerves on overdrive, but my gut tells me this is trouble. I should've remembered, Willem Botha, my fiancé —no, ex-fiancé—isn't just one person. He's an institution with plenty of minions, and one of them has compromised my safety, even in the dead of night.

I reach for my phone to call Morgan, but it slips out of my grasp and falls behind the car seat. I keep driving, merging into the highway, only to realize the car is following closely behind. If I stay on this road, they will eventually catch me. I can't risk leading them to the other car I've prepared, where everything I need to survive is stored, and I definitely can't lead them to Morgan.

The only way to shake them off is by leading my pursuers on a wild goose chase through a city. I've been driving since I was fourteen, thanks to my rogue mother, who was a taxi driver. I've learned all there is to know about navigating city streets and alleys. Tonight, though, I've got to handle it with care.

"Hold on, Quinton," I call out. But my baby is asleep.

I take the exit to Salt Lake City, stepping on the gas pedal. It's an unfamiliar place, but I trust my instincts and head into areas with traffic sparse enough to allow me to weave my way through.

My eyes switch rapidly between what's ahead and what's behind me. Finally, I gain some distance, and this is when the party begins.

Determined to outmaneuver my chaser, I leave the main road and venture into the labyrinth of alleys, taking whichever path I come across. Elmo barks while Quinton, the usually alert one, doesn't even stir.

"I believe we're in the clear, Quinnie-Bear." My baby has been given numerous nicknames, but this particular one coined by my mom seems to have stuck.

Certain that I've lost the pursuing car, I turn back south, heading to where I've hidden my other car. Still reeling from the pursuit, I stop about a mile from the destination at a clifftop that probably hasn't seen a living soul except me.

"Stay, Elmo. Stay," I try to calm the nervous pup as I unload.

I place Quinton in a portable cradle and leave it on the ground, away from the edge. As I make my way back to the car, ready to release the handbrake, I suddenly realize that the giraffe is missing.

In the darkness, I fumble around and miraculously locate the giraffe teether on the car floor. Quinton won't be able to survive without it. It's not just a toy or a gum soother. He genuinely loves that giraffe. As his mother, it brings me a sense of calm knowing he has it.

Wasting no time, I muster the strength and push the car over the cliff. Then I pull out my engagement ring, throwing it into the abyss. The tale of Willem Botha and me has truly crashed and burned.

I put Elmo on a leash and carry Quinton in a front carrier, along with his diaper bag. "You have to walk now," I tell Elmo. "I can't carry both of you!"

I search around for my phone, hoping to use its light. Much to my dismay, I recall that my phone had slipped out of my pocket during the drive, and now both it and my car are lying at the bottom of the cliff. I press on, guided by the faint glow of the moon.

With Quinton snug in the cradle and Elmo tugging at the leash, I follow the path, shielding Quinton from the rain. I've been here a few times. I've memorized the way until it's like I was born with a map. Elmo seems to know, too.

It's dark, but it's peaceful. The only load I'm carrying is an abundance of hope.

2

JACK REDLEY KELLEHER

Oahu, Hawaii

PERCHING on a hill concealed behind a row of ferns, I peer through my binoculars, observing a squad of Marines approaching a compound where four hostages are held. Humidity is at a stifling ninety percent, and the temperature continues to rise, reaching the high seventies.

I bet these jarheads would rather be sipping cocktails in an air-conditioned bar, listening to the strumming of a ukulele. But they're here on a mission. While they are trained, they still have much to learn. None of them have experienced the chaos of battle or the intense pressure of a life-or-death situation.

"Staff Sergeant Mitchell," I instruct, asking for an update on the time elapsed.

"Sir, they have five minutes until they reach the extraction point."

Concern fills me. They haven't even located the hostages.

I continue to observe until the squads depart from the

compound. Now, a dense jungle lies between their current location and the extraction point.

"Let's go," I say to Mitchell, and we leave our post to join the Marines at the edge of the Kahuku Range.

I look into each Marine's eyes, watching sweat covering their faces, their shoulders rising and falling with each breath.

"Sergeant Perry reporting, sir," the squad leader says. His face paint fails to conceal his worry. The trainees are familiar with my reputation on this island, and this one clearly wasn't expecting to meet me today, thinking Mitchel was in charge. He then announces, "We have successfully retrieved all four hostages, sir."

I acknowledge the sergeant, then inspect the squad with a stern expression. "Welcome to week three of your AIMC!" I declare. AIMC, or Advanced Infantry Marine Course, is a rigorous seven-week training program designed to refine the squad's infantry skills in a realistic setting. "Today was your lucky day. You got me whooping all your sorry asses."

I pace in front of the line-up, then stare at the leader. "You're three minutes behind schedule, Sergeant."

"We faced a counterattack and found two wounded Marines separated from their squad."

"They're a vital aspect of the mission, not a pretext."

"Yes, sir."

I then deliver the fate of the Marines. "The air support designated for your unit's extraction faced fuel constraints, and their location was jeopardized, so the pilot received orders to terminate the extraction. You exceeded the permissible time for maneuvering the path to the target, and you failed to secure the property within the specified timeframe."

"Understood, sir. It won't happen again."

"You're all dismissed," I order.

Mitchell takes charge, barking, "Debrief in fifteen!"

Despite the additional three minutes, the men performed better than expected. The mission parameters Mitchell and I established were practically impossible, but today's most important lesson is that they upheld the principle of leaving no Marines behind. And that makes me proud.

As the day comes to an end, I make my way to the waterfront. Finding a comfortable spot on a smooth rock, I retrieve a folded sketch from my wallet. The lines on the paper are well-crafted, a testament to Ava West's exceptional talent as a courtroom artist. Not only does she possess the skill to capture an image, but she knows how to reveal the essence of a person —which is exactly what she did when we were in Bozeman.

The relentless Montana wind messed up her hair the night we met, and I tried to get the wild strands off her face. The silkiness of her blond curls left my fingertips tingling as her azure eyes and peaches-and-cream complexion became visible. God, how I wanted to kiss her. Only Ava could drive me to act with impulse like that, although I kept my self-control.

Our introduction was brief because neither of us enjoyed small talk. We were both there to support Morgan, her best friend, after she narrowly escaped a murder attempt. Despite that, Ava and I managed to find time for one-on-one conversations. We discussed the books we love. Mine being *Helmet for My Pillow* by Robert Leckie, a memoir written by a World War II Marine veteran, and hers being *The Help* by Kathryn Stockett, a novel set during the civil rights movement.

Time flew by beautifully when we talked, whatever the topic—the military, visual art, psychology. Despite her girl-next-door appearance, she exuded intelligence and maturity. Our six-year age gap seemed irrelevant. There was a profound depth in her heart that hinted at the ability to carry weight, perhaps both mine and hers. It was evident when our conversation innocently veered toward the topic I dreaded the most —birthdays. In that moment, I realized she was unlike anyone I had ever met.

Believe it or not, I didn't have a real birthday on my actual birthdate until I hit thirty. There is no relation between my pessimistic view of birthdays and parental neglect or anything of that nature. It's all because I was abducted at the age of seven.

I was born in New York, but a significant part of my childhood is missing from my memory. Nothing made sense when I found myself inside a Florida monastery, a nun feeding me, asking me my name. I had no idea who I was—it was like my braindead self watching my body doing its own thing. Only thanks to my brother's perseverance, I was reunited with him and my dad three years ago, and I had my first real birthday celebration. It felt peculiar, but I experienced it nonetheless.

When people hear my story for the first time, pity is usually the first reaction I see in their eyes. But not Ava. She was surprised, naturally, but instead of offering apologies or trying to understand what I had gone through, she showed belief. 'You may not have all the answers, Jack, but you've got all the fight within you. Take a moment to give yourself credit for who you are now,' she said then. That brought me comfort, and it felt as if we were connected even before we met. Still, there were many things I chose to conceal.

Now, the more I look at the sketch, another impression starts to emerge. People say that every artist leaves a piece of themselves in their work. Perhaps it's merely my imagination, but I see her presence behind my own face.

Holding onto the sketch, I gaze ahead. The sun is at its prettiest when it sets. I've seen sunsets all over the world, and I can say the best ones I witnessed are in Montana—especially in Bozeman when I was with her. But there's something undeniably captivating about the vibrant hues of the Hawaiian sky at this time of day.

Just as the sun sinks behind the horizon, I fold the sketch and tuck it back into my wallet. I've accepted that she will never be a part of my life. Sooner or later, I'll need to erase her from my thoughts or face the consequences of holding onto a hope that will never come to fruition.

Suddenly, my phone buzzes. Sam. Why on earth would my older brother call me at this time? Most likely, he's going to try persuading me to come to Helena again and join his company, Red Mark Rescue & Protect. It's an organization specialized in rescuing missing children. A cause close to home and the reason why my brother founded it. While I've been considering the idea, for now, I still feel I belong to the Corps.

"Sam, brother, wassup?" I answer.

"Hey, you've got a minute?" His tone is neither persuasive nor friendly. "Morgan wants to talk to you."

This is unusual. Morgan and I rarely speak to each other. In fact, I haven't talked to her at all this year, and it's the end of summer already.

"Jack?" She's only calling my name, but I can tell she's really shaken up.

"Morgan, what's going on?" Warning particles flutter in my gut.

"Ava is missing."

My stomach buckles. "What do you mean she's missing?"

"She left her fiancé and was supposed to meet me here in Helena yesterday. I tried to call her, but she didn't answer."

She left her fiancé? I don't know much about him, only that he's an asshole.

"How about Quinton?" I ask.

"Quinton was with her the last time we spoke. At the time, she was just outside L.A. She should have been here ages ago. Ty has been searching with a few Red Mark guys, but there's no sign of her."

Tyler Hunt, Morgan's husband, is the head of operations at Red Mark. If he hasn't found her, that means Ava isn't in Helena. Besides, Morgan and Ava are like sisters. They seem to be able to sense each other.

My answer is easy. "I'm on my way!"

I speed back to base. Fortunately, the traffic flows smoothly despite the bustling activity of both tourists and locals as dinner time approaches. I manage to catch my captain just as he's leaving.

"Please, sir. This is an emergency."

The captain flashes a displeased smirk, but he about-faces. "Come on in." He opens his office door. "What can I do for you, Lieutenant?"

"I request a leave of absence, sir."

"Have you uncovered another lead about your kidnapper in Florida?"

I was only transferred to Hawaii a year ago. I spent most of my career at Camp Lejeune in North Carolina. The captain has obviously heard about my pursuit.

I have made several requests for leave in order to uncover the truth about what happened to me, but my efforts haven't yielded any results.

"No, sir," I answer.

"If you need to be in that part of the country, I can put in the good word so you're transferred to Panama City. You're a trained combatant diver, are you not, Lieutenant?"

"I am, sir."

"They surely need a diving instructor like you there."

"I appreciate the offer, but I must go to Montana."

The captain's expression turns perplexed. "Montana?"

"It's an emergency involving a friend, sir. A very good friend."

In the eye of the military, 'a very good friend' is not a compelling reason to call it an emergency, and I can sense my captain's disapproval through his gaze. Ava is more than just a dear friend, but I'm at a loss when it comes to explaining this to him.

Ava and I only spent a few days together. When we parted, I tried to play it cool. But inside, everything in me throbbed, like I was driven to the point of desperation. I wish I'd given her more than just my jacket or a friendly hug when she looked to need extra warmth. Sadly, we only used the weather as an excuse to get close to each other—nothing more.

The captain raises his eyes to me, expecting further clarification. I could've pretended the emergency concerned Sam or my father, my only family, but I prefer to handle the situation without lying to my superior.

Realizing I'm not going to even defend myself, the captain continues. "You haven't taken leave in over a year, and you're one of the most dedicated Marines I've known, maybe even obsessed. However, I have a knack for reading minds, Lieutenant. Is this friend of yours the one who's been distracting you?"

"Sir?"

"Granted, you were never distracted while on duty, and you haven't put a foot wrong in any given mission. I heard about your actions in Kabul when the city fell. You were offered a flight out, but you declined, letting your men depart instead. You were one of the last few to leave."

"Any leader in my position would have done the same. Those men had a family back home."

"Here's the thing, Lieutenant. To me, you act like you're on duty all the time. And don't deny it. You try to hide the fact that you've been thinking of *her*."

A creeping warmth makes its way up the back of my neck, leaving me uneasy. Seven months ago, I discovered that she had given birth to a baby. That means she was pregnant when we met. It was painful, but I still care about her. Perhaps more than just caring, but less than love, because love cannot simply blossom in a matter of days.

My captain knows how to read me, but I attempt to deny him anyway. "With all due respect, sir, that's not true."

He narrows his lips as he reclines against his leather chair. "How long do you need, Jack?"

He calls me by my first name only when we're off duty or when he softens his stance during a disagreement. I know he will understand, but something shifts in me. I feel a sense of belonging to the Corps, but what I feel for Ava surpasses that loyalty. For *her*, I'll do anything.

"The whole thirty days," I respond.

"You've dedicated your life to the Corps. It wouldn't be right for me to deny your request. But if there's a chance you may exceed your allotted time, you must inform me beforehand."

"Understood, sir."

"You're dismissed."

"Thank you, sir."

I rush back to my apartment at the base, where the boxes containing my research on my abduction await me, like pets welcoming their master home.

It has become a routine for me to dig into the photos, maps, and leads after a long day in uniform. Night after night, I tirelessly piece together the fragments—attempting to reconstruct my childhood and identify the man who destroyed it—

only to reshuffle them and start over. I collect scattered visions from my dreams and nightmares and combine them with solid evidence, yet they never quite align.

But tonight, it's not about me. It's Ava who I need to find, and I won't rest until I do.

3
____

AVA

Helena, Montana

EVERYTHING THAT COULD POSSIBLY GO wrong seems to go wrong. I'm running incredibly late and with no means of communication, Morgan must be worried sick. My new phone's battery got fried during its very first charge. By the time I realized it, it was too late to get a replacement because I ended up getting lost in the middle of nowhere. Even worse, my on-and-off breathing problem has made me stop more than I wanted.

This morning, I have no choice but to arrive unannounced and apologize for ruining my best friend's honeymoon. I feel guilty as hell, but I know Morgan wouldn't go without knowing I'm safe.

"We're almost there, baby," I try to comfort Quinton. Crying is a recurring theme for him this morning as he bawls once more.

While I can manage the exhaustion and the drive itself, the constant need to be on high alert is taking a toll on me.

But we all have to arrive in one piece, so I'll just have to prop myself up and make it.

"Where's your giraffe?" I'm on a narrow stretch of road, and I can't stop. So I just have to rely on Elmo to comfort my boy. Elmo nuzzles at him, persisting to cheer up his little boss even though the pup is clearly worn out.

Despite all the commotion, a smile finds its way onto my face as I admire the scenery spreading before me. The first rays of sunlight slowly pierce through the horizon, casting gentle shades of pink and golden yellow onto the Montana sky as if painting a fresh masterpiece. A reward, a greeting, a much-needed reprieve.

I crack open my window, letting in the crisp air and the fresh scent of nature. The gentle touch of the breeze brushes against my skin. This may not be the typical 'me time' that people talk about, but it's enough to convince me today's going to be alright.

The address that Morgan gave turns out to be a small house several miles outside Helena.

As soon as I pull over, my best friend runs to me, screaming my name. She pats me all over as if looking for injuries. "You're okay? What the hell happened?"

"I'm fine, Morgie," I reply, concealing my panting. "Long story. But... I'm sorry I've ruined your honeymoon."

"Don't be silly! Nothing is ruined! Where's baby Quinton?" Morgan looks around.

"He's in there." I gesture at the back seat. "Word of caution, he's been very cranky this morning."

"Hey, Quinnie-Bear!" Morgan greets him, trailing her fingertips along his rosy cheek.

Quinton gapes, unsure what to make of my best friend.

"Do you remember Aunty Morgie?" I tell him, starting to unbuckle him from his baby seat. He wriggles impatiently. I won't blame him if he doesn't want to see that mini-throne in the near future. He's been sitting there too long. I wrap my arms around him as Morgan gently touches his thin hair—it's so soft, with long strands here and there, almost like candy floss. "Say hello to Aunty Morgie."

"Mo!" he says.

"Yes! I'm Morgan." My best friend erupts in excitement. "Of course you remember me."

"Don't get too excited, Morgie. He's calling the dog," I say with a laugh.

Morgan glares at me playfully, then helps Elmo out.

We unload the car while the dog explores the space, and Quinton plays on his favorite mat, which he hasn't seen in three days. Toys that Morgan bought seem to interest him, but as usual, the giraffe teether isn't far from his reach.

Finally, I have time to hug my best friend. "I would've been trapped with Willem forever if it wasn't for you. He sent the invitations already without me knowing."

"What an ass!"

"And he sent me some ideas about my hair—you know how he always wanted me to straighten my curls. He thought they were old fashioned."

"No, no, no! Your curls are the eighth wonder of the natural world. I'll kill whoever dares tell you to straighten them! You only do it if you want to."

My hair isn't in the league of the Grand Canyon or Mount Everest, but for sure, I won't let anyone tell me what to do with it.

Morgan adds, "Well, you're out of the house. That's your Neil Armstrong moment."

I watch Quinton, grateful for our safe arrival. "You're a little warm," I mutter as I check on him. "You're tired, aren't you?"

Morgan proudly announces, "I've prepared a room for him if you want to let him sleep there." She scoops up Quinton, and he looks at her like someone has just sounded a stranger alert. "You really don't remember me, do you?" Morgan says disappointedly. "And here I thought you inherited your mother's hyperthymesia."

"Well, Mrs. Biologist, you're not doing yourself any favors using words like that. He'll think you're Aristotle's daughter," I chuckle.

Quinton trails his fingers across Morgan's cheek, bringing a smile to her face. "What about your mommy's *memoria eidetica*? I'm sure you have it."

People say I have a photographic memory, but I see it as a tool for my art rather than a superpower. As for hyperthymesia, that's just my friend exaggerating. I've never been diagnosed with it, and I don't remember every detail of my life as the condition suggests. I simply have a strong recollection of things.

Suddenly, Quinton starts crying.

"Quinton, it's Aunty Morgie. It's okay," I try to coax him to stay with Morgan, but the boy rebels, trying his best to get to me.

"I guess your mommy's right. You can't stand Latin," Morgan remarks, handing Quinton over to me. "Or maybe I look like an evil clown—the worst company for any baby."

"Nonsense!" I deny. My best friend is gorgeous, with her big brown eyes and a classic, elegant smile like Sophia Loren's. "He's just a fussy baby. Apart from me, my parents, and my babysitter, he doesn't want to be with anyone else."

Morgan ponders. "So he remembers me?"

"Of course," I reply.

"But he doesn't like me?"

I shake my head and laugh. "He likes you. It just takes time for him to show it. He'll warm up to you," I reassure her. "You can speed up the process if you're willing to wear the *Paw Patrol* sunglasses for him."

"What's that?"

"It's his favorite show, and those sunglasses have dog ears on the sides," I laugh. "Although they're buried somewhere in there." My hand gestures toward the bags scattered on the floor.

"I doubt it'd make a difference. It's me—proof that I'm not cut out for motherhood yet." She shrugs casually. "Anyway, come on in. This is Quinton's room."

I gape in awe when she leads me into the smaller of the two bedrooms, which she had converted into a nursery. "Morgie... you didn't! See, Quinton. Aunty Morgie did all this for you."

"Everything is there. Diapers, powder, sheets, blankets, bottles—you name it. Oh, and that's your glider. The lady at the store assured us it's the best."

With its plush cushioning and tall backrest, there's no doubt that I'll be able to breastfeed Quinton comfortably there. "And you think you're not cut out for motherhood?" I comment. "Really, are you sure you and Tyler..."

She smiles. "Not yet, Ave. Remember, I'm five years younger than you. I've still got the advantage of youth. Ty is on the same page. He's happy to wait."

Sometimes, I forget our age difference. Because it's never mattered, even when she was three and I was eight when we first met. Now I'm twenty-seven. I never thought I'd be a runaway fiancée, ever, at any age, but the blessing of baby Quinton outweighs all the downsides of my choice to stick with Willem. And my bestie is the one who keeps me sane and optimistic.

"You and Ty are a match made in hea—Helena," I quip.

"Well, speaking of my husband, I should let him know that you're here."

While Morgan makes the call, I take the time to settle Quinton in the crib, singing to him, and his eyes finally shut. "Sleep tight, baby." I kiss him, then rejoin Morgan.

"Tea?" Morgan offers.

"Please."

Morgan leads me into the kitchen. "I've stocked up. You've got everything you need here. No chamomile tea, though." She winks and then reaches for two bags of Lipton.

I chuckle appreciatively. No, I won't have to smell chamomile ever again.

We make ourselves comfortable on the two-seater couch in the living room.

Morgan starts, "This is a stupid question, but I need to ask, Ave. Are you sure no one is following you?"

If anyone else had posed that question to me, considering all the effort I had put into ensuring my own safety and protecting Quinton in the past few days, I would punch them in the face. But my friend has every right to ask. She has put herself on the line for my sake. And she has experienced her own share of danger, having been pursued relentlessly after surviving a murder attempt. She understands firsthand what it's like to be on the run, constantly trying to stay one step ahead of those chasing her.

"Someone tried to chase me when I was entering Utah," I admit. "But let me tell you, I drove like Max Verstappen at the Miami Grand Prix." That makes Morgan cock her head. "Well, actually, I drove like my mother!"

We laugh. We both knew she was the epitome of L.A. taxi drivers in the nineties—efficient, talkative, and slightly insane.

I glance at Quinton's room and add, "With passenger comfort in mind, of course."

"I trust you know what you're doing."

"They lost me, Morgie. I was sure of that. I went the long way around, always checking if anyone was on my tail."

She responds with a hint of pride, perhaps reminding me of the valuable tips she once gave me. "I'm proud of you." She pauses, then asks another question. "And you didn't tell any of your work friends?"

There's a special bond among courtroom artists. I'll miss them. But I couldn't risk it, considering the close connection between the media, the justice system, and Willem. His company plays a crucial role in the California Department of Justice database network and has won a bid to expand to the federal level.

"No one, Morgie. I told absolutely no one," I answer.

She acknowledges me with a nod, then sips her tea.

As I look out the window, all I see are vast green fields. I can't help but wonder, "Do I even have a neighbor around here?"

"Um... about half a mile on each side."

I quirk my lips sideways. "Okay."

"Ave, you're not in California anymore. You have to get used to seeing more cattle than humans."

"Hey, I'm not a city brat, you know. I can handle rural!"

Morgan giggles. "The next town is only four miles away. The stores there are pretty good. And you're not that far from the city. By city, I mean the Red Mark HQ. Ty has arranged for the guys to come check on you every day."

"I don't think that's necessary."

"You can never be too careful. Willem will suspect you're in Helena with me, but I rented this house under a fake name. So there's nothing that ties this place to you or me."

"Thanks, Morgie."

"Besides, I won't be here. So there's no chance of Willem kidnapping and interrogating me."

Fright and confusion drive me to frown. Frightened because I can't bear the thought of my ex torturing my best friend and confused because I'm not sure what she means by 'I won't be here.'

Morgan laughs, perhaps noticing my expression. "I mean, damn, I'm still going on my honeymoon!"

I ambush her with a joyful hug. "You managed to rearrange your bookings?"

"Ave, good things happen to good people!" she teases me. "When you didn't show up two days ago, Ty and I took a chance at rescheduling everything instead of canceling. We gave ourselves until today. If you hadn't turned up, we would've canceled everything because it would mean you were in serious trouble."

"Are you still meeting your researcher friend in Antarctica?" I ask. It seems that my best friend, who's a wolf researcher by trade, can't resist combining wildlife with romance, even on her honeymoon.

"Hell yeah. He's stationed there long-term, so getting there a few days late won't matter."

"Luckily, there're no wolves in that part of the world. Imagine all the penguins!"

Morgan laughs. "Nature knows how to take care of itself."

Suddenly, Morgan gets a call. She answers. "Yeah? Oh, good... She's here. Yeah. She's safe." She then waits for a while to listen. "No! No, don't you dare turn around! You hop on that plane, and we'll see you soon." She raises her eyes to me, sparkling like her wish-upon-a-star has just come true.

"Who's that?"

"Your babysitter."

"What?"

"Not Quinton's. *Yours*."

This is the second time my friend confuses me in a matter of minutes.

Morgan laughs again. "After all, you were right. There won't be any need for the Red Mark guys to check on you."

"Morgie, who was that?"

"It was Jack, silly!"

Warmth fills my chest as if sparked by crackling firewood. Yet, amid these sensations, strange numbness consumes me. This wasn't part of my plan. The man who has haunted my dreams, the man I never expected to reenter my life, will soon be standing here beside me.

"Jack? Why?" I murmur.

"I called him when you didn't show up as planned."

"And he's still coming even though I'm here?"

"He is still coming *because* you're here! As we speak, he's boarding a plane bound for Helena after a layover at LAX. So he should be here this afternoon."

"Morgie, tell me, what did he say when you gave the sketch to him?" I finally have the courage to ask her the question. When I drew it, it was really my heart that penciled every stroke. It was how I saw him, how I remembered him. The fear of rejection held me back from ever discovering his reaction.

"He asked why you were too chicken to give it to him yourself."

"Come on, I'm serious."

"He didn't say anything. But his eyes did. He was torn. I tried to nudge him, hoping to change his mind about moving to Hawaii. I sought his brother's assistance to convince him to join Red Mark so he could be in Helena and have a chance to reconnect with you. But his loyalty remained with the Marine Corps."

I let out a hopeless sigh. "I miss him. But life is life. I have to put Quinton first. Jack is just a dream."

"Well, he won't be for much longer. He'll walk through that door in a few hours. And when he does, tell him. Don't make any excuses, like you won't do it because the guy has to express his love first. I know you're not that kind of woman."

I shake my head. "There's something about him that makes me kind of...sad. Not just because of the tragedy he had to endure as a child." I pause, unable to fathom his plight, being taken away from his family when he was only seven. "There's something else. I'm usually good at reading people, but with Jack, I don't know what to expect from him."

"You'll never figure out a man, Ave. You just have to take the ride and navigate every turn with him, impromptu."

"Geez, Morgie. You sound like you've aged ten years! What has Tyler done to you?"

"In a good way, right? Ty has done wonders for me. He annoys me sometimes, especially with his tardiness. I understand, though. His job isn't the nine-to-five kind. And neither is mine, for that matter. But I love him—everything about him, including the surprises—good or bad."

"I don't know if what I have for Jack is love."

"That's another thing you won't figure out until it's too late."

I pause for a moment, then reach a conclusion. "Perhaps it's already too late."

It's true. The moment was brief, but it was love. I loved him because he made me feel safe even though I didn't know what to expect from him. This feeling wasn't solely a result of my dismal choice with Willem. It was because I felt a sense of rightness with Jack. There was no one else in the picture, and that remains true even today.

"It's just us now," I say to Quinton, who is now wide awake after Morgan leaves for the airport. "Do you like your new home?"

He turns away from me.

"Oh, don't be like that." I rub his back. "I know it's not as big and colorful as your old room, but we'll find a new place soon. And I promise I'll paint those animals on the wall again for you."

"Ma.... ma... ma..." He hasn't quite mastered the word 'mama' yet. Random sounds like that only happen sporadically.

"What is it, baby?"

Once again, he avoids me, crawling away.

"You don't want my company?" I tickle him with the giraffe teether, and he giggles. If he had a dad, I would've called him right away, giving my baby a break from seeing his wearied mother. As if the words are drawn out of my throat, I whisper, "Jack will be here. Can you say 'Jack'?"

Quinton grimaces. His distress tells me it's not because he's responding to Jack's name. My little boy starts kicking around in discomfort.

"What's wrong, baby? You're still tired, aren't you?"

Despite cradling him for an hour, he still refuses to calm down.

I give in and opt to switch on the TV, hoping it will divert his attention. Just in time, Quinton becomes engrossed in his favorite show, *Paw Patrol*. I can't recall how he grew to love it, especially since the show is usually targeted toward kids two years and older. I guess it's all about the colors and the dogs.

"Po po po," Quinton babbles, pointing at the cartoon

canines in their helmets, flying around using their superpowers.

In the meantime, I find the missing dog-ear sunglasses and start to play peek-a-boo with him.

But he loses interest in the show, and my funny faces behind the shades don't amuse him anymore. His complaints turn loud, but then he abruptly falls silent and lies limp on the mat.

"Quinton?"

He's never been like this before, and he's burning up with a fever.

My chest tightens. I wish I could absorb whatever is troubling my baby, but nothing seems to work. This must've been what my mother went through when she took me to the hospital one night. I was only five, but I vividly recall her distress and the sensation of my head ready to explode. Despite her meltdown, she rushed me to the emergency room. And it saved my life.

I bundle Quinton in a blanket and get ready to take him to the hospital. Elmo sprints to catch me at the door, but after hearing my command to stay, his paw nails click against the floor as he tries to stop himself. The pup then sits and watches me with a pitiful expression as I leave the house.

I buckle Quinton in his seat, and he retaliates, crying loudly. I guess it's better than silence. "I know you don't want to be in this thing, but just one more time, okay?"

He keeps crying all the way to the emergency room.

A doctor immediately tends to Quinton.

After being given some acetaminophen, the boy begins to drift off to sleep. According to the doctor's assessment, it appears that Quinton is having difficulty adjusting to the change of weather.

"Give him plenty of fluid," the doctor advises. "Also, you

can put him in lighter clothing. I know it's Montana, but we do have warm days here. Like California in spring."

I thank the doctor and leave the hospital in relief. With Quinton sleeping soundly, I think I'll finally be able to steal a nap until Jack arrives.

On the way back to my car, I spot two men sauntering along the garage. They are dressed in casual attire, but something about their demeanor makes me feel uneasy. They seem to be walking aimlessly at first, but then they approach me. One of them has a beard, while the other is taller and more muscular. They both wear baseball caps pulled low over their foreheads, obscuring their features.

As they get closer, I instinctively tighten my grip on Quinton while hastening my steps.

But they follow, and soon, the taller one glues his back against my car door, blocking it.

"Are you Ava West?" he says, his tone unnerving.

"No. You've got the wrong person."

"We couldn't help but notice your little one. Is that baby Quinton?"

The bearded man, who has remained silent, hooks his arm around my elbow. Finally, he speaks. "Don't be foolish, woman. If you do, you and your baby will end up in the ICU. Well, I guess you're already in the right place, but I'm sure you wouldn't want to toy with that possibility."

The men drag me into their van, shoving me inside. All I can think about is protecting Quinton.

"You put something in your fiancé's drink before you left, didn't you?"

This can't be! I knew Willem wasn't just one man, but to be caught so quickly, with Quinton in my arms? I don't know what I'm going to do.

"Well, your fiancé is dead," he continues. "So you better

keep your mouth shut, or you'll spend the rest of your life in jail for murder."

My blood runs cold, and my throat constricts. Willem is dead? That's impossible! I measured the dose carefully. It couldn't have killed him!

"If you breathe a word of this to anyone, baby Quinton will suffer the consequences. Stay silent, and we can negotiate."

Although still wearing their caps, the men seem to have let their guards down now that we're on the move. They don't even bother hiding their faces. The bearded man bears a resemblance to Zach Galifianakis from *The Hangover*, but sinister. On the other hand, his taller companion has a distinct set of rounded features.

As if realizing that I'm studying them, the taller one strikes me on the head.

Everything blurs and disappears, only to reappear as if it were a trick of the light.

I find myself lying on the grass. Alone.

"Quinton!" I call out in panic, only to hear my own voice echoing through the park. With every attempt to rise, I feel the weight of my throbbing head dragging me down. A metallic tang fills my nostrils, the scent of my own blood. I ignore my body trying to tell me to slow down. I scour the park, screaming out his name. But my baby is nowhere to be found.

"No..." I sob.

I don't know where I am, but I can see the Capitol's dome in the distance, so I'm not far from the city. Overwhelmed by dread and despair, only guided by instinct, I slowly make my way to the one place where I might find hope—Red Mark.

4

JACK

The drive from the Helena airport feels surreal, as if I'm still in the sky. Seeing Ava again has got me all jittery, but my body is slow to bounce back from my accidental nap on the plane. I woke up scratching the armrests of the plane seat, my spine burning as if my skin had split. The elderly woman next to me gawked as if I had some sort of phobia or PTSD, perhaps noticing the USMC pin attached to my bag.

I've served in the military for more than a decade. The stigma of PTSD is often linked to our experiences, regardless of its accuracy. Even with all the research conducted, our understanding of it remains surprisingly lacking.

Nevertheless, my mid-air terror has nothing to do with PTSD, and I do not have a fear of flying. It's a story about a place and a person, dark but vivid. If it holds any truth, those visions would be the fleeting moments I was face-to-face with my kidnapper. Nonetheless, I won't have certainty until I find solid evidence.

As I approach my destination, thoughts of Ava fill my mind, drowning the haunting images and convincing my body that I'm back on solid ground.

The rest of the journey leads me through undulating hills. Morgan's idea of seclusion takes me by surprise, but I guess she had to make sure her best friend was safe.

I arrive at the address Morgan texted me earlier, hoping to find her husband Tyler at the door. Despite knowing Morgan and Ava, I will feel much better if I don't have to face the ladies alone—especially the latter.

Now that I'm at the doorstep, the prospect of seeing Ava again frightens me. What the hell am I going to say to her? What does she think of me? How will I feel? It was easier when she was only present in her sketch, while the real her was hundreds of miles away.

"Tyler!" I call. But there's no response. The only sound I hear is barking, followed by noises from behind the door. Curious, I peek inside. The dog seems friendly, but then it disappears.

"Morgan?" I try calling again.

It occurs to me that the two might've orchestrated a prank, leaving me with no choice but to spend time alone with Ava. But somehow, it doesn't seem likely.

Moments later, I hear more scratching, and the dog reappears outside, holding a toy in its mouth. It's a long, yellow-and-white toy, which I recognize. I bought it from a specialty shop in Honolulu when Morgan told me about Ava giving birth. I can't believe Ava had kept it. And judging by the marks along the giraffe's neck, I'm sure it's been well used.

"Where're your parents?" I ask the dog as it sits at my feet, and it barks in response. For a few seconds, we appraise each other. The dog cocks his head, and his ears flap. He resembles a Labrador, but his legs are short and stubby.

I go around the back of the house, calling out for Tyler and Morgan once more. But there's no sign of anyone.

Thinking the gang might be at Red Mark, I call Sam. "Hey, is Tyler there?"

"Why would he be?" my brother answers. "He's on the way to his honeymoon with Morgan."

Honeymoon? Why didn't anyone mention a honeymoon?

"Where are you?" Sam asks.

"At the house."

"Ava should be there. I mean, not Ty's city house, but the one that Morgan rented for Ava. Have you got the address right?"

"Yeah. I'm here."

"Ava should be home. Is her car there?"

"No," I answer, then shift my attention to my welcoming party. "I've only got a dog here."

"It must be Ava's. Morgan and Ty's dog is in Bozeman with Ty's parents." Then he pauses.

My former Navy SEAL brother rarely runs out of ideas regarding someone's whereabouts. Something is amiss.

"Damn it! I'll find her," I resolve, returning to my car.

The dog refuses to let me go, wrapping his short front legs around my ankle and nipping at my sock. Unable to resist his adorable face, I pick him up and let him ride in the back.

The deserted streets around the neighborhood make me increasingly desperate. I keep my eyes peeled, checking out other properties and then hitting up the nearby town with all the stores. But there's no sign of Ava. With a sigh, I head to the city to meet up with my brother.

As I approach the Red Mark office, I spot a figure stumbling toward the same building. Even from a distance, I recognize who it is. I accelerate, then stop at the curb next to her.

"Ava! Ava!"

I jump out of the car, my hands reaching out to catch her faltering body. The dog goes berserk, whining as if knowing his master is in trouble. As I hold Ava in my arms, the crimson hue stands out vividly against her ghostly skin. Her disheveled hair brushes against my fingertips as I wipe the blood off her forehead.

"Ava, talk to me." I tap her cheek. "It's me. Jack."

"Jack…"

That soft voice.

The last time I heard it, she was saying goodbye. Now, she's calling out to me because she needs me. It's different but equally painful.

"Take a breath. Just breathe," I try to calm her down as I scoop her up and rush into the Red Mark building. Once I'm in the lobby, I immediately call out for Sam.

Ava chokes as she sobs silently. As if trying to swallow a clog in her throat, she struggles out, "They took my baby."

"Where did this happen?"

"I went to the hospital. Then they took him." She gasps for air, her breathing labored.

Perhaps her struggle to get here has taken its toll, but her breathing becomes even more strained. And then she faints.

Sam finally arrives. "Jesus, Jack! What the hell?"

I lay Ava on the floor, ready to give her mouth-to-mouth to help her breathe, but my brother has a better idea. He returns with an oxygen tank. I know there's a training facility here, and Red Mark personnel are often pushed to their limits, so it's no surprise that the office is equipped with medical apparatus.

"Sweetheart…relax," I reassure her, placing the mask over her nose and mouth. "Breathe slowly."

"Call Dr. Tripp!" Sam instructs one of the staff.

"Your doctor?" I question.

"We have our own medical team now."

The oxygen seems to provide some relief for Ava. Once her

breathing stabilizes, Sam suggests, "Come with me. We have a bed upstairs. She'll be more comfortable there."

The dog follows us faithfully as we take an elevator up.

"Jack..." Ava murmurs as I cradle her in my arms.

"I'm here."

She rests her head against my chest, her curls brushing my chin. Her body smells of baby powder, evoking an unexpected surge of emotion—something that has never entered my reality. It's as if I'm enveloped in a realm of abstract tenderness, purity, and innocence.

Ava nuzzles into my shirt.

Disbelief washes over me, erasing my doubts about her presence in my life. Even though more than a year has passed, she's still part of me, and her responses affirm our unbreakable connection. We are picking up where we left off in Bozeman despite the punishing circumstances.

I hold her tight, feeling the weight of her body against mine. As she hooks one arm over my neck, her need for closeness moves me deeply. How does one console a mother who has lost her baby? There's no comparison, but the closest I can come is to imagine the pain of losing her now. With this empathy, I hope to offer her a sliver of comfort.

"Quinton," she huffs. "He had a fever."

"We'll find him," I assure her. "I promise, we will. For now, you must get better first."

Sam whispers to me, "Her baby?"

"Someone took her son, Sam! He's only seven months old!" My fury wells up at the thought. I've accepted that evil is part of life, but I wish it would stay the hell away from children and stop making mothers cry.

"No way, he's far too young to be separated from his mother!" Sam's voice remains low, but anger is written all over it.

I, too, am fighting the eruption of my rage. Quinton may

not be my son, and I may not have met him or know who his father is, but he has become a part of me, just like his mother. Whoever is responsible, whatever the reason may be, if it affects Ava and her child, I'll take it upon myself to fight the battle.

As I lay Ava on the bed, she whispers my name. Her lips gradually turn rosier, but her breathing becomes labored once again. Sam hands me the oxygen, and I quickly place the mask back on her face.

With a tired sigh, she closes her eyes. There is a blanket resting at the foot of the bed, and I spread it over her, covering her legs. I wish I had something softer to offer her, but she's got to feel me. For now, my denim shirt will have to do, so I drape it over her chest, leaving me in just a T-shirt. She grips the crumpled shirt, bringing back memories of our time in Bozeman—me giving her my jacket, which she wrapped around herself.

Just then, the doctor arrives. Ava's weak voice calls out for me, her hand searching for mine. I grasp her palm, assuring her, "It's the doctor, sweetheart."

Ava looks at the doctor and nods when she introduces herself as Celine. Ava looks to be at ease in her company.

"I'll be right outside," I whisper.

Sam and I step aside, allowing the doctor to examine Ava in private. I pace anxiously in the hallway, my mind racing with worry. "It's her fucking fiancé," I whisper to Sam. "I'm going to mush his ass, man!"

"I can't agree more," he concurs.

"She mentioned bringing Quinton to a hospital."

The doctor exits the room and joins us in the hallway, reassuring us that Ava will be okay. "Firstly, she's suffering mild concussion because of the blow to her forehead. With plenty of rest, she should recover in no time," she explains.

"And her shortness of breath is caused by her previous battle with leukemia."

I'm taken aback by this revelation. "I didn't know she had leukemia," I admit, feeling guilty for not being aware of her condition.

The doctor flashes a glance of surprise, perhaps assuming I would've known, being a man who keeps calling Ava 'sweetheart.'

"You're her family?" she asks.

Sighing, I shake my head.

She continues, "I'm sorry, Mr.—"

"Kelleher. I'm Sam's brother," I answer, and she tries to hide her surprise.

Sam and I don't look alike. He takes after our father while I'm apparently a spitting image of my mother—if only I'd known her.

"I'm sorry, Mr. Kelleher." Dr. Celine Tripp looks at Sam and me. "I shouldn't be discussing this. It's patient confidentiality. All I can say is that she'll be okay. She mentioned leaving her medication at home. Perhaps you could fetch it for her and call her family?"

Sam instructs one of his men to retrieve Ava's medication.

I tell the doctor, "With all due respect, she is *my* family. I need to know!" I change my statement about who I am to Ava. I might come across as pushy, but Ava's health is my responsibility.

"Please, Doc," Sam insists politely.

She hesitates but then reveals, "Ms. West has an underlying lung condition because of her previous battle with leukemia. She's cancer-free now, but this is a lingering side effect of her chemotherapy. She had to go through the most aggressive treatment."

"She will be okay, right?" I need to hear it again.

"Yes. Just keep her relaxed and comfortable."

The doctor leaves us, and I check in on Ava. Her head is bandaged, and she looks so weak and fragile.

"Ava, which hospital did you bring Quinton to?" I ask gently.

"St. Peter's," she replies in a whisper.

"Can Sam come in?"

She answers with a nod.

I tell my brother about the hospital, and he says, "I'll get one of the guys to check the CCTV."

"No, please," Ava begs. "They said they'd hurt Quinton if I told anyone."

Her panting returns.

"Ava, calm down," I say, caressing her back.

"We'll be careful, Ava," Sam assures her. "We won't let anything happen to Quinton."

Ava looks at me, silently begging for action.

"They're the best at what they do," I emphasize. Although I feel an overwhelming urge to take matters into my own hands, I know my anger and personal biases may cloud my judgment. One careless move and everything could go horribly wrong. "You can count on them," I say firmly, holding her hand.

She nods, exhausted, and soon falls asleep. While Sam and his men swing into action, I stay by her side. The dog stands guard, ever vigilant. I look at his name tag and give him a gentle pat. "Good dog, Elmo. Good dog," I whisper, determined not to move from my spot. I will not leave Ava's side until I uncover the truth about what's going on.

5
___

AVA

Squinting my eyes open, I find myself in an unfamiliar room. The tightness in my chest is suffocating. It feels like an elephant has taken residence on top of me. As I turn my head to the right, I'm greeted by the outline of a familiar figure. A sense of comfort shrouds me upon seeing him.

Elmo.

My loyal companion is with me. But where the hell am I?

Behind Elmo's fuzzy image and his enthusiastic licking, a shadowy figure emerges. It's a man. I should run or seek help from Elmo, but instead, I allow the man to approach me. Is this some kind of dream? The kind where you desperately want to flee, but your body refuses to respond? Strangely, I feel no threat, no urge to escape.

The man takes my hand, shaking it gently. Is he calling me 'sweetheart?'

My eyes focus, my mind wavering between acceptance and disbelief at the sight before me.

"Ava? Can you hear me?" His voice is crystal clear, cutting through people's chatter outside my room. It's steady, asserting its authority as though he's the only one with the rightful claim to my name.

Although I have no recollection of how I got here, this isn't a dream. That man, he took me here. When we bid farewell in Bozeman, his hair was wavy and thick. Now, the ash-blond mane is neatly cropped, the signature haircut of a Marine. His face is clean-shaven, accentuating his sharp features. My goodness, he looks breathtaking.

As I sit up, pressure converges in my head. Jack tries to persuade me to lie back down, but now I understand why I'm here. My admiration for the Marine should be the last thing on my mind.

"Have you…" I struggle to finish my sentence, coughing from my dry throat.

"Here." Jack offers me a glass of water.

Elmo attempts to join me in bed, but as usual, he fails. Seeing this, Jack gives him a push so the pup can lie next to me.

After a few gulps, I ask, "Have you found my baby?"

"No," he murmurs as if he doesn't want to deliver the news. "We've analyzed the CCTV from the hospital parking garage. We saw two men, but their faces were obscured, and the van registration number was fake. Do you remember anything about them?"

"I remember their faces. Give me a pencil and paper."

Jack leaves the room and soon returns with a drawing pad and an HB pencil. My hand can barely grip them. Stroke by stroke, shaking as if I'm possessed, I manage to draw something.

My fingers unfurl, the pencil rolling down to the floor.

That face. It's faint, but…

"I can't, Jack. I can't."

"It's okay. Forget about the sketch." He tries to take the

drawing pad away from me, but I hold onto it. "Ava, we'll do it another time."

I sob, staring at the black-and-white, faded impression of Quinton. My Quinnie-Bear is out there alone, and who knows what those men are doing to him!

Jack wraps his hand around my trembling fingers as I grip the paper tightly. But finally, I let it go.

"I do remember their faces, Jack. I just can't put them on paper."

"It's fine." He puts a hand on my shoulder, the other rubbing my hand. His eyes radiate with concern and kindness that my slowed-down brain can still perceive. "Can I get Sam to join us?"

I nod. Sam then enters and discreetly hides the pad and pencil, but not before he takes a quick glance at his brother, perhaps surprised at what I've drawn. Sam then passes me a strip of pills. "Your medication."

"Thanks."

Jack helps me pop the blisters and take out two pills.

Seeing the two brothers side by side, my attention is drawn to their contrasting appearances. Jack, the younger but taller brother, is more serious and reserved. His complexion is naturally light but appears tanned, hinting at days spent under the scorching sun.

By contrast, Sam the ex-Navy SEAL epitomizes the phrase 'dark and handsome,' with his brunette locks and dusky skin. He's also the more laid-back of the two. Despite their physical disparities, a common trait unites them. Beyond their rugged masculinity, they radiate a gentle demeanor. From what they do and how they do it, it's clear the men possess an innate ability to nurture and care for others.

After taking my time to swallow the pills, I confess, "I think I killed my fiancé."

Jack and Sam stare at me intently.

"Did you really do it?" Jack asks, his tone implying he's not taking my statement literally.

"I put a sedative in his tea. I just wanted him to sleep so I could escape."

"How did you find out that he died?" Jack presses.

"The men who took Quinton, they knew what I did. They told me my fiancé was dead. So now, when they make their demands, if I don't comply or if I go to the police, they'll hurt Quinton—or at least take him away from me forever—and expose everything. I'll spend the rest of my life in jail, Jack!"

He holds me firmly, his face burning like hell has just put down its roots in him.

I add, "I swear, I measured the dose carefully. I just wanted him to sleep until the morning. Enough to give me time to disappear." I pause, thinking about what could've happened. "He never did drugs. I didn't smell alcohol on him. So there's no way he died from complications. No way!"

"Those men lied to you!" Jack bellows, full of certainty.

In the silence, I try to recall the kidnappers' expressions. I should have been able to read them, but at that moment, all I could think about was my baby.

"Maybe his body couldn't handle it," I reason. "We were going to get married. He sent out the invitations without me knowing. I couldn't bear the thought of living another day with him, let alone forever! Maybe I accidentally gave him the wrong dose. I don't know..."

"He's trying to manipulate you," Jack adds. "Don't let him. Trust yourself. The sedative you put in his tea didn't kill him." He says it with such conviction that I almost believe him.

But no matter what I've done, I've put my baby in danger. "I just wanted to get away from him. I want Quinton to grow up free from such a controlling and violent man. And now, my baby isn't even safe!"

Jack kneels in front of me, holding both of my hands. "Listen, if it's true that your fiancé is dead, it's because those men killed him. Whoever they are. Not you, not your tea."

While Jack tries to comfort me, Sam says, "He's right. You shouldn't blame yourself. You're not just a case, Ava. You're our family. But let me tell you, I've seen how families get torn apart under pressure because they either blame each other or themselves. Blame is your worst enemy when you need to find your loved one."

"Ava," Jack interrupts, restarting the conversation. "If I'm correct in thinking that those men were lying and your fiancé is still alive, it means you won't go to jail. And he won't harm baby Quinton."

"You can't know that," I reply.

Jack let out an exasperated huff, his eyes widening in disbelief. "Are you suggesting that the father of your child is capable of hurting his own flesh and blood?"

The intensity of his gaze is so intimidating that I instinctively look away.

"He... um, he never hurt Quinton. But he had a temper, and I was always there to protect my son. So I never really tested him," I explain.

The air thickens with unresolved anger as Jack, his face flushed with fury, abruptly stands up and marches toward the corner of the room.

"I'll talk to him," Sam offers, apparently trying to ease the tension.

Jack hears him and shouts, "I'm fine! Just give me a minute."

Jack Kelleher, a Marine who has likely witnessed atrocities that most people can't even fathom, is shaken by the idea that

Quinton's own father could harm him. After another stretch of silence, he turns back to me and apologizes. "I just never thought I'd hear it. I'm okay now."

Sam carries on. "Your fiancé must've suspected that you'd escape to Helena because of Morgan."

I respond, "But he wouldn't have known the place she had prepared for me. If only I hadn't gone to the hospital."

"You did what you had to do!" Sam reassures me.

"I just panicked," I mention. My mother's voice echoes in my head again, although not as loud as when I saw Quinton lying in silence. I rue my lapse of judgment. "Quinton only had a slight fever. I should've simply given him acetaminophen, and everything would have been all right."

Jack embraces me, stroking my back lightly as he whispers, "Stop blaming yourself. Please."

I'm used to fighting my battles alone, but in the midst of chaos, I now know what it feels like to have someone by my side. And it's not just anyone. It's a man who has stolen more than a piece of me and one who will go to any lengths for me.

The security in his hold and the way he props me up when I have nothing left within me solidifies the truth in my secret declaration of love for him. If only I could surrender myself completely, allowing him to bear all the burden. But I can't. I'm a mother. For the sake of Quinton, I'll set aside my despair and remain strong for my baby.

I indicate that I'm ready to continue the conversation.

"Do you have any idea what their demand might be?" Sam asks.

I reply, "I have no idea. Willem is a wealthy businessman. A tech guru. If he's really dead, maybe one of his rivals wants something from me. But since I'm not married to Willem yet, I don't have access to his estate."

"And if he's still alive?" Sam asks.

"I don't know. Maybe he just wants his heir back," I speculate.

"His heir? That's how he saw Quinton?" Jack mutters, at a loss for words.

Sam adds, "No doubt your fiancé is aware of your connection with Red Mark."

"I'm sure he is, yes," I confirm. It's a no-brainer since my best friend is married to the head of ops.

"And Willem Botha has the means," Sam suggests. "He could've staged anything."

"Willem Botha?" Jack looks at me intently. "Willem Botha is your fiancé?"

I whisper a 'yes,' too embarrassed to even hear that name. When I first met Willem, his name stood out and made me think of his Dutch-Afrikaans background. However, now, it carries an unfortunate connotation that has tarnished its uniqueness.

"Is that the AI chip guy?" Jack still doesn't believe it.

Although Willem's primary business is database technology, he recently made a significant breakthrough in microchip research. It caused quite a stir in the news not too long ago, and obviously, Jack knows about it.

"That's him," I confirm.

Jack's eyes narrow as he asks, "Did he know about me?"

"No."

"Are you absolutely certain that you never mentioned me to anyone in Cali?"

It feels unjust and hurtful. As if I've wiped him out of existence. But I answer, "Nobody knows."

"In that case, we should split up," Jack says, looking at his brother.

"What do you mean?" Sam asks, puzzled.

"I don't believe Willem is dead," Jack repeats. "You and Red Mark can investigate the kidnapping here. He's too clever to think that Ava won't turn to Red Mark just because those men threatened her. So, let's play along. But we'll keep the police out of this. Meanwhile, I'll go to Cali and find out what's really going on."

"Jack…" I tremble, worried that he's doing this without thinking it through.

"You go with my brother. You'll be safe," Jack insists.

"I can't involve you in this, Sam!" I say.

"Of course you can," Sam responds lightheartedly.

"You have a family!"

"Who will gladly welcome you into our home. Look, Ava, if eyes are still following you, they'll know you're with me. And that's all right. My house is secluded and secure. I won't let anyone follow us. Trust me, I've been in this line of work for a long time. I understand the risks and how to handle them. And remember, you're family, Ava."

Jack nods, offering reassurance.

I absorb the moment with quiet awe as I gaze at the Kelleher brothers. Their smiles reflect genuine acceptance— I'm no longer an outsider.

But before I can fully revel in this newfound belonging, Jack's voice breaks through. "I'll be back as soon as I can. I'm going to use my…um, previous name, Jack Benedict." He mentions the name heavily.

"You had another name?" I ask.

"After drifting from street to street, not even knowing my own name apart from 'Jack,' a nun from a Florida monastery took me under her wings. She was part of a Benedictine sect, hence the name."

Sam observes him. "It's a good idea, but are you sure about this?"

"Yeah. I'm good. I'll get a new phone, okay? I'll let you know as soon as I get there."

"I'll give my second phone to Ava," says Sam. "And Jack." He looks at his brother from head to toe. "Have you got a suit in your bag?"

"Why?"

"If you want to blend into Willem's environment, you've gotta look California rich. Cargo pants and a T-shirt won't cut it."

I cringe and nod, agreeing with Sam.

He advises Jack, "Go and see Ben before you leave. He's your size. He's got spares in his locker."

Morgan has shown me photos of Tyler and his colleagues. For sure, the Red Mark men know how to work a suit. It's like an unwritten rule.

"Yeah, all right," Jack concedes, brushing his pants and T-shirt as if realizing he's far from looking presentable. Although for myself, I don't care. He looks as handsome and rugged as my dream hero.

Sam mentions, "Gloves, masks, and ballistic vests are in room 201."

Jack gives him an 'if I must' stare while Elmo circles the Marine as if questioning what the fuss is about.

"He's so adorable," Sam remarks, lightening the mood slightly. "How old is he?"

"He's six, but he'll forever be a puppy. He has skeletal dysplasia, a form of dwarfism," I reply with a smile.

"Bless him," Jack says, bending his six-foot-six frame to pat Elmo. "Take care of her."

"Can Elmo come with us?" I ask Sam.

"Of course!" Sam responds. "I have a German Shepherd named Maximus who's constantly trying to challenge my authority in the house. He only has three legs, but I'm sure he'll get along with Elmo. That dog is just a big ball of fluff and overflowing with love."

"Maybe he'll finally get to be the alpha to someone," I glance at Elmo, who lets out a few soft barks.

"Oh, he gave me this, by the way." Jack takes something from inside his cargo pants pocket, handing over Quinton's giraffe teether.

Fingerprints graze the dirt-covered toy. No doubt they are Jack's. It's a small thing, but the moment signifies that our worlds have truly merged now.

My hand quivers as I hold it, feeling the smooth texture beneath my fingers. I know I can clean it later, but right now, I can't help but imagine how my baby is coping without his cherished toy, possibly still feeling under the weather, too. And he's without me, his mother! The hurt in my chest intensifies, threatening to unleash a sob. I lift my gaze to Jack, my eyes filled with gratitude, but the words get caught in my throat.

He draws a breath, his exhale a faint sound separating us. "I've got to go." He looks away as his eyes start blinking rapidly. With a swift turn, he pats Sam's shoulder, the impact audible as a soft thud. I strain to hear his whispered words, just loud enough for me to catch, "Never leave her side."

Sam responds, "You can count on me, brother."

Jack departs without a backward glance. Unable to utter anything, I watch his every move until he disappears from sight.

6

JACK

As soon as I arrive at LAX, I purchase a new prepaid phone using cash to avoid leaving any unnecessary traces. Having only been to California once, to San Diego, I can say I know Kabul better than Los Angeles. I need to give myself a crash course on this city so I can look and think like a local.

Operating under pressure is ingrained in every Marine. It's how we survive, endure, and excel. But now, I'm facing an unforgivable kind of pressure, even fear, which should never be in my vocabulary.

Every life is valuable, but nothing else takes precedence when it comes to innocent children. My connection with Quinton goes beyond knowing his name. It stems from the special bond I share with his mother.

Is this fear the price you pay for love?

I don't believe so.

Love must be earned. The giver has the right to know who you are before granting it to you. However, love doesn't come with a price tag. You don't have to pay for anything to be loved. When it's meant for you, it's yours.

As a Marine, I'm a weapon—I'm the danger.

With Ava, as a man who's capable of feeling, fear becomes a part of me. I have a choice to make it my enemy or my friend.

Ava's pain draws me to her as if she has been mine forever. Whatever danger she may be in, it's my responsibility to shield her or anything or anyone that's hers. And it's my responsibility to wipe those tears and bring a smile back to her face.

I take the deepest breath I can, resetting myself.

Fear is the bridge to perseverance.

And I'm crossing it now.

To match my borrowed suit, I pick a sleek black BMW from a high-end rental near the airport and head to the city. It doesn't take an experienced traveler to recognize the palm-lined streets or the ridiculous opulence that define Beverly Hills. Mansions as big as castles, along with their immaculate gardens, dot the landscape as I drive by. Willem Botha's house is no different. I slow down to give it a passing glance, then continue until I reach a small hill a few streets away. The elevation allows me to have a vantage point into the complex.

Parking the car, I position myself behind a tree and use binoculars to survey the area. The house's pristine facade reveals no hints of life inside.

I call Ava, and she answers with a soft but alert voice. "Jack, where are you?"

"I'm looking at your house. Well, Willem's house."

"Are there police there? Like... have they turned the house into a crime scene?"

"No. No sign of that. Trust me, he's still alive."

"Or it could be that those men have hidden his body somewhere..."

"They want you to be the killer, remember? They wouldn't want to disturb the scene."

"I guess..."

"Ava, how do I get in without setting off anything."

"Is there anyone outside? Today is Wednesday. Perhaps the gardeners are still there? Or do you see any movement behind the windows?"

"There doesn't seem to be anyone around."

Ava sighs. "If Willem is still alive, he must have changed the alarm code. So there's no way for you to get into the house itself. But there might be a way to access the gardens. You might get a better look inside from there."

"I can easily climb up the gate, but will it trigger anything?"

"There's a more discreet way."

"Ben will thank me for not ruining his suit."

She gives me a chuckle. I can picture her face lighting up as she explains, "Willem puts motion sensors everywhere. But there's a path leading to the back gardens that Elmo liked to use. The dog often ran away from home, and it drove Willem mad, so he decided to switch off the sensors around that area. For our sake, I hope he hasn't remembered to turn them back on."

"Is there another gate or something at the back?"

"There's a patch of hedges that have come loose. It started with Elmo digging and playing with the plants, but it has gotten bigger. I even saw a deer go in one day. I never told Willem. I didn't want him to kill the animal. I think you may be able to squeeze into it."

"Good to know. I'm on my way."

"Do you think Quinton is back home with Willem?"

"I don't know, Ava. If he is, I'll bring him home."

Keeping a safe distance from the estate, I disguise my face behind a pair of Ray-Bans and a face mask as I stroll along its boundaries. Eventually, I come across a broken section of hedge. It's a bit of a tight squeeze, but I manage to slip through.

The path Elmo has carved out is small but obvious. I shake off the dirt and grass stuck to my suit and pants. As I continue further, I spot disc-like devices scattered throughout the gardens. At a glance, they look like outdoor lights.

"Nice try!" I scoff.

As a highly trained FORECON, the elite Force Reconnaissance unit within the Corps, I'm not easily fooled by their glassy, high-tech appearance.

I make my way around the mansion's perimeter, pondering what life must have been like for Ava and Quinton in this expansive place. It's so vast that people could easily go days without crossing paths if they so desired. But I doubt Willem is that type of person. Being the man of the house, he likely wants to be aware of and involved in everything that goes on here.

Having explored as much as I can without getting too close to the house and finding no signs of life, I return to my car and give Ava another call.

"I don't think Quinton is in the house. It's way too quiet here," I inform her, earning a disappointed sigh in response.

"Did you see the babysitter?"

"No. No sign of anyone there."

She stays silent.

"Ava? I'm not gonna give up."

"I know you're not. It's just... it's hard. I've never been without Quinton. Ever."

Hearing her like that, it's like needles tunneling through my veins. "I know." I pause, trying to somehow cheer her up. "Hey, have my brother taken good care of you?"

A soft cackle escapes her, giving me hope.

"He and his family have been so amazing to me," she

rasps. "I didn't want to eat anything this morning, but their daughter Grace was so sweet. She made me a hot chocolate, you know, with a heart in the froth. I couldn't say no."

Sam and Cass have done a great job as parents. Grace is Cass' daughter from her previous marriage, and Sam and Cass have a son together. Although I haven't had the chance to spend much time with them, I've only heard wonderful things about their children.

I tell Ava, "You have to take care of yourself. We can't have you getting sick, too."

"I promise I'm taking care of myself." She inhales, then asks, "Where are you going next?"

I open the email from Cora-Lee Rancic, the head of tech at Red Mark, which contains a list of properties in California associated with Willem Botha personally or his company, 'W-Bot.'

"I'm going to survey the other properties that Willem owns. Maybe if I find him, I'll get some clues about Quinton's whereabouts. I'll call you later, okay?"

Willem Botha's portfolio consists of the typical mix of houses and commercial buildings, nothing out of the ordinary. I begin exploring the addresses that are within my reach. All the commercial properties are currently occupied, with the exception of one in southwestern L.A., which is still under-going construction. The residential estates appear to be occu-pied by families, evident from the flurry of activities that I observe.

Determined to find Willem, I head back downtown to visit W-Bot's headquarters. While I am on my way, Sam calls.

"How is she, Sam?"

My brother hums. "Didn't you talk to her just now?"

"Yeah. But I want to hear it from you."

"She's still in her room. I don't think she got any sleep, and she hasn't eaten much. But Cass is checking on her regularly. And don't worry, my wife will get her to eat, or my kids will."

"I appreciate it, brother."

"You know, Jack, I didn't think you were that close to her until I saw how you looked when she was with you."

"I didn't know I was, either," I reply, contemplating. I guess I can't hide from myself. But that makes me wonder. Closeness is like a double-edged sword. It exposes both sides of you, the dark and the light. When Ava sees all the baggage I carry, what will she do? Will she be scared off by how broken I am?

God help me!

I can't even spare a brain cell to process that right now. My focus is on finding baby Quinton.

Sam's voice brings me back to what's at hand. "Hey, listen, we just got hold of the CCTV from around the park where Ava was left unconscious. It looks like the two men went their separate ways. The van drove off, while one man carried Ava and left her in the park. We caught him on the street camera, driving a different car."

"There's got to be a woman involved, Sam. You can't just abduct a seven-month-old baby with only a male kidnapper. Plus, it wouldn't be easy to travel by air with a baby and go unnoticed. I think they're driving. Maybe to Cali. But so far, the suspected properties around L.A. are duds. They're either normal or empty."

"Damn. What are you gonna do?"

"I'm heading to the W-Bot headquarters. I may come face to face with that cockbag."

"You know what I'm going to say, right?" my brother croaks.

"What, Sam?"

"You're very close to the heart of this beast. As your big brother and someone who has been in this rescue business for years, may I remind you? Love can sometimes be your undoing when you desperately want to save the one you can't lose."

"Damn it, Sam. So you think my judgment is clouded?" I challenge him. "Let me ask you this. How close were you to the heart of the beast when you were trying to find me?"

My big brother was only twelve when I was abducted at a fair in Syracuse. Yet he never gave up on finding me. He left home at fifteen to take matters into his own hands. The police closed my case after discovering my bloodied clothes, but he knew it wasn't over. He believed because he's my brother.

"That was different," Sam denies.

"No, it wasn't. It couldn't have been more personal. I was missing, presumed dead, with no leads, and practically an amnesiac. But you trusted your instincts. And here we are."

"Fuck it, Jack. You're getting really good at kicking my butt."

"We both have a tendency to get emotionally involved with people we rescue—rightly or wrongly. But we also know how to separate our personal feelings from the facts when the time comes. It's in our genes, Sam. I still have that Marine mentality running through my veins, so I'm solid."

Sam sighs, giving in. "All right. Let me know if you need anything."

The call ends. Time to face the beast.

7

JACK

The W-Bot headquarters stands as a six-story structure in downtown L.A. On the outside, the building maintains its nineties aesthetic, which is not typically associated with innovative companies these days. According to some news articles, the building is bursting with W-Bot's rapid growth, so they're planning to relocate.

I step inside. The atmosphere is that of a typical tech company office—clean-cut, modern design, with open spaces adorned with eccentric, futuristic furniture.

I approach the receptionist, pretending to be interested in a job in building security.

"Do you have any experience?" the lady asks. "This is a senior role that requires at least five years of field experience."

"I worked as a PSC at various US installations overseas."

"Impressive." The lady nods, although her tentative face says she's unsure what PSC means. I guess it can refer to anything from Private Security Contractor to Paranoid Snake Charmer. She hands me a tablet and gestures toward the screen, saying, "Scan the QR code for the online form."

I pretend to scan it while studying the big, backlit W-Bot

logo behind her. "Has the company rebranded?" I ask casually.

"What do you mean?"

"The logo. It looks different."

The receptionist chuckles. "You have a sharp eye! Well, actually, the logo did change a few months ago."

"The background, does it represent a microchip or something?"

"Good guess, but not quite. You see, behind the 'B,' there's a faint sketch of Mr. Botha's profile. His fiancée drew it."

I squint, attempting to discern the lines. A company logo often reflects its owner as much as its philosophy. My question about rebranding would always be relevant—either the answer was a yes or a no. It was more sophisticated than asking bluntly, 'What does your logo mean?'

So, W-Bot not only bears Willem's name but also encapsulates his face. He is the central figure in everything, serving both the symbol and the substance. I wonder what Ava must've gone through when she decided to leave him. First, she chose freedom instead of riches. Second, she showed remarkable courage by breaking the chains of his control. She's stronger than steel, yet she's as delicate as a rose.

Acting like I'm completing the form on my phone, I take in my surroundings and listen to conversations. Willem is currently out for a lunch appointment. So, it seems the departed man has returned to satisfy his hunger, possibly craving his favorite sandwich.

I inform the receptionist that I've submitted my application, then leave the building. I immediately call Ava and tell her, "Willem is alive."

She gasps. "Oh, thank God!" She pauses to catch her breath. "Where is he?"

"I haven't seen him, but I just left the W-Bot headquarters and overheard his name being mentioned."

"Jesus, Jack. Don't let him see you."

"He's not there. But I'm applying for a position as a security guard."

"You didn't get the job on the spot, did you?"

I chuckle. "Look, he's apparently out for lunch. Do you know where he usually goes?"

"Either Flavio's or Mamasita, around the corner. Or, if he's with a client, he usually takes them to Fountain, two blocks away," she explains. Then she sighs, "Jack..."

"Yes, Ava?"

"I managed to sketch the kidnappers."

"Good job!"

"Sam has seen them, and he'll try to use face recognition to identify them. I'm going to send them to you now."

I open the message and gaze at the sketches. Just like her other works, the faces are astonishingly lifelike. The person has a thick beard and beady eyes, which are nearly engulfed by his equally bushy eyebrows. The other has a round face and full lips, giving off a strong, imposing vibe.

"We'll find Willem, and we'll track down these men. Then, we'll bring Quinton back home, I promise," I say through gritted teeth as I walk around the locality to investigate the three restaurants she suggested. At Fountain, I spot Willem walking through the door alone, then taking a seat at a table set for seven.

"Hey, I have to go," I say and end the call.

Dressed in a pinstripe suit, he blends in with the other businessmen in L.A. He's fit, probably a testament to his gym membership, and has a clean-shaven face with sleek black hair. He walks confidently, although he appears shorter than I initially imagined—maybe even shorter than Ava.

I enter the restaurant and request a table. After being presented with a few options, I choose one that provides both privacy and the ability to eavesdrop on their conversation. Without flinching at the steep prices, I place my order just like any ordinary customer. I suppose a prestigious three-star Michelin restaurant in the heart of Los Angeles is allowed to command such premiums.

While observing Willem, I fiddle with my phone, pretending to be engrossed in something important. Then, a new sketch arrives from Ava.

This time, it makes me smile.

I text her in response.

ME

So Sam's dog didn't eat your Elmo?

AVA

LOL. They're besties now.

My food arrives almost at the same time a group is arriving. Three men and their partners are being guided to Willem's table.

They exchange handshakes, and it becomes evident that Willem is the only one dining alone. His discomfort is palpable, especially as the conversation revolves around his upcoming wedding. He insists everything is going according to plan, but his repeated quick movements to hide his face tell a different story. He can hide from his guests, but from where I am, I can see his shattered ego.

The final blow comes when one of the guests asks about Ava's whereabouts. This man seeks revenge. It's why he took Quinton. It must be devastating for such a proud man to be deceived by his supposedly obedient fiancée.

By stirring the conversation to business, Willem seems to

have weathered the storm brewing inside him. He wears a friendly smile, occasionally showcasing his control. If it were just me and him, I would take pleasure in obliterating his skull, wiping away any trace of a smile. But the reality is, until Quinton is safe in Ava's arms, I can't lay a finger on him.

Willem seems even more relaxed as they discuss the development of W-Bot's new headquarters in Hawthorne. So that construction site I visited earlier is destined to be the new home for the company.

He casually remarks, "Well, it'll be more than a state-of-the-art facility. Even those powerful dark web mobs backed by the Russian oligarchs will pale compared to what we'll be capable of. I could hack the whole AT&T network like it was child's play."

The table falls into silence, all eyes fixed on him.

"Of course I'm only joking!" Willem exclaims, prompting laughter from everyone.

I take photos of the table and send them to Ava with a question.

ME

Do you know who those couples are?

AVA

The one wearing a purple dress is his architect, with her husband. The other guy is the city of LA's director of planning with his wife. The couple closest to him is the lieutenant governor of California and his wife.

ME

Nothing suspicious to you?

AVA

No. They meet regularly. Willem is building a
new HQ in Hawthorne. His future research
facility and factory. He used to joke that we
shouldn't be so reliant on Taiwan for
microchips. So far, they've only finished the
basement. But it's one of the most important
parts of the building.

ME

They were asking about you.

AVA

What did Willem say?

ME

You were busy preparing for the wedding.

It takes her a while to respond this time.

AVA

Soon, the world will know the truth.

Following a lavish three-course lunch and free-flowing
champagne, Willem pays the bill, and the group heads toward
the exit. I maintain a safe distance while monitoring their
movements, being cautious not to attract attention.

I quickly update Ava that they're leaving.

AVA

Tell me he doesn't recognize or suspect you.

ME

No. I'm clean. But since I know where Willem
is, I'm gonna give the house another shot.

AVA

Be careful, Jack. <3

I don't do emojis, but receiving that heart is inexplicably satisfying.

I lean against a pillar and continue to observe as Willem's guests depart in their separate cars. When Willem is alone, a man with a thick beard approaches him, the very same man depicted in Ava's sketch!

I capture several pictures of the encounter. Determined not to lose sight of them, I hurry back to my car and trail behind. Soon, I discover their destination is Willem's Beverly Hills residence. As they enter the complex through the front gate, I retreat to the broken hedge with my shades, mask, and gloves on. As if I had rehearsed my moves, I manage to get close enough to see the code to open the house's front door. I slip into a corner and wait, almost mimicking a potted tree towering beside me.

Finally, the two individuals return and depart from the estate. Armed with the acquired code, I cautiously enter the mansion. So this is how the other half live—or rather, the privileged two percent of Americans.

Numerous studies, living rooms, and libraries spread throughout. I don't have to imagine that this property belongs to Willem Botha; his presence is evident in every corner. The walls are adorned with exhibits showcasing his awards, framed photos capturing his achievements, and a dedicated wall displaying the chips produced by W-Bot, resembling a museum devoted to himself. Among the displays, there are also prominent photos of him with Ava and Quinton, carefully arranged like pieces of art in a gallery.

I head upstairs, where I discover even more libraries and a room equipped with a telescope and astronomy gadgets. The whole house feels so detached from reality that I don't even know what to make of it.

Next, I search the master bedroom, disregarding the fact

that it used to be Ava's when she was with Willem. I set my emotions aside and scan their belongings, including those in the walk-in closet, which is almost as big as my entire apartment in Oahu. But just like a meticulously cleaned five-star hotel room, Willem hasn't left anything useful behind.

Adjacent to the master bedroom is a door that remains locked. It doesn't use a conventional lock. Access requires the use of a swipe card.

Feeling slightly irritated, I move on to the next room—Quinton's nursery.

It's the first time I sense a touch of humanity in this house. The walls around me are adorned with charming murals of African animals, most likely Ava's creation. In every corner, colorful furniture and storage boxes light up the room. And that unmistakable baby powder scent...

Was Quinton here when Ava served Willem his tea? What went through her mind, carrying her baby for the last time in this house? Yet, there are no remnants of those moments. Like the rest of the house, everything appears impeccably neat, as if untouched by any past events.

My attention then falls on the twin-framed photos resting on a dresser, bearing the words 'before' and 'after.' One captures Ava heavily pregnant, while the other shows her cradling Quinton in a hospital room. Her face and hair are wet with perspiration, and Quinton still bears the mark of newborn blood. It must have been taken shortly after she gave birth.

My gloved fingertips trace the glass covers, and a new sense of responsibility washes over me. I've always envisioned my future solely with the Marine Corps until the day I die. My duty has always been to my country and the brave men ready to defend it. A woman, let alone a family, has never factored into that equation.

I gaze at Ava's radiant face in the photos. People will call it a mother's glow, but to me, it's like a lighthouse guiding me out of the darkness. When I'm out of here, when Quinton is safely back in his mother's arms, I've got to rethink the straight path I've carved before this moment. Because I know this paternal instinct that I never thought existed in me will not go away.

I call Ava. "I've searched around the house. I can't find anything. Is there a basement here?"

"No. The garage is the lowest level."

"An attic?"

"Neither. The highest room is Willem's stargazing room."

"I've already checked there," I murmur. "By the way, the W-Bot receptionist mentioned your sketch of Willem in the company logo."

Ava lets out a frustrated sigh. "He made me do it. But to his credit, I think the logo looks tasteful."

I chuckle. Suddenly, I hear noises. "Shit! He's back."

"Just hide, Jack. As long as you're not in the bedroom or his study, you'll be fine."

"I'm in Quinton's room."

"He may or may not go there. There's an extra bedroom next to it that the babysitter used. Try hiding behind the corner armchair there."

I quickly make my way to the suggested hiding spot, barely managing to fit myself. Fortunately, whoever is inside the house doesn't even venture up to the second floor and leaves shortly after.

With no new discoveries in my search, I trace my way out empty-handed but filled with fresh nuggets of emotion.

I report back to Sam, and he then fills me in on his findings based on Ava's sketches of the kidnappers. The round-faced man, who has been identified as a resident of Helena, has a history of being involved in kidnapping cases in Montana, Utah, and Wyoming.

"How about the bearded one?" I ask.

"We're still looking for him."

"He's here with Willem. I'll send you photos. My guess is he's from California. He seems close with Willem."

"Every powerful man has his puppet."

"Sam, I don't believe Quinton is in L.A. The round-faced man and Quinton are still in Montana. Most likely, they have more accomplices, probably including a woman."

"We'll keep working on it."

I explain, "I think they're planning to make a demand soon, but they want to do it outside of California. Willem and Ava may not be celebrities yet, but they are recognizable here. But in Montana? Ava is unknown—and you can easily find a location where you can commit a murder without anyone knowing. Plus, it would simplify the logistics. Ava is already there, so she doesn't have to travel and risk being seen."

Sam agrees with my analysis. He then asks, "When are you flying back?"

"It's late. I probably won't be able to catch a flight tonight. I'll follow Willem some more. See what he's up to. Tell Ava I'll call her soon, and I'll see you all tomorrow."

Ava is currently surrounded by people who genuinely care for her. Staying here another night wouldn't make much of a difference. But she's a mother desperately waiting for the safe return of her baby. Reflecting on my own mother's inability to cope when she lost me, I know that even one night matters greatly. I'll make sure she doesn't feel alone tonight, even if I have to be on the phone with her till morning.

8

———

AVA

My eyes are wide open, as if I just downed six cups of coffee in one go. I have been without my baby for three days, and I'm losing my mind. Without the weight of his little body against me, life feels devoid of any goodness. I feel numb, unable to hear his laughter or see his face scrunch up when he cries. The absence of his soothing suckling has left my breasts aching with emptiness.

Jack tried to console me last night during our call, but there was only so much he could do. His voice, though he meant well, only served to make me miss him more.

"He's coming," Sam assures me as I repeatedly sit and rise from his living room couch in the past hour. "Once his plane has landed, I'll drive you to Belgrade, your new safe home. And he'll meet you there."

I nod, still worrying about Quinton and thinking about Jack.

"You know he'll do anything for you and Quinton," Sam continues.

"That's comforting, Sam. But to be honest, that worries me too," I admit.

"He knows what he's doing, and you have no reason to feel guilty about it," he tells me as if he can read my thoughts.

"I just don't want him to think this is the only way to redeem himself."

"Maybe he does. But that doesn't mean he'll be careless."

I mentioned it because I can see how desperate Jack is to prevent what happened to him from happening to anyone else, especially my baby. Honestly, Jack doesn't have anything to redeem for.

Silence falls. My mind is like a restless pendulum, swinging back and forth between Jack and Quinton. Sam has reassured me countless times that it's unlikely for Willem to harm Quinton, and I believe him. But there's still that small 'what if' lingering in the back of my mind. Besides, there's no one else who can look after my baby as well as I can. Quinton should be with me, not with some random person hired by Willem. On the other hand, I don't want Jack to sacrifice himself for us.

In a bid to distract myself, I ask, "What happened to him, Sam? I mean, Jack had told me about his kidnapping, but he didn't tell me exactly how. When we were in Bozeman, we mostly talked about the aftermath, like how we perceived birthdays differently. I had fond memories of mine, while he didn't have any recollection at all."

Sam sits beside me. "I'm surprised he talked about his birthday with you. He hated it. It took some convincing from me, Cass, Grace, and our father, but he finally agreed to have his thirtieth celebration with us."

I scoff. "He told me that, too."

Sam then laces his fingers in front of him. "Well, to be honest, a lot still remains unresolved. I'll tell you what I know. As you're aware, we're originally from New York. That day, we were in Syracuse, just being kids at the fairground over Labor

Day weekend. We both wanted to go on a rollercoaster ride, but he was too short."

"He was too short?" I say in disbelief. How did he grow to the size of a tower?

"Yeah," Sam chuckles. "So, I rode alone, and he stayed with our father. When the ride was over, I couldn't find either of them. I searched and searched, only to find my dad surrounded by police, but Jack was nowhere to be found."

He pauses, his hand trembling as he clears his throat, then waves at me to wait. The event, though it occurred when he was a child, is still clearly raw for him. He rises from the couch, facing the window, searching for the sun as it peeks over the landscape surrounding this country house.

His voice is slow and deliberate as he recounts, "Jack slipped from our father's grip while the old man was busy taking photographs of me. Someone in the crowd just grabbed my little brother and dragged him away, maybe even sedated him so he couldn't scream or fight back."

Jack could have been sedated in many ways, but my mind instinctively deduces it, and my neck pulsates involuntarily, as if a syringe pierced my jugular vein.

After a moment, Sam returns to my side, saying, "Years passed, and the only evidence we had was Jack's bloodstained clothes. The case was eventually closed, and he was presumed dead."

"That must've been devastating."

"I never believed it, and I was goddamn right. We still don't have much information. Jack's memory is practically non-existent. But I know he was wounded, maybe even tortured. And he was definitely drugged, mercilessly."

The revelation hurts me. "I don't know how he copes. God... he's done well to absorb all that. If you spoke to him, you wouldn't have known, would you?"

"He still has a lot to reconcile with himself. Be gentle with him."

Suddenly, Sam's phone rings, interrupting our conversation. He doesn't say much, but I understand. Jack has landed.

AFTER A COVERT TRANSFER from Sam's house to our new safe house in Belgrade, we wait. Elmo paces around us like a satellite, his nails clicking against the hardwood floor, in rhythm with our own nervous energy. Jack should have arrived by now.

Then, the distant hum of a car reaches our room, causing Sam and I to spring to our feet. Though I know the car is there and the engine has stopped, my surroundings are taken over by the jumbled voices of the two brothers, blended with Elmo's barks.

In a blur of movement, I find myself enveloped in Jack's arms.

"Ava, you okay?" His voice is as gentle as his hold.

"Jack... you're back," I whisper, the words more for my own solace than for him. I press against his chest, needing to feel him to confirm his presence. And there he is, as tangible as flesh and muscle, despite the darkness of his suit jacket.

"Come inside," Sam urges, breaking the spell.

In response, Jack guides me in while never fully releasing his grip. We settle in the living room of the safe house, and Jack helps me find a seat. As my mind gradually quiets, I can finally take in the full sight of Jack before me. A different kind of whirlwind holds me captive.

I'm compelled to momentarily set aside the grim reality we've been facing and immerse myself in the breathtaking scene that unfolds before me. Jack stands tall, his hands resting on my waist. His face is marred with concern, but boy, his whole body exudes handsomeness that can only come from the Kelleher genes. He's wearing a borrowed suit, with the absence of a tie, but he looks as if he's stepped straight out of a scene from the TV show "Suits."

"What took you so long!" Sam opens the conversation.

"Taxi got a flat tire," Jack reveals.

Sam peeks out, rechecking the vehicle Jack drove to get here. "But you took that car from the motel I told you about, right?"

"I'm not an idiot, Sam! I took a cab to the motel and drove here—wasn't that what we discussed?"

"You're here," I say. "That's all that matters." My fingertips glide over the damp fabric of his chest as his restlessness grows amid the tension between him and his brother. They're both tired, I can tell.

"I guess the suit makes up for your tardiness," Sam jokes as I help Jack remove his jacket. Sweat clings to his shirt, evidence of the physical and mental strain he carries.

Sam heats up some pre-made meals from the fridge, and we have a late lunch.

He then packs his things, saying, "I've left a laptop in the bedroom. If you need to revisit any CCTV footage, that's your go-to machine. Call me if you need anything else. And there's still plenty more food in the fridge and pantry. Don't order pizza!"

With that, Sam waves us goodbye.

Jack inputs a security code at the door to lock it. Obviously, he has been briefed. He then turns to me, "You need some sleep. I thought you were going to pass out when I got here."

I simply plop myself on the couch. "I don't even know where the bedroom is. And I don't really want to sleep."

"Rest here then." He guides me to lie flat across the long

couch. Then he spots Quinton's giraffe teether resting on the side table. He pauses but stops short at showing his reaction.

My body sighs in anguish. "He must be anxious to play with it again. He must be crying." Those words make me wither as if life drains out through my pores.

Jack reaches for a throw blanket, draping it over me. He leans closer, and his fingertips caress my arm. "Hang in there."

I bring my hand to my tired face, trying to compose myself. Jack rises from his seat, but I reach out and grasp his hand, halting his departure.

"I need to change," he says.

If it were any other man, I would have requested a shower. But with Jack, his scent pulls me in. Somehow, his perspiration becomes a symbol of his unwavering dedication to me. He has earned his place in my heart, the whole him—blood, sweat, and tears.

"Please, stay," I implore meekly, shifting myself in to give him room on the couch. He settles down beside my legs, his hand caressing my thigh.

"You know, Ava, when we were in Bozeman, you told me how after a day in court, sometimes you'd spend the night reflecting on the faces you drew," Jack recalls.

"That's right."

"And you didn't enjoy cases where it was a David versus Goliath battle. Especially during long trials when you noticed the expressions of the innocent ones deteriorating. Didn't you say, sometimes, you wished you could tell them not to give up?" he adds.

I chuckle, impressed that he actually remembers. Then I explain, "I never allowed my emotions to interfere with my work. It was my job to separate my thoughts from what was presented to me. Occasionally, I sympathized with some of the people. I'm only human. But it only happened when I was away from my pastels and paper."

Jack nods understandingly. "What I wanted to say is... that's how I feel right now. I want to be the one in your corner, telling you not to give up. I know it's easier said than done, but you can't lose faith," he says earnestly.

I rub his arm, grateful for his support. "We had some interesting conversations back then," I muse.

"We did," he murmurs, gently stroking each of my fingers. "Remember when you said tall men have slower reflexes?"

"It's true!" I insist. "The longer your limbs, the longer it takes for signals to travel from your brain."

"No, Ava. Come on! I defeated you in every game of ball toss!" Jack defends himself, playfully reaching over to tickle me. "See!"

I attempt to repel his rapid attacks, but I find myself unable to keep up. I let out a giggle and wriggle around. "Alright! Alright!"

A satisfied smile spreads across his face as he looks at me. "That's what I wanted to see."

We laugh some more, and then I remind him slowly, "I almost fell asleep in your room that night."

"Why did you move?"

"I was pregnant, you silly!"

His 'yeah' is barely audible, but the intensity in his eyes speaks volumes. "Did you wish you had slept in my bed? That maybe... we had gone further?"

I sigh. "I did."

"My kidnapping didn't bother you?"

"Why should it?"

He tilts his head, exhaling. "Well, I've succeeded in distracting you, haven't I?"

I give his hand a squeeze. I do feel better, while he's apparently ready to move on from where our conversation in Bozeman has left off. I steer our chat to the more current matter. "Hey, what else did you find in L.A.?"

"It wasn't exactly a new discovery," he says with a hint of frustration in his voice. "But being there, sitting just feet away from Willem, I managed to gather some clues."

The mention of that name sends an involuntary shiver down my spine. "What are those clues?"

"I don't believe Quinton is anywhere near him. He looked far too casual, and he didn't go anywhere else apart from his office, some restaurants to eat and meet people, then home."

"I think you're right. Not that he's a hands-on father anyway."

"Look, I've seen cases where very young children were taken. The kidnappers usually hired female help."

Anger surges through my muscles, causing my body to jolt upright as if I were a corpse suddenly brought back to life. "Another woman is taking care of my child?" Frustration fills my voice. If Willem were here, I would have punched him square in the face!

But Jack, ever the calming presence, soothes my racing emotions. "We haven't had a hit with that round-faced man. It has to be a woman showing up in various places—buying diapers, milk, food, gas, anything they may need for the trip, and the baby," he explains, his tone understanding. "Yes, Willem's men may have left L.A. well-prepared, but with young children, there's always something you need to get, isn't there? Am I right?"

His words placate me, as if he's already been a father before, an empathetic figure to his child's mother.

"Yes," I reply, my voice softening. "But how have they managed to remain hidden? Quinton is a fussy baby. He doesn't warm up to people easily. Even Morgan struggled to handle him."

Jack nods, lost in his own thoughts, until his phone suddenly buzzes in his pocket.

"Hang on, Sam," he answers. "I'm going to put you on speaker."

I stoop forward as if I would miss a thing if I'm too far, my stance rigid. Then we hear Sam. "Jack, Ava. There's a development. Completely unrelated, but it might be one of our strongest leads so far."

"Sam, tell us!" Jack's voice is low and concise.

"The police have found a seventeen-year-old girl from Wyoming with a baby boy who's about the same age as Quinton."

The possibility makes my stomach churn, but something concerns me. "I thought we agreed not to involve the police!" I protest.

Sam carries on, "She was reported missing three weeks ago. It's an ongoing Red Mark case, and the police have been in on it from the beginning. The girl insists it's her son. But as far as we know, there was no mention of a baby with her until today."

I grip Jack's hand, begging, "Take me there!"

"No, Ava!" Jack stops me from getting up. "Calm down."

My body has become a mass of fatigue and disarray. I can't feel my own existence or even the presence of Jack. The void of sensation bears down on me, and I collapse onto the couch.

"Ava, stay with me," Finally, Jack's voice brings me back from my state of detachment. His hand envelopes mine, clinging like my digits are wrapped in a snug glove.

"You two wait there," Sam instructs. "I'll have Cora-Lee stream Ben's body cam footage to your phone."

Jack opens an app on his phone and starts streaming. It's

like watching a police operation on a TV show, except it's real. My heart pounds intensely, but so far, all I see is a group of police officers.

"Ben, we need visuals on the baby," Sam relays. Ben is part of the Red Mark team and is also Sam's brother-in-law, Cass' brother.

Ben replies, "The baby is safe. He's with child services. They haven't given him a name yet." We watch Ben sprint outside the house, urgently calling the paramedics as they prepare to shut the ambulance doors.

I close my eyes, drowning out all other sounds, focusing solely on the cries of the baby. My lips purse, the sound confusing me.

Ben persuades the child services lady to reveal the baby's face. "I just want to make sure he's okay, please." His desperation latches on me. "I rescued him. I need to know."

The lady presents the baby to Ben, the camera capturing the delicate features.

I release a sharp breath. "It's not Quinton," I utter in despair. The anticipation, so immense, causes bile to rise in my throat. I sprint, miraculously stumbling upon the bathroom in this unfamiliar house. And then, I retch, emptying my stomach.

"Ava..." Jack rushes to my side. He gently gathers my hair, holding it back from my face, while his fingertips trail soothingly along my spine.

My ass rests on the cold bathroom floor while Jack takes a damp towel and wipes my mouth.

"I'm so sorry," he murmurs, his voice filled with genuine remorse.

"I can't... I can't go on without him, Jack," I quaver. "He's a part of me. He's my entire life!"

"I understand, sweetheart."

I would ask 'how could you possibly know?' but his words carry so much pain that I wonder if he has absorbed mine and truly understands.

"You know, Jack. Many cancer survivors struggle to have children. I'm one of the fortunate ones who's blessed with strong fertility despite my leukemia."

He gives my hand a tender squeeze. "You were meant to be a mother."

"And I need to be with my baby," I shoot him a desperate look. "One more day without him, and I'll lose my sanity."

With a gentle gesture, he brings my hand to his chest, placing it over his left pec as if offering me his strength. "I promise I will do whatever it takes to bring Quinton back into your arms." His voice breaks with emotion.

Trembling, I reach out and grasp his other hand, squeezing it tightly against my left breast. His presence brings a rush of darkness and light at the same time. Foreheads pressed together, his lips so close, I can almost taste the oasis in this desert of despair. With half a breath, our lips meet, and it becomes more than just a kiss. It becomes a necessity, a lifeline.

In Bozeman, I had yearned for this moment, imagining the heat and passion of our connection as I admired his physique from afar. We didn't sleep in the same room, only letting out our affection like we were just friends. Now, this kiss exceeds my wildest dreams. It is a primal need, a salvation for my shattered soul. It grounds me, keeps me alive. And he willingly gives it to me.

Every girl wishes their first kiss to be romantic, earth-shattering. But my first kiss with Jack is more than just a physical act. It's magnetic, binding us together on multiple levels.

Jack's hand cradles the back of my neck, and I reciprocate, pulling him closer. As we break the kiss, our breath coming in ragged gasps. We don't need words to communicate; we feel each other's pain and determination. When my own strength wavers, this man reminds me of the indomitable power within every mother.

This brief respite allows me to gather myself. Then, like a bolt of lightning, a thought strikes me. "Jack...you said there was likely a woman involved?"

"Yes."

"My babysitter."

His hum whirs low in his throat. "Who paid her?"

"Willem. And I remember. A few weeks before I left L.A., she asked for a raise and more hours. She said her brother was in debt. Could it be her?"

"Damn... we should start looking for her instead of that round-faced man!" he asserts.

I press my forehead wearily. "How could she..."

With a concerned look, Jack suggests, "Why not rest while I have a conversation with Sam?"

"I don't want to sleep alone."

His expression changes. "Wait for me in the bedroom. I won't be long."

Why do I sense he's not comfortable with the idea of sharing a bed with me?

I speak hesitantly, "Jack, you don't have to—"

"I won't be long, okay?" His head whips around as if trying to hide the fact that he's terrified.

9

JACK

My hands press against the damp wall, its rough texture grazing my skin. A tangled garden surrounds this underground space, and the relentless rain has turned the soil into a muddy barrier, blocking the only ventilation. As I inhale the rancid, mold-filled air, the door creaks open, revealing a silhouette. The wind disturbs his long hair as he reaches up to the back of his neck, concealing something.

I frantically scratch at the peeling paint on the wall, the gritty surface grating against my fingertips. In a matter of seconds, the figure engulfs me, and a searing pain shoots through my shoulder blades as if my spine is being exposed. I squirm, desperate to scream for help.

In a gasp, my eyes fly open to the sight of daylight. A friendly canine face greets me, a pink tongue eagerly licking my face. I let out a relieved huff, grateful that I didn't reach the part where my screams would have roared and woken up everyone.

When Ava invited me to sleep with her in the same bed, I felt honor and joy. Yet, this nightmare is the one thing I dreaded.

"Good dog, Elmo," I whisper, patting his head, which only fuels his enthusiasm to lick me more. "All right, all right. You don't want to wake her up now, do you?" I glance at Ava, who's still sound asleep.

Slowly, I lift myself, catching my breath. *Damn you, Scalpel!*

Elmo fidgets on my lap, his fluffy tail wagging like the spinning wheel of an express bus. Meanwhile, Ava starts to stir, turning toward me with her arm reaching up to my shoulder. "You okay?" she rasps.

"I'm fine. Go back to sleep." I brush her hand aside, but as she feels the dampness on my palm, she wakes up fully.

"You're sweating!" she exclaims, patting my body. Her gaze then falls on a patch on my tank top. "Is it too hot in here?"

Not really, but I certainly look like a man who just stepped out of a gym. "I'm fine, Ava."

Elmo leaps onto my chest, his nose pointed at my face, ready to lick me again.

"Elmo, come on, go easy on him," Ava says. "How did he manage to get onto the bed?" She stretches to see my side and realizes the dog used my bag as a launching pad.

"Let him stay." I pat Elmo's head. "Good dog."

Resting against the bedhead, Ava smiles, observing us. "The vet at the shelter said Elmo wouldn't live past four. I had the option to cancel his adoption, but I loved him too much. He's six now, and he's still going strong."

I wipe my face, clearing the remnants of Elmo's kisses, then help the mutt off the bed.

"I guess it's proof that love can keep anything alive," I quip.

Ava's azure eyes lock with mine, her love radiating like a lifeline that will sustain me for a hundred years. With restrained lust, I lean in to kiss her, wanting to confirm that yesterday wasn't a fleeting moment. Oh yes, she craves more. Yesterday's kiss was pure bliss, a taste of heaven. Now, as our lips meet again, a subtle dance of tongues ignites an irresistible heat.

Her body slowly sinks down until her back meets the mattress. I hover over her, propping myself up on my elbows. Our lips stay locked while her hands eagerly run over my abs. Then, they trail behind my back, gliding up along my spine until they reach the spot between my shoulder blades.

I arch my back. It doesn't bother me that she's touching my scar, but the moment feels tainted as my mind wanders momentarily to the dark figure in my nightmare.

Ava pulls away slightly, her expression reflecting the realization that we've rushed into things. She has a lot on her mind, more than what I'm trying to conceal.

"Sorry," she murmurs.

"Yeah." I roll over to her side.

"I wanted it, Jack, but I don't think the timing is right," she explains.

I stroke her cheek, feeling a tingling sensation from the contact. "I wanted it too, but you're right."

She lifts herself a little, just enough to reach my lips.

"You up for breakfast?" I offer.

"I don't feel like eating anything. You go."

I hold her. "Ava Belle."

She cocks a brow. "Ava Belle?"

"Look. You promise to take care of yourself. You didn't have dinner last night."

"Okay. I'll have a banana." She gives in. Then she tilts her head. "Why did you call me Ava Belle?"

I nod toward her T-shirt featuring Belle from *Beauty and the Beast*. "I didn't know you were into Disney."

She lets out a giggle. "It's Cass' tee."

Of course. When Sam took her to his place, they didn't bring anything with them.

Ava adds, "Apparently, they had a Disney-themed Christmas a few years ago at the request of Grace. This one looked comfy, so I picked it from the pile Cass offered me." She pauses then mutters, "Ava Belle, eh?"

"You don't like it? I'll stick to the standard 'sweetheart' then."

She twists her lips. "Have you ever called me sweetheart?"

"Haven't I?" I have, many times, but perhaps not when she's fully awake.

A grin accentuates her cute morning face. "I like it. I mean, both Ava Belle and sweetheart."

I peck her soft, pink lips before throwing off the covers and moving myself to sit at the edge of the bed.

Ava caresses my bare skin, prompting me to quiver. No doubt she has found my scar again, but as if she understands, she doesn't ask.

Years of my life have been devoted to the Corps and to finding the man responsible for ruining my childhood. My encounters with women have been purely physical, lacking any emotional attachment. But now, a force named Ava West has stripped me bare. In her presence, beyond a few sentimental photos, my yearning to commit myself to her deepens. And it feels damn special.

Some may argue this is simply a man's instinct to protect, a trait that has existed since the beginning of time. But for someone who barely survived the horrors of abduction, tortured and turned into a shell of a human, my dedication to Ava goes beyond natural. It's extraordinary.

We sit at the breakfast table, and Ava agrees to share a banana smoothie with me. As she takes a sip, she asks, "Why is Willem doing this? If he wants me back, just take me. Why make Quinton go through this?"

Her eyes search mine for answers. At that moment, a vivid image of Willem's smile at that restaurant flashes before me.

I reply, "He wants revenge. Firstly, *you* left him. Imagine the humiliation. His own fiancée ran away with *his* baby? And when people discover that *his* wedding isn't going to go ahead? Ava, his ego will stop at nothing."

She shakes her head as if she's found an answer—a painful one. But even so, her eyes still look so stunning. "Maybe it's more than ego." Her face is full of thoughts. "And he may not want me back. You know, Jack. Willem's mother left him when he was six. His father remarried and had another child with his new wife. Willem left home shortly after that to live with his grandfather. He never explained what really happened—whether his father didn't want to take care of him anymore, or he was simply jealous."

"So Willem wants to teach you a lesson for leaving?"

She sighs deeply. "What do we do now?"

Last night, the Red Mark men scoured possible areas where Quinton's kidnapper might have taken him. They also tried to find any sightings of the babysitter, but so far, they've found nothing.

"We'll widen the search," I assert.

"Willem hired the babysitter because of her glowing reviews. I agreed to hire her because I thought she was good with Quinton and she was tidy. She was really tidy. Perhaps that made her able to cover her tracks every time."

"Maybe. And, we may need to start thinking about involving the police."

She shakes her head adamantly. "No!"

"Look, I heard from Sam that Red Mark has a good relationship with the Helena PD captain. They work together many times. We can trust him."

Ava nods. "In that case, we just have to trust that Willem won't do anything to Quinton."

"He won't." Despite my initial assessment of Willem and how much I hate that man, he's not Scalpel. I don't believe he's capable of hurting his own son.

Ava's fingers tap at the empty glass where the smoothie was. She then asks, "Jack, can I see those photos you took in L.A.? Those of the bearded man talking to Willem?"

I scramble for my phone and show her the photo she requested.

Ava squints at the image and questions, "Is that his car? Way in the background?"

That gets me thinking. "I didn't see him coming from or going into that car, but why did you think so?"

"In some of the CCTV footage that Sam had, you know, when I was dumped at that park. He drove a similar car."

Realization strikes me. I reach for the laptop Sam has left in this house, analyzing the footage Ava is referring to. "My God, you're right." Comparing it to the photo on my phone, I catch a rental car sticker on the windshield. And even though it's blurry, I can make out the registration number on the photo I took. "Ava, you're brilliant!"

10

JACK

Sam and I meet at the Red Mark headquarters while his wife Cass stays with Ava at the safe house. Although I've heard about the facilities here, I've only seen a small part of the complex. The meeting room we're in is impressive, with a large glass table and luxurious leather chairs. It's equipped with electronic boards and teleconference gadgets that would make the military green with envy. Red Mark is backed by two wealthy investors—the very people Sam and his business partner, Mark Connor, protected when they still worked as bodyguards in New York. But beyond the finances, my brother has done well.

Sam brings up a map on the screen and starts marking a few locations digitally.

"What am I looking at?" I ask.

"I checked the rental car company. The car had been returned to their depot in L.A. And these are the places where the bearded man refueled." Sam's finger glides across the glassy surface of the screen.

I look at his tired eyes and ask, "You found all this by yourself?"

"Of course!" Sam responds with confidence. "Although I wish Cora-Lee was here. It's been like working with one arm tied behind my back without her."

"Where's she?"

"She's in the hospital for sinus surgery."

"I hope she's okay," I express my worry. Cora-Lee is a tech genius who can locate anything as long as it's stored digitally.

Sam refocuses on the map and adds, "All these places are en route between L.A. and Helena. Except this one." He puts a red circle on Townsend, a town about thirty miles southeast of Helena.

I praise him with a pat on his shoulder. "I'm gonna check it out."

"Be careful, and keep your distance."

"As far as our enemies are concerned, I'm Jack Benedict. I don't know Ava, I don't know you."

"Good." Sam nods, gesturing for me to go.

I ask, "Do you have men on standby in case Quinton is there?"

"I've got your back, Jack. Call me when you find something."

Grabbing my jacket, I leave the meeting room. I make my way toward the basement exit, the same way I entered earlier today. This exit leads to an adjacent building where I parked my car, trying to preserve my dissociation with Red Mark for as long as I can. As I drive out cautiously, my eyes dart around, constantly on the lookout for any signs of someone following me. Satisfied, I head straight to Townsend.

Upon arriving, I question my enemy's choice of this hiding place. Townsend seems more like a holiday destination than a suitable location to conceal a baby. The Big Belt Mountains envelop the town on its west side, and the Missouri River flows nearby. Nonetheless, just like a lot of spots in Montana, the isolation of a place can make it an advantage for criminals.

I decide to stop by the town center to fill up with gas. The old man behind the counter has a boat-captain look that reminds me of a face from cruise advertisements back in Oahu. He quotes the price, "Thirty-five fifty." Then he makes eye contact. "Visiting today?"

"Um...yeah. Actually, I'm not really sure where I'm going. I'm looking for my sister, she's just moved here. But we lost contact, and I don't really know her address."

"Hmm. We're a small community, and there aren't that many newcomers here."

I show him a photo and ask, "Have you seen her? She would be with a baby."

"I'm sorry, young man, I can't remember." He glances at me as he puts away the cash I just handed to him.

Deciding that the man at the store was unlikely to cooperate, I leave without asking any more questions. I keep driving around, and eventually, I come across a bookstore that also sells toys. If Quinton is here, maybe the babysitter bought something from this store.

As I gaze at the friendly face of the cashier from outside, an idea springs to mind.

Before entering the store, I create a new contact on my phone using the photo of the babysitter that Ava helped me find. There's nothing out of the ordinary about her. Greta Hall is a twenty-five-year-old college dropout who has spent her whole life in L.A. Her primary source of income has been babysitting, supplemented by occasional work at supermarkets and hotels.

The bookshop lady greets me with a wide smile. When she offers assistance, I politely decline, stating that I'm just browsing. I peruse the shelves, but none of the books catch my attention. However, determined not to leave empty-handed, I pick up a plush toy from a basket.

"Isn't it adorable?" the lady says. "It's your lucky day. This is the last one!"

"Very popular, obviously."

"Well, I actually just ordered two of them. They're these beautiful handmade items from Kenya. The first one got sold right away to a lovely lady who wanted it for her baby."

"I'm actually buying this for my nephew. Coincidentally, my sister has recently moved here! Maybe I'm buying it for the same baby?"

"Oh, that little boy absolutely loves giraffes, doesn't he?"

"Was he upset when he was here? I heard from my sister they lost his favorite toy—and no surprise, it was a giraffe."

"Maybe you're right." The lady chuckles as she wraps the toy.

I continue the conversation. "I'm from L.A. I have no idea where I am, and my sister isn't answering my calls. I'm looking for this address." I show her the babysitter's contact I just created, purposely exposing the photo and the name and address I made up.

"Well, I don't know where she lives, but that address doesn't look familiar. No wonder you couldn't find it. But look, Townsend is a small place. Maybe if you just drive around, you'll find her."

I thank the lady and continue. I meticulously search every street in town, but nothing jumps out at me. My last option is to venture toward the outskirts, closer to the river.

There's not much out here, mostly farms. However, my attention is drawn to a small, worn-out house. Behind a pile of discarded items on the front porch, I notice the handle of a stroller peeking out.

Since there's no one around, I step into the front yard to

investigate the house's exterior. All the windows are covered with newspaper from the inside, allowing me only a small gap to peek through.

Goodness gracious!

There is a crib with a neatly folded blanket and carefully stacked pillow. If there was such a thing as five-star house-keeping for a baby bed, this would be it. But my eyes lock onto the giraffe plush toy in the corner of the mattress, the twin to the one I just purchased. The back door is unlocked, and I let myself in.

No one's here. That could mean Quinton had been transported somewhere else, or they were merely out. I believe the latter as the house doesn't feel abandoned.

I could wait for the group to return, hoping that Quinton would be with them. But I don't know the exact number of people. There are no indications regarding how many pairs of shoes or the amount of plates and glasses that have been used. The junk out on the porch looks to belong to the previous owner or someone else. It's old. Everything inside is tidy.

Ava mentioned that the babysitter was meticulous, potentially possessing an obsessive-compulsive tendency to ensure everything is in order, or else she would become unhinged. Maybe this has been one of the reasons why the group has been moving around undetected.

I've never held a baby in my life, let alone rescued one. Everything will become that much more delicate when a tiny human is involved. Quinton will be completely defenseless while I fight the kidnappers. It's likely that Quinton will stay with the babysitter, and I can't just overpower her as I would an adult criminal. So there's a high chance she could escape with the baby, and then I'd be back to square one.

Feeling uneasy, I decide not to leave any evidence of my

presence and drive away before calling Sam. Almost at the same time, Sam contacts me.

I start, "They're here, in Townsend."

"Is Quinton with them?"

"No one's in the house, but I know it's their hiding place."

"Well, we've received a demand from Willem," Sam reveals.

There's a thump behind my chest, echoing like the resounding finale of my beating heart. We've been waiting for this, yet it's unsettling me to my core. "How?"

"While Ben was investigating in North Helena, a passing motorcyclist threw a bag at him. Inside the bag was a letter demanding that Ava go to an address between Clancy and Jefferson City."

"Where is that?" I question.

"It's about time you familiarized yourself with Montana!" Sam says. "It's fifteen miles south of Helena."

"I'll check it out."

"No. Come back here, and we'll plan this carefully."

My brother is right.

Since Sam found me, when I'm not on duty, I have dedicated every waking moment to finding the person responsible for destroying my childhood. I haven't succeeded, but in the process, I've aided in the safe return of three missing children in unrelated cases. I knew my efforts were not in vain. However, now that it's my duty to rescue the flesh and blood of the woman I love, it's a different situation. Failing myself is one thing, but failing her?

Failure is never an option as a Marine. With her, it becomes even more imperative.

11

AVA

The safe house feels more like a gloomy jury room, filled with indecision as deliberation stretches beyond ordinary hours. Sam, Jack, and I still haven't reached a consensus on how to approach tomorrow. The brothers express their concerns about me facing Willem's men or even Willem himself. They're proposing alternative strategies, but for me, there is no other option.

"I have to be there!" I insist. "We're talking about my son's life here. I'm not being impulsive or deluded. Willem wants me, so I will be there. And I will find a way, even if the two of you try to stop me."

Sam says, "Ava, I understand, we're all behind you, but—"

"I'm heading to Clancy to meet whoever is waiting for me there," I determine. I can feel myself becoming confrontational toward Sam, who has always been the voice of reason.

Jack steps forward and manages to calm me down. He takes a moment, then determines, "Ava should go alone."

The statement leaves Sam speechless, his eyes locked on Jack. I can't believe what I'm hearing either, but I know Jack will support me no matter what.

He explains further, "That property is away from the town itself. Yet it's open. If we send too many people, it will only raise suspicion. Our best chance of rescuing Quinton is if Ava goes alone."

"Are you crazy?" Sam protests.

"Crazy enough that our enemies would never guess what we're up to," he counters. "Ava should go alone, but we'll wire her."

"Okay," I agree despite being rattled inside. So many things could go wrong, but this solo mission is something I absolutely cannot mess up.

Jack then adds, "And one of us should stay close enough to reach her and Quinton if things go wrong."

"What do you mean one of us?" Sam inquires.

Jack takes a seat beside me, his fingers steepled. "Willem is not going to make this easy. When I was in L.A., I sat just a few tables away from him, and I could taste his thirst for revenge. He'll make sure he's the only one winning. He's a man who believes everything revolves around him. I bet he's going to deceive us. It's possible that you won't see Quinton in Clancy tomorrow."

Sam inhales, contemplating. He reluctantly nods in agreement. "So what's the plan?"

"The house in Townsend is their real base. That white van caught by the cameras from the nearby farm is the same as the van that took Ava and Quinton at the hospital. While the rental car used by the bearded man had been returned to a depot in New York, the group is still using the same vehicle. It's how they transport Quinton around."

Sam nods repeatedly while listening to Jack's explanation.

Jack adds, "Yes, that Clancy property is quiet. No one would know if you committed a murder. But that Townsend house is surrounded by a forest. Missouri River is nearby if they want to escape another way."

Sam seems impressed by Jack's newfound knowledge of the areas, especially after teasing him about not being familiar with Montana. It's amazing how much Jack has learned in just a few hours.

"I trust your instincts, Jack," I say, showing my support.

"Now Willem's men have two places to take care of. None of them are aware that we know about Townsend, so it's likely that the place won't be as heavily guarded as Clancy.

"So, who's going where?" Sam asks.

Jack glances at me, heaviness hanging on his face. He tells his brother, "Give us a minute, won't you?"

Sam smiles. "Take your time." He brushes his brother's shoulder and duly leaves the room.

Still seated beside me, Jack turns toward me, his expression tense. "I have a bad feeling about this deal. He will stop at nothing to hurt you. My life and career depend on my ability to read people, and I know I'm right about him."

"He can hurt me all he wants, but not Quinton."

I shift my gaze away from Jack, reminiscing the extent of violence Willem can carry. When that wretched man proposed to me, he painted a picture of an everlasting, unparalleled love between us. I had run away from him once before, but he seemed like a new man when he made that promise. It made me question if that was what true love meant—a man was willing to change for me, for us. But it wasn't love, and I accepted his proposal because I needed help with my pregnancy.

Jack, who has patiently waited for me, finally speaks up. "I've never seen a man with such bitterness in his expression when talking about his woman. He hid it from his guests, but he couldn't hide it from me. He will try to hurt you in the worst possible way."

There's no question that Jack is right. "Then we need to prepare for the worst. So, you suggest we cover both areas, meaning you and Sam will split up?"

"As much as I wish I could be in two places at once, I can't. The decision is yours. Do you want Sam or me to accompany you?"

I want Jack by my side. But if Quinton won't be in Clancy as Willem had promised, I want Jack to be with my baby when I cannot. I decide, "You go to Townsend. I'll go with Sam. I'll feel better knowing Quinton will be with you."

Jack gently squeezes my hand. "There is no one I trust more than my brother. He's just as good as having you with me."

His hand is so massive that mine feels like a child's when I return his squeeze.

We then inform Sam about our decision, and he's fully on board.

Then Jack makes a request to his older brother, "Give me someone."

Without hesitation, Sam replies, "Comet will be with you."

"Comet?" Jack frowns.

"He once saved a toddler from certain death in Colombia, and he's saved my ass a couple of times." Sam pats Jack's shoulder. "Good night, brother. Night, Ava." Finally, that man gets the opportunity to go home.

I make my way into the bedroom. Elmo, who has been quietly observing us, follows me with his tail wagging.

"Elmo, bed," Jack points to the doggy bed outside our door. The mutt gazes at Jack, begging for permission to sneak past and join me. "Let Mommy sleep." Elmo obeys and settles down as Jack strokes him.

When I see the bed, my eyelids get heavy. A good sign. After all the sleepless nights, I'm on the verge of losing my ability to function.

"Baby Quinton will be with you tomorrow," Jack says as he joins me in bed. "Believe that."

I stare at the crib in the corner of the room. I'm sure Sam had included it in the house because he believed that, too.

The impending moment looms just hours away. Despite my sleepiness, my emotions are in disarray, raging inside every corner of my body. Icy numbness seeps into my bones, a reminder of the stakes at hand. I trust Jack with all my heart, but my mind betrays me, unleashing a torrent of doubts that twist my stomach into knots. Thoughts of Quinton, vulnerable and in harm's way, haunt every second that ticks by. I am a wreck, shattered and broken, longing for the one person who can bring me solace. I imagine the warmth of his embrace, as it is the only remedy that can ease my torment.

After what feels like an eternity, I shift myself, sitting up with my face buried in my hands. Jack rises as well, his touch gentle upon my arm. But for the first time, simply being in his presence isn't enough, and I struggle to find the words to convey it. If he were to ask, I wouldn't be able to articulate anything other than begging him to fuck me.

To fuck me.

The rawness of my own words takes me by surprise. What happened to 'comfort me' or 'make love to me?'

He leans closer, seeking perhaps a glimpse into my troubled mind. "You need to get some sleep, Ava."

I turn to him. "I need you. Please." My plea comes out more civilized than my thoughts. Aching for him, I press my palms against his smooth, bare chest. He hesitantly runs his fingers through my hair as if afraid of what he might discover.

I interrupt his hesitation and tilt my head toward him, capturing his lips in a kiss.

He responds by kissing me deeper. Overcome by hunger, I let greed take over, sucking his full lips ferociously as if trying to devour his essence to sustain myself through the night.

"Sweetheart..." His voice, barely a whisper, breaks our connection. His hand soothingly rubs my back as if attempting to soften the growing separation between us.

But my desperation refuses to be quelled. "Jack, I need you," I growl, determined to bridge the distance that threatens to pull us apart.

He halts my advance, his voice filled with tenderness, "Lie down."

My breath quickens as I obediently fall back onto the mattress. My lungs take in air as if my life has just been renewed. The mass of his body envelops me, pressing on my distended breasts, making a moan escape my lips. His hand glides beneath the Belle T-shirt, eliciting a pleasant ache in my hardened left nipple with each tender caress. Giving in, I discard my T-shirt, granting him unrestricted access. When his mouth latches onto my other nipple, every nibble ignites a fire within me. This should be the moment I surrender control, letting him burn me as I've been wishing.

But the heaviness of my conscience bears down on me like a punch to the chest. It's impossible to resist the allure of his skilled hands. Yet, my tears flow for the wrong reason. Guilt.

I release a pent-up breath, feeling his body retreat from mine.

Jack appraises me. "I'm sorry. Did I..." His words trail off.

I sit up, the sheets slipping from my body. *What am I doing?*

My face contorts, and my chest tightens.

"Ava, have you taken your medications?" Worries hinder the warmth of his touch.

I rub my sternum. "I'll be fine. Just give me a minute."

"Take it easy, sweetheart. You need to save up your strength for tomorrow."

I turn to face him, feeling exposed as if standing naked in the snow. "I'm so sorry, Jack. I never meant to play with your emotions." My guilt multiplies for both Quinton and him.

"Stop worrying about me." His voice is firm yet filled with understanding.

"I don't know where I am... I don't know what I'm doing!" I slide out, leaving the bed. But Jack's long arm stretches out to keep me in place.

"I understand," he murmurs.

I shake my head, unable to believe his patience.

Jack pulls me close, burying his face in the back of my neck. "When I say I understand, believe me. I've known what it's like to be trapped in a state of desperation when it felt like there was no way out. You never play with me, Ava. You're being honest with me."

"I want this nightmare to end, Jack."

"You've got to believe," he whispers in my ear as if casting a spell. "Quinton will be with you tomorrow."

I try, but the darkness remains like a suffocating black net. "I'm scared."

"Me too," he admits. "But think about your fear as a bridge. Once you've crossed it, you will gain the strength to persevere. On the other side, there won't be anything stopping you."

My rigidness thaws. If fear can touch a man of his caliber, then my own fears are justified. Still, I need him to walk the bridge with me. "Hold me, Jack."

He lies down, pulling me with him until I'm nestled against his chest. Then his arms swirl around me. So soothing that I'm weakening under his spell.

My lips press against his warm, gleaming skin as I add, "Hold me until morning."

"My arms will still be right here when you wake up."

Closing my eyes, I immerse myself in the comforting support of his broad chest. The rhythmic sound of his heartbeat resonates in my ears. His natural scent lingers in the air, drawing me into a state that's as close as I can get to peace for now. At this moment, I understand why God created men. To shield and safeguard the delicate vulnerabilities that reside within every woman, no matter how tough she is. A good man recognizes this need and channels his inner strength to allow his woman to fall apart under the safety of his wings.

12

JACK

The morning arrives as the hours fly by like mere minutes. It feels like just moments ago she was in my arms, and now, we find ourselves standing face to face, ready to say, 'stay safe.' Or perhaps, 'I love you.' That's what I would've said, but it's not the time.

The Montana sun casts a glow on Ava's hair, creating a display of sparkles. The bright rays make her blink instinctively as she tries to maintain eye contact with me. We exchange a kiss, and as if we had rehearsed this moment, we both pivot away from each other simultaneously. I don't look back, letting the sound of gravel crunching beneath our shoes be a clue of how far apart we are. Until we enter our respective cars. This is our plan, and Sam is following her, but I can't help feeling a twinge of unease as the reality sets in—I won't be by her side.

"Let's roll!" I tell my partner, who's been observing me since the moment he got here.

Sam has entrusted me with Huxley Cometti, or 'Comet,' a twenty-seven-year-old former SEAL. Despite his celestial nickname, he hails from Montana, and I let him take the wheel so I can focus on our comms and the mission at hand.

"Should've gotten a bigger car," he remarks, observing me fidgeting in my seat as we hit the road. "You're packed tighter than a bull in a chute."

What was Sam thinking pairing me with this whipper-snapper?

I give him a death stare. "Don't start, or I'll throw your balls in the ring."

He lets out a bark of laughter, surrendering with a raise of his hands.

Over the radio, Sam's voice is a constant, coaching Ava. "Keep up that speed if you can. And, if you don't see me, don't freak out. I'm always close."

The cab is quiet for a while. Huxley locks his gaze on the road, wise enough to not sneak in another provocation. But silence can be just as trying when you're looking to bond with your partner in the trenches.

I start, "So, what's your story?" I'm not just talking about the scar that runs a harsh line down his face, although I'm curious if he's willing to share.

"Well, I joined the Navy when I was nineteen. Did it for college money," he answers, his tone unapologetic.

"It may not scream patriotism, but that's perfectly alright."

He settles back, a smirk playing on his lips. "And to get a chick."

I can't help but let out a short, sharp laugh. "You couldn't get laid?"

The man is like a baby rhino—solid but not overdone. He's got a chiseled face, but his eyes have this innocent vibe that'll surely make the ladies swoon.

He gives me a side glance, quizzical. "What about it?"

From that angle, he resembles friendly danger, like a

classic World War II aviator poster boy. How could he ever struggle to woo a girl?

"If you want a chick, you go to a Pilates class," I advise.

He lets out a hearty laugh, shaking his head. "Ranch life is a solitary gig."

"A rancher, huh?"

"Born and raised. Had to step up when my dad fell ill. Mom was up to her elbows with the ranch and my kid brother."

"And your dad, is he doing better now?" There's a careful tilt to my question, respectful.

A shadow crosses his face. "He left us when I was twelve."

"Sorry to hear that."

The car rolls on, and for a moment, he's lost in thought. "The ranch keeps me grounded. It's my piece of heaven, near Seeley Lake. It's me, through and through, and it's not going anywhere."

We round a bend and we catch our first glimpse of the Missouri River.

"So you kept the land in the family?" I ask.

He nods, pride lighting up his features. "Yep. The kid's running it now. Nineteen and bossing like a seasoned ranch hand. I taught him all he knows."

"You taught him?" I press, genuinely impressed.

He looks straight ahead, conviction in his voice. "Had to be the man of the house. Teach him how to stand tall."

Turns out, Sam knew what he was doing when he partnered me with Huxley today. He might've seemed all bravado and brawn at first, but the Comet's got layers—made of tough stuff. I think about my own path, how I had to relearn everything after being taken by Scalpel. But even if the kidnapping had never happened, I doubt I could've shouldered the world like Astro Boy did, all before he was old enough to drive.

"So, did the Navy bring you closer to finding your one and only?" I venture, trying to keep the talk light, not probing too deep too fast.

"Girls, yes. Soulmate? That's another story. I signed up for the bonus bucks, not for valor or heroics. But, you know how it is, you get out there, into the thick of it..." His voice tapers off, a hint of harshness seeping in.

The man beside me shifts, a small motion, but one laden with unspoken memories. "Living on a razor's edge, it gets into your blood," he says. "Made it through BUD/S, wore my Trident, and stayed in the game until my last op."

He draws a breath, and I can feel the weight of whatever is on his mind.

"Listen, if this is going to stir up the ghosts, we can cut it right there," I say, keeping my voice steady. Everyone has got their demons, be it from the battlefield, the operating table, or just life's cruel twists. "I want you to focus on Quinton, do you hear?"

"You're the one who poked the bear," the baby rhino reminds me, not unkindly, just stating facts.

I crack a half-smile. "I was just trying to make conversation."

His eyes flick to mine, a glint of something—appreciation, maybe—before he returns to the path ahead.

There are still a few miles left to kill, and after all, I started the conversation. Experience has taught me that sometimes, things left unsaid can be more distracting than those we let out. I concede, "All right, what happened in Colombia?"

He smirks, knowing the question burning in me. "We were in a jungle down south, extracting a CIA operative whose cover had been compromised. The intel was spotty—classic CIA's spook style, keeping us in the dark on half the game.

Two members of our team got seriously injured. Well, three if you count me." He gestures to his face.

Now that he's given me permission, I examine the deep scar.

He continues, "My face was hanging out, and my chest was a wall of shrapnel. But I suppose it wasn't as bad for me since I didn't lose any limbs. But you know, Jack. What shook me was the fact that I failed to protect someone. Even though technically, we rescued the only person we were tasked to bring home safely." His confession hangs between us.

"An innocent victim?" I murmur.

"A very innocent victim," he reveals. "I was shielding a two-year-old girl who was standing at the door just as the house behind her exploded. Her twin brother didn't make it. We never knew they were kids in there." He shakes his head. "My chief got court-martialed for what happened. It should've been the CIA's asses."

"That was fucked up."

"Very fucked up. When I held that girl, I made a promise that when my Navy days were over, I'd dedicate the rest of my life to the well-being of children. I considered joining UNICEF, but I felt like I should start closer to home."

"Well, it's our gain."

"You know, that girl. When she opened her eyes—" I catch a glimpse of a smile forming on his profile. "She held me tight and called me 'Papa' for some reason," he shares, gripping the steering wheel tightly as if he's reliving that moment. Then the smile fades, and he gulps. "I mean, we were the ones who took her father's life, and I swear, I don't look anything like that murderer. Honestly, with my messed-up face, I should've looked straight out of a horror flick."

You don't have to spend a lot of time with a guy to know what he's like. Huxley may not be an open book, but underneath his tough exterior, there's a tender side to him. Considering he helped raise his younger brother, it's no wonder the girl saw him as a father figure.

"Maybe you smelled like her old man," I tease.

"He was a millionaire drug lord, so I'm sure his cologne was some top-notch Parisian product. Let's see if Quinton calls me Papa."

Now he's getting cocky. "Don't you fucking dare provoke him!" I warn. "Even if he says something that sounds like it, it won't mean anything. Nothing that boy says to you is binding."

"Yet the smell will linger," Huxley jokes. "So what's your story, Jack? You're an active Marine. How come you're here?"

"I'm on leave."

"So you're on duty while off duty?"

"Well, I thought it was my duty to be here. Until that thought got here." I tap at my chest.

As if in sync, my senses heighten when we enter Townsend. Instead of heading toward the town center, we veer west, choosing a path leading to the farm area. Our objective perches on a slight elevation, a strategic vantage point that provides a clear view of the surroundings. This was why Willem's men chose the house. If we drive further, even before they spot us, they'll know fury is coming.

Determined to remain undetected, we opt to park in the recess of an alleyway concealed behind a row of mulberry trees. We proceed on foot, using the overgrown bushes along the road as our covers.

With our radio on, hooked to a headset each of us wears, we make our approach to the house from the rear. Upon first glance, the surroundings appear unchanged from yesterday.

Huxley and I split up, each of us conducting a quick survey of the exterior. My eyes flit from window to window, tracing the outlines of the structure. The glass remains covered with newspaper from the inside, and the gap in the bedroom window is still there. As I peep in, my heart sinks like a stone in murky water.

There is absolutely nothing inside. The crib is gone, and the room is empty. I step onto the porch. The random junk is still there, but no sign of the baby stroller that was parked here when I came yesterday.

Huxley and I rendezvous at the back door. "It smells like a baby!" he whispers, unaware of the storm brewing inside my head. From the side he inspected, I don't think he would've seen anything that reveals a baby is around. I can't detect the scent from here, but I wish my partner were right. Perhaps it's just a lingering scent that the group moved on not that long ago.

Convinced that the house is empty, we exchange a wordless glance. Slowly, I open the door, allowing Huxley to enter with a wide stride, his Glock firmly gripped in his hand, aimed forward. We search the house, finding no trace of anyone. Most rooms are empty and have been cleaned thoroughly. There are only the unmade beds in the bedrooms and a few furniture scattered around the living room.

"Fuck!" I gripe.

As I settle behind the cover of an old leather couch, Huxley positions himself beneath the window, keeping a vigilant watch on the outside.

I contact Sam. "Where are you?"

"I'm in position. Ava is almost here."

My heart races as I picture her venturing into the unknown alone. But I can't dwell on it now—she knows what she's doing.

Sam then asks, "How's Townsend?"

"The house is empty," I respond in dismay. Meanwhile, Huxley remains composed in his observations.

I ask Sam, "Can you spot the white van?"

"Negative." Sam pauses, then adds, "Actually, I don't see any cars here either." He gets quiet once again. I sense that he's on the move. Then he relays, "Two motorbikes park at the back of the house."

That will allow them to navigate through narrow passages inaccessible to cars.

I acknowledge him, and he instructs, "Give me an update in five."

My eyes roam the room, searching for any remnants of baby Quinton. They scan the air as if attempting to catch a whiff of that distinct scent Huxley had detected. Yet, all that lingers is the aroma of cleaning products.

Perhaps I've been relying on my instincts too blindly. The urge to leave and join Sam in Clancy rises, but something keeps me anchored here. As Sam told me, those men in Clancy arrived on motorcycles, and transporting a seven-month-old baby on a motorcycle is highly unlikely.

Suddenly, Sam's voice crackles through the radio. "Ava's here."

I switch to her frequency. "Ava, talk to me."

"Jack. Have you seen Quinton?"

"Not yet. We've got to be patient, and you have to focus."

I can hear her pulling a breath. "I'm ready."

"You listen to whatever Sam says, okay? If he says get out, you get out. Not a second after."

"Understood, Jack," she responds, composed and direct. "I'm going in now."

The radio falls silent, leaving us on edge. Minutes later, Sam updates us. "She's reached the door. I'm closing in."

Just then, Huxley and I hear an approaching car.

Clutching his binoculars tightly, he reports, "It's a white van with a male driver."

"What about the babysitter? And Quinton?"

"Negative. Only the driver."

Not the answer I wanted. Huxley and I get in position, flanking the door, ready to shoot.

"Are you sure there's only one man?" I ask Huxley.

"Positive, boss."

While I could leave Huxley to hold the fort, considering we're only facing one person, I decide to stick with the plan. I trust Sam to keep Ava safe and have faith in my own intuition that Quinton is still nearby.

The sound of the engine is getting closer. When I listen carefully, something remains in the distance. It's a cry. It's faint, but it's unmistakably a baby's cry.

My persistence has been rewarded. Quinton is here, and he needs me. Besides, I can't allow that Comet boy to claim that Quinton has called him 'Papa.'

13

———

AVA

Like many small towns in Montana, Clancy possesses the old-world charm that transports you back in time. But away from town, my intended destination is anything but charming. I have never encountered a more desolate place. You can scream to your heart's content, but your cries will go unheard, save for the occasional birds soaring by. The landscape surrounding the property is devoid of any significant features except for a few scattered trees. As Sam and Jack foresaw, executing an ambush with a group of men would be a disastrous decision.

Standing alone on the porch, I watch as the door gradually opens with a hesitant creaking sound. Then, it stops, creating just enough space for me to slip through. As I step inside, a hand seizes me, forcefully pulling me in while the door slams shut behind me. I hear the distinct sound of at least two heavy locks being engaged, followed by the sliding of a bar.

Blocking my path stands a man I've never seen before. His face is bloated, resembling an overfed raccoon with dark circles around his eyes.

The room is bare, save for a solitary table and chair positioned at its center. A stack of paperwork and a pen rest neatly upon it as if deliberately arranged for my arrival. Quinton and my ex-babysitter are nowhere to be seen, but a doorway leading to the rear of the house catches my attention. When I arrived here, from the outside, this old wooden house appears large enough to be a three-bedroom dwelling. There is also an outbuilding at the back. If Quinton is here, he could be anywhere.

A figure emerges from the doorway, revealing itself to be Willem's lieutenant, the bearded man. "Ava West. We meet again," he utters, his voice exuding confidence as if he owned this estate.

"Where's my baby?" I approach him, only to be held back by the raccoon man.

"I trust that you came alone?" He brandishes a gun, pointing at me while motioning to his comrade to check the outside. Then he bends down and whispers in my ear, "He won't find any of those Red Mark bitches out here, will he?"

"I'm here alone!"

Just a few minutes seem to stretch out into an hour when the raccoon man comes back. "She's clean," he confirms.

"I'm impressed," the bearded man says, withdrawing his gun. "I guess a mother knows. Quinton is here. Sit down."

As the raccoon man pushes me down onto the chair, I strain my ears to catch any sounds that might be coming from the other side of the house. At the same time, I listen intently to Sam's voice in my earpiece.

"Stay calm, Ava," Sam assures me. With a microphone discreetly taped behind my shirt, he can hear everything that's happening.

"Let me see Quinton," I demand, my eyes piercing through him. "He's just a baby. If you and your minion here want something, then take me instead," I emphasize.

I hear Sam's voice again, "Understood. There are two men present with you."

Meanwhile, the bearded man shuffles through the stapled papers on the table until he reaches the last page, then pushes it toward me. "Sign it," he commands, handing me a pen.

I refuse to take it, choosing instead to read the contract from the beginning. It's an agreement between Willem and me, a document that would strip me of full custody of Quinton, denying me any visitation or contact.

"So he's not dead," I mock the bearded man, pretending I didn't know.

He chuckles, a twisted smile forming on his face as if he's pleased to have fooled me. "Well, the tale of his death by tea was just a scare tactic. Of course he's alive!"

My unblinking eyes lock onto his as I firmly slide the paperwork back in his direction. "Tell Willem to go to hell. I'm here to take my baby, not to surrender him."

He tuts, regretting my response. "Between the two of us, Willem informed me that if you agree to this, he might be willing to negotiate with you. It's a slim chance, but still a chance, that he might allow you to visit Quinton. On his own terms, of course. And you know, it's better than nothing."

I hear Sam whispering in my earpiece, "Ask to see Quinton. The outbuilding is clear, but the windows into the house are all barricaded. I'm just outside, next to the front door."

I quickly respond to my adversary. "Let me see Quinton."

With a sneer, he counters, "Sign the paper first."

"Well, I'll talk to the coward later if he has the guts to meet me. I'm Quinton's mother, and I will do anything to get my baby back!"

He casually remarks, "I've been warned that you won't give up easily. Here's the thing. If you refuse to sign this paper, someone will testify that you've been abusing Quinton."

I stand up, trying to lunge over him, but the raccoon man holds me back. "Don't you dare!" I move my body in wild motions, trying to break free, but the man's strength overpowers my will.

"Willem's death was a trick. But this time, there won't be any trick. Your babysitter is fiercely loyal to her employer. And I don't mean you. She'll do anything to maintain her retainer from Willem and prevent him from revealing more incriminating evidence against her brother. You do know that your babysitter's brother is in trouble, right?"

"And that will make her an unreliable witness."

"You're familiar with court procedures. I'm aware of that, Miss West. However, with the reassurance of a respected man like Willem Botha, who has made significant contributions to the city of Los Angeles, the court will believe her over an unstable mother who took his baby away to disappear in this forsaken land." He then grabs my shirt collar. "By then, rest assured, you won't ever see your baby again."

Jack said yesterday Willem would try to hurt me in the worst way possible. I never thought this would be it. "I won't sign this paper until I see Quinton healthy and unharmed."

"Maybe you believe a witness alone isn't enough to bring the abuse case to court. You think there needs to be proof, right? Perhaps a bruise, a cut, or even a broken bone?"

Suddenly, I hear a cry coming from behind the doorway.

Reacting to the distressing sound, I rush toward its source, retaliating against the raccoon man. "Don't you hurt him!" I call out desperately. "Quinton, Mommy is here!"

The first two bedrooms I come across are empty. I keep running. At the back, behind the last door, I'm startled to see another man stooping into a crib, a smirk on his face as he holds a knife in his hand.

My cry echoes through the room, blending with the sound of Sam's voice saying, "I'm coming in!"

Despite the chaos, I reach the crib with neither of the men making any attempt to stop me. It doesn't take long for me to understand why.

It's not Quinton's cry. It's only a recording of it. And it's not my baby in the crib. It's a fucking doll!

14

JACK

A loud, high-pitched cry forces me to take off my headset.

That cry can only mean one thing: Quinton is not here. He's in Clancy!

As I recover from the piercing noise, a cacophony of voices emanates from the radio, painting a vivid picture of chaos.

"Sam! What the hell is going on?" I whisper-shout as I maintain my position.

However, my brother isn't responding, and neither is Ava.

Regret swarms around me like an army of ants. I should've been there with Sam and Ava. This is so fucked up! I'm too close to the heart of the beast, I've become shortsighted, and I'm paying the price—or rather, Ava is paying the price.

Maybe Quinton is, too.

As I ponder a way to correct my missteps, I'm reminded of the sound I heard coming from outside this house just a moment ago. Did I misinterpret that faraway cry? Or did I merely imagine it?

Positioned near the door, Huxley grabs my attention, signaling for me to look outside. There, I spot the driver of the white van we've been observing making his way toward the house. It's the round-faced man.

I block out all other thoughts and concentrate on apprehending the enemy in sight.

Now that the car engine has stopped, all I can hear are the round-faced man's footsteps. He climbs onto the porch, and in the background, I hear the distant cry once more. I remove my headset, allowing it to hang around my neck. I can't hear anything but static coming out of it.

The man takes another step, and suddenly, I hear it loud and clear. That cry is not coming from the radio. The voice is physically present here! Even Huxley hears it this time. He gives me a signal to quickly exit the door and leave him to handle our lone enemy.

Meanwhile, the footsteps outside come to a halt. The round-faced man bends down to pick up something while grumbling, "Stupid fucking toy!" It turns out he's picking up the plush giraffe that was left behind among the junk.

At my command, Huxley and I barge through the door. The Comet swiftly grabs his arms, locking them behind his back while simultaneously covering his mouth—clearly, our enemy is about to alert someone. But he's no match for Huxley and me. While my partner ties his hands, I gag our captive.

Now that we're outside, the cry becomes clearer. It's still distant, so there's no way it's coming from inside the van that's parked just a few yards away. With just one glance, Huxley understands exactly what I'm thinking. He's like a younger brother I never had.

"I've got him!" Huxley grits out, determination in his voice.

Without hesitation, I sprint toward the source of the cry. It's coming from along the street. As I turn the corner, my eyes catch sight of some movements. There, just outside a park, stands a man who is impatiently gesturing to someone. And then, as if out of nowhere, a stroller glides into view from behind a cluster of trees.

Slowly, a woman emerges. I'm still a distance away, but I'm certain it's the babysitter trying to comfort the crying baby nestled in the stroller. I know the rules. One of them is never to assume. But even without visuals, I know in my heart that it's Quinton.

Suddenly, my attention diverts as the man catches sight of me. He raises his weapon and begins firing. The babysitter's scream pierces through the chaos, her figure vanishing into the depths of the park, frantically pushing the stroller away. Even in broad daylight, the surrounding area is cloaked in shadows thanks to the dense, towering trees. It could well be a forest.

The man's relentless barrage of bullets forces me to seek shelter, but I can't lose Quinton. I have to finish the gunman before the babysitter runs too far. He's about a hundred yards away, and I only have a pistol with me. But it's my trusty SIG, known for its accuracy over long ranges.

I take aim and squeeze the trigger, bringing down the assailant in a single shot. His body crashes to the ground. After detecting no movement, I approach. Sweat drips down my brow as I kneel beside him, ensuring he is no longer a threat.

The immediate danger has passed, but my next action will make or break the mission—and the stakes are the life of a baby. I sprint toward the spot where the babysitter disappeared, my eyes scanning the surroundings for clues. As I venture further, a trail comes into view, a faint imprint amid the underbrush. My heart quickens at the sight, propelling me forward. Not far in the distance, I catch a glimpse of them.

"Stop!" I yell. "Hand over the baby, and I swear I'll let you go!"

But the woman refuses to give in. I continue chasing after her. Knowing it's a matter of time before I catch her, in panic, she releases the stroller. At this time, the crying has stopped. If she has harmed Quinton in any way, I swear I will take matters into my own hands and end her.

As we race a downhill slope, the stroller becomes a runaway train, heading straight for a creek! The babysitter runs in the opposite direction, but I pay her no mind. My focus is on the stroller's path.

From where I am, I can see Quinton's legs hanging out. He's slipping through the straps! I could jump and reach for the stroller's handles, but abruptly stopping it might make Quinton fly out. In a split second, I leap over the stroller, using my body to cushion its impact and ensure Quinton doesn't fall on the rocky ground. My shoulder takes the brunt of the fall, but Quinton escapes the tumbling stroller and lands safely in my arms.

My heart races, sweat covers my face. When I look down, I'm met with Quinton's scrutiny. I'm certain he's on the verge of crying.

"Don't worry, baby. You're safe. You're safe." I cradle him.

The baby wriggles—not in distress but driven by curiosity. I loosen my hold, and he reaches for my Ray-Ban sunglasses, nudging them up to let him peek at my eyes. He giggles as if I was the funniest thing he's ever seen. "Po po po," he babbles.

I gently pat him all over to ensure he's not injured. It's my first time holding a baby, but his joyful expression and ability to move freely assure me he's in good health.

With sweat oiling my nose, my sunglasses slip down. When I lift them, Quinton laughs even harder, repeating, "Po po po!"

"I don't know what you're saying, baby. But I'm glad you like me."

The pain throbbing in my shoulder, possibly dislocated, is forgotten as his laughter numbs the ache. The stroller lies overturned by the edge of the creek, its wheels spinning lazily. I retrieve a blanket from it, wrapping Quinton snugly to shield him from the breeze.

I remain on high alert, scanning the surroundings for any sign of Willem's men, but all I see are leaves rustling in the wind.

Adjusting my headset, I pique Quinton's curiosity, his tiny fingers reaching for the microphone as if eager to join the conversation. "Sam, I've got him. I've got Quinton," I announce, my voice crackling through the static-filled radio. Unsure if anyone can hear me, I persevere, determined to keep them informed.

Quinton eagerly sinks his teeth into the microphone's rubbery tip. I pull it away from him. "You need that giraffe teether, don't you?" I remark, a hint of amusement in my voice. I urge him to speak. "Say Mama."

"Mo."

"Mo? Are you calling Elmo?"

"Mo!"

I chuckle. The bond between Quinton and Elmo must be strong, perhaps even rivaling Ava's position as his number one. "Don't worry, and I won't tell her," I quip.

Leaning back against the trunk of an elm tree, I take a moment to catch my breath. Quinton crawls along my lap, his grip surprisingly strong. Perhaps he sees me as nothing more than a mattress. I slide down, making myself as flat as I can, allowing him to reach the top of me. His tiny hands brush against my Ray-Bans, eliciting laughter as I play peek-a-boo with him. If this was a military operation, it'd be by far the best debrief I've had.

Amid Quinton's innocent laughter, reality sinks in. I have fulfilled my promise. Now, all I need is the safe return of Ava and Sam.

15

———

AVA

Staring at the doll in the crib, my shoulders slump, and my body teeters on the brink of surrender. I've fallen for Willem's ruse. All I can hope for is that my baby is in Townsend, just as Jack has believed from the beginning.

Among the mocking laughter from the men, I realize that my hasty move to check the crib has caused my earpiece to slip.

The raccoon man yanks me away from the crib, eyeballing the bean-shaped object resting on the mattress. He pushes me into a corner. In his rage, his hands tear through my shirt, uncovering the microphone taped to my bra. "You're fucking wired?" he growls, crushing the device beneath his boot.

Where is Sam? I thought he was coming in.

Seeing what's unfolding, the bearded man collects the speaker-like equipment emitting Quinton's fake cry. "Kill her!" he orders and then disappears from the room.

Suddenly, a loud crack echoes from the back of the house. It's Sam. He has deliberately chosen the rear entry, likely aware of our presence and the fortified front door.

I maneuver past my two captors, only to be stopped by

the one who had been standing by the crib. With an iron grip, he grabs me, using my panicked body as a shield. The knife he had waved earlier is now pressed against my neck. He used it to threaten fake Quinton, but the weapon is anything but fake. Its steely blade grazes my skin while I watch the raccoon man aiming his gun at Sam, his finger poised on the trigger.

My neck tenses, pressing against the sharp edge of the knife. I feel a distinct line breaking on my skin, a sharp, stinging sensation that causes me to squeeze my eyes shut.

The room falls into an eerie silence, but not for long. A shot rings out, emphatically signaling a turn of events. Almost simultaneously, I hear a thud next to my ear. The raccoon man sways toward me, his lifeless body sliding down against my shoulder and onto the floor. Sam's bullet has found its mark in the man's chest.

The captor holding me tightens his grip, one arm wrapped around my waist while the other keeps pressing the knife against my neck. My eyes widen in terror as he lifts me, using me to cover his face and upper body.

"Release her!" Sam orders. This is the first time I hear the Red Mark leader's voice so low and menacing.

But my captor keeps dragging me back, his ragged breath blowing against my nape. I struggle to inhale as the tight grip restricts my chest, trying to release the fear that fills me.

Sam stands still in the doorway, blocking any escape route.

My captor warns Sam, "I've been given permission to kill her." I feel the blade dig deeper into my skin. I take it as a sign of desperation—he knows he's trapped, and I'm his only lever-age. "She'll just be collateral damage."

But Sam doesn't wait, rapidly changing his aim and firing low, hitting the man's foot. A scream escapes my captor as he releases me. Seizing the opportunity, I duck and sprint toward

Sam, seeking safety. As he shields me, Sam takes another shot, ending the man's life.

"Ava, Ava, are you all right?" I hear Sam's worried voice, his grip steadying me as I struggle to regain my balance.

"I'm fine, Sam," I pant. "But Quinton isn't here. Did you hear anything from Jack?"

The silence that follows fills me with unease. I'm too afraid to ask again, so I simply watch him slipping off his jacket, draping it over my tattered shirt. He then guides me toward the front of the house. The wide-open door invites a rush of air and the distant sound of a revving motorcycle.

Sam lets out a growl, clearly displeased that the bearded man has managed to escape. But he looks at me, offering a reassuring nod. I know that I am his top priority. "Come on, let's go," he urges me forward.

We run toward my car parked outside the fence, but the tires have been slashed. We have no choice but to head toward Sam's car, which was left in a spot away from the house.

Adrenaline fuels our steps, and I finally see his car, hidden behind a dense thicket of bushes. Sam remains vigilant, constantly scanning our surroundings, ready to defend us if anyone should approach. We jump in without wasting a second, and he floors the accelerator.

"Please call Jack," I beg. "You haven't heard from him, have you?"

"No, not yet, but we will soon," he mumbles, his eyes scanning the surroundings. "We're heading to Townsend now."

I gaze at him, silently urging him to make the call to Jack.

"Ava, I haven't heard from him, but that doesn't mean something bad has happened. My headset went haywire earlier, around the time you got close to whatever was making that crying sound."

Ah, that digital speaker. It wouldn't surprise me if Willem

had designed it using some sort of voice cloner. It sounded exactly like Quinton's cry. So real, as if he was in the room.

"I'm sorry," I sigh, feeling guilty for potentially causing the disturbance.

"Hey, don't apologize. It wasn't your fault." Sam grips the steering wheel with one hand while his other hand adjusts his radio.

Around the corner, a familiar figure catches our attention. It's my former babysitter, Greta Hall, running along the road like a fugitive. The woman showed nothing but trustworthiness, order, and gentleness when she first introduced herself. I can't believe she's capable of doing this. But that's the nature of humanity—it can both amaze and shock you.

Sam slams on the brakes and swerves to the right, blocking her path. As soon as the car comes to a halt, I step out.

"Ava, wait!" Sam yells.

I march on. It doesn't take much to corner her. Her face is flushed, and her legs wobble. It looks like she's been running for a while. The image of her caring for my baby, as if she were his real mother, ignites a surge of anger within me.

I throw a punch, my knuckles landing on her nose. Then I push her to the ground.

"Where's my baby?" I shout at her.

She cries out helplessly, then pleads, "Miss West, I can explain..."

"Where's my baby!" My fury intensifies, and I raise my leg, ready to stomp on her pitiful face.

Sam intervenes, stopping me in my tracks.

"Step away, Sam! This is between me and her!" I protest, my anger directed solely at Greta.

"No, no!" Sam persists, restraining me while pointing his gun at her, even though she appears too exhausted to flee.

"Ava, Jack has Quinton," he announces, halting my fight instantly. "I just heard from him," he asserts.

My body goes flaccid as if letting go of all the strain. Those are the words I've been desperately longing to hear.

He releases me and takes charge of Greta, allowing me the time to compose myself. When I turn around, I find Sam has tied her up, and she sits on the side of the road, still sobbing uncontrollably.

"It's over," Sam whispers. "The sheriff's coming."

I give him a heartfelt thank-you hug. He has been there for us from the beginning, risking his safety and opening his home for me, and now, saving me.

Shortly after, the sound of sirens permeates the air as the sheriff and his men arrive at the scene. They grab Greta without any pushback. She walks on, not even sparing me a glance.

The weight of the situation lifts as Sam and I head back to the car.

"Ready to see Quinton?" Sam says behind the wheel.

Just as my ex-babysitter takes a seat in the back of the sheriff's car, out of nowhere, a motorcycle passes by, the rider aiming his gun through the open door. He's so close that it stuns everyone. Two quick shots ring out, causing panic among the sheriff's men. As the smoke clears, we see Greta's limp body slumped in the deputy's arms.

The motorcycle, a blur of speed and agility, disappears into the distance before anyone can react. It effortlessly evades the attempts of the sheriff's men to take aim and fire.

It's as if something is obstructing my airway. I struggle to comprehend what I'm witnessing. Greta Hall, the woman I despised for her greed and betrayal, now lies completely still on the ground. A spike of guilt pricks at my gut, wondering if there could've been a different outcome.

The sheriff instructs us to wait, but Sam explains how urgent it is for us to be in Townsend—citing that my baby is there. After assuring the sheriff that we will provide our statements as soon as we can, Sam is given permission to leave with an escort.

As we drive away, thoughts of reuniting with Quinton consume my mind, gradually erasing the unfolding events.

We veer onto a path off the main road, the tires crunching on the gravel, and it becomes apparent that our destination lies along the Missouri River.

"Shortcut," Sam remarks with enthusiasm, glancing at the trooper's car trailing behind us.

My only concern is reaching Jack and Quinton, so I don't care how Sam does it. Yet, I'm confused. Why the river?

I silently implore my handsome driver to explain with a gaze.

He smirks, a glimmer of mischief bouncing in his eyes. "Quinton is apparently a big nature lover. He grew weary of the Townsend house, so Jack decided to treat him to some R&R at a riverside location."

His response amuses me. I never knew my little one was an outdoorsy baby!

I notice Sam is driving without a GPS. "You seem to know this area well."

"Red Mark's first office was in Townsend. Not on this side of town, but the east side near the center."

The path narrows, sandwiched by tall trees on our left and right. The scent of fresh pine seeps into the car.

Finally, we reach the trailhead, excitement bubbling in my gut. As the path opens up, the blue waters of the Missouri River come into view, its surface sparkling under the rays of sunlight. With every step, my eyes search for any signs of Jack.

And there it is—the man is seated under the shade of a

tree, gazing at the horizon with my baby contently sitting on his lap. My heart leaps with pure happiness at the sight of my two precious dears together. With his sunglasses on, Jack looks like a man who's enjoying a break. From here, I wouldn't have any idea what he had gone through to rescue Quinton.

I yell Quinton's and Jack's names. My voice bounces against the trees as if following me as I sprint toward them. Kneeling next to Jack, I reach out to Quinton, my fingers tingling. A contagious squeal of delight escapes the boy's lips, his face lighting up with a smile that etches lines of honest joy. It's a sound I couldn't bear to live without. "Are you okay, baby? Mommy's here," I whisper.

"He's okay," Jack affirms—calm and proud as if telling me he has shielded Quinton with his life and emerged victorious.

Holding Quinton close, I plant gentle kisses on his forehead, stroking him tenderly as his cotton candy hair tickles my palm. "I love you, Quinton. I love you more than anything," I quaver. "I won't let anyone come between us ever again, you know that, right, Quinnie-Bear?"

Quinton trails his fingers along my cheek as if trying to wipe away my tears. I can't resist kissing him again, savoring the sensation of his tender skin against my lips.

I then glance up at Jack, my other baby. His sunglasses are perched on his head, and I notice a wince clouding his face when I rest against his shoulder. "Are you hurt?"

"I'm fine," he reassures me, quickly regaining composure and planting a kiss on my lips. His touch is like sunlight, radiating warmth that reminds me of something I can't live without.

Quinton wriggles, prompting us to break the kiss. Jack's sunglasses slip down from his head, and that seems to excite the boy as he points at Jack. "Po po po!"

I giggle almost as loudly as Quinton.

"He's been saying that all day," Jack says. "What is it?"

"*Paw Patrol.* That kid's show." I look at him, still laughing. "You, in your sunglasses."

Jack smiles, his lips curving into a heartwarming arc. The sweetness of the moment compels me to lean in and press my lips against his once more.

"Are you all right, Ava Belle?" he murmurs, gesturing at Sam's jacket, the fabric bearing the remnants of a recent altercation.

"Your brother made sure I was," I explain, glancing at Sam, who's patiently standing a few paces away.

Jack's eyes meet Sam's, a silent understanding passing between them. With a face filled with gratitude, he says to his big brother, "What are you doing? Come here."

The four of us come together, embracing tightly, as relieved sighs escape our lips and blend with the sound of Quinton's babbling. It takes adversity to arrive at this point, but this is one of the best moments of my life.

Sitting on the grass, we encircle Quinton as we let him crawl on a blanket.

I glance around, searching for a glimpse of the infamous Townsend house. "So, where did you find Quinton? I can't see a house anywhere here."

"The house is a bit further away, on the other side of the forest," Jack answers. "I saved Quinton near a creek. There's a path that runs from a park not far from the house."

"A creek?" Anxiety creeps into my voice. What could have possibly happened?

Jack rubs the top of my hand, calming me. "Your babysitter panicked when she tried to escape. But Quinton seemed to take it all in his stride. Probably thought it was just a grand adventure."

"Oh, baby." I hold Quinton close, my hands carefully patting his small body, searching for any signs of harm.

"He's all right," Jack's voice breaks through my thoughts. "But —don't be mad—I did make him cry." His innocent smirk melts me as he explains, "I believe he thought I was taking him back to the house. So I wandered back into the park, strolling along the tree-lined path until we ended up here. Quinton looked content, and I thought it'd be the perfect spot to wait for you."

I caress Jack's cheek. He is my hero, the one who saved my precious child. This will be a story I'll share with Quinton time and time again, as well as with our future children and their children.

Then Quinton starts to fuss. I gently bounce him up and down, but he continues to squirm. His tiny hands reach out, grasping at the air as if trying to communicate something.

"He may be hungry," Jack says.

I glance at him, my eyebrows raised in surprise. My potential baby daddy is absolutely spot on. Sam looks at him, too, perhaps thinking the same question—how does the Marine know?

Sam smiles crookedly, then gets up, his footsteps rustling the grass as he walks away. "I'll go check on Comet and handle our escort," he said, nodding toward the trooper standing nearby. "Are you two okay here?"

"Yeah," Jack responds. He watches Sam's retreating figure.

"We both owe him," I murmur.

Meanwhile, Quinton continues to squirm in my arms, interrupting my attempts to prepare for his breastfeeding. "Hold him, please?" I hand him over to Jack, at the same time stealing glances at his muscles straining against his snug T-shirt. I can't wait to lay my body down on those carved abs.

Quinton cries. Jack holds him close, his large hands

shaking him gently in an attempt to soothe him. I take off Sam's jacket, revealing my torn shirt, a stark reminder of the events that unfolded.

"What happened?" Jack's eyes widen.

"They found out I was wired, but Sam took control of the situation. I'm okay, Jack." I remove my shirt and unclasp my bra, letting my boobs spill out.

I reach out to Quinton, my fingers brushing against his soft cheek. "Come here, baby." The warmth of his tiny body brushes against mine as his lips latch onto my nipple. How I missed this.

"Must feel good to be a mother," Jack whispers.

"I wouldn't trade it with anything else." I softly chuckle as Quinton's sucking becomes more pronounced.

Jack kneels behind me, and his body presses against my back, his strong arms enveloping me. I can feel his chin perched on my shoulder, his warm breath caressing my earlobe.

"I love you, Ava," he whispers, his words like a gentle river flow.

Emotion fills my chest. I tilt my face, meeting his gaze as I accept his declaration and his kiss. "I love you too, Jack."

16

JACK

The doctor at the hospital popped my dislocated shoulder back into place. Despite managing to ignore the pain while I was with Ava and Quinton, the doctor's touch served as a harsh reminder of my injury. But I've been mended and allowed to go home. Baby Quinton has also been given a clean bill of health, although the pediatrician has asked us to monitor his behavior, particularly his reaction to noise and being in a stroller for an extended period.

Sam and I are convinced the bearded man is the motorcyclist who killed Greta Hall. Unfortunately, the elusive villain has managed to erase any evidence of Willem's involvement in the Clancy house, including the paperwork Ava was coerced into signing and the sound machine that supposedly imitated Quinton's cry.

What is left looks like a scene from a bad prank, with the crib and doll—not accounting for the two dead men that Sam took down. The most troubling part is that nobody knows the bearded man's identity, almost as if he were a creation of Willem's artificial intelligence. But we all know he is flesh-and-blood.

My partner for the day, Huxley Cometti, was able to keep the round-faced man under control in the Townsend house until the police arrived. But the criminal has been stubbornly keeping mum about implicating anyone. The only thing he told the police was that he and his group were planning to leave town this morning, but Quinton wouldn't stop crying. They believed the baby wanted his giraffe. So, while the round-faced man returned to retrieve the missing toy, the babysitter was attempting to calm Quinton by taking him for a walk—a move that ended up changing everything in our favor.

I am certain it wasn't the toy that made Quinton cry then. When I showed him the matching one I bought from the bookstore, he threw it to the floor and never wanted to see it again. So, in Townsend, he cried because he was afraid of going back to the house.

Huxley is driving us to the safe house, and we've welcomed him to stay and be our bodyguard tonight.

"You're good back there?" I swivel in the passenger seat to see how Ava and Quinton are doing. She hasn't let him out of her sight, not even for a second.

After sleeping for most of the afternoon, Quinton has been vocal throughout the journey. There's no sign of his *Paw Patrol* calls. Instead, he's been uttering different sounds as if singing a story.

"I think he's saying he's happy to have his favorite back," Ava says while Quinton gazes up at me with wide eyes. His tiny fingers grip his beloved giraffe teether.

I feel pride and humility, realizing that my gift has remained his most cherished possession.

As we arrive at the safe house, Quinton's content expression crumbles into tears.

"Do you think he's afraid of this house?" I query,

concerned that the repercussion of today is starting to manifest itself in him.

Ava shakes her head gently, her fingertips tracing circles on Quinton's belly. She appraises him, then coos, "No, I think he's hungry again. Yes, baby?" She cradles him close, peppering his belly with sweet kisses and making playful sounds to distract him. Quinton's cries grow louder. "That's definitely his hungry cry."

As soon as we open the door, Elmo greets us. The mutt jumps up at Ava's leg, seemingly wanting to comfort Quinton. When he doesn't receive any attention, he starts barking.

Quinton's cry softens into sobs, his hand reaching down to Elmo.

"Good dog!" Ava praises as she settles on the sofa and gently rocks Quinton on her lap, suggesting, "Let's feed him formula tonight."

"I can help," Huxley offers, eager to raid the diaper bag he's just set on the kitchen bench. That shifts Elmo's attention, and the pup starts circling the Comet, sniffing him. "Just tell me how many mils and scoops."

Ava is amazed and amused. "I didn't know you had kids! No wonder you got everything on my shopping list right."

"No, ma'am," Huxley chuckles. "I used to help my mother take care of my brother, that's all."

"That's all?" Ava exclaims. "That's remarkable!"

"Thanks." He blushes.

"All right. Two hundred ten mils, with seven scoops, please."

"On it," Huxley replies and begins fussing in the kitchen.

I'll let the Astro Boy steal the limelight for tonight, but I need to step up my game and learn more about the culinary needs of infants.

Then Ava approaches me. "I think he wants you." She hands Quinton to me, and I happily oblige.

Ava watches as Huxley prepares the bottle and checks the temperature while I cradle Quinton. The baby is calm now but keeps gazing at the bottle. I'm glad it wasn't trauma that prompted him to cry just now. A mother always knows.

I give Quinton the bottle while Ava observes me with a smile. He feels so right in my arms, as if I was meant to be with him, and I'm honored by his trust.

"Why don't you go to bed?" I suggest to Ava, her eyes heavy with exhaustion.

Hesitating for a moment, she locks eyes with Quinton, her gaze filled with tenderness. She whisper-kisses him, "I won't be far. Be good to Jack, okay?" Then, she turns her head toward the open door of the bedroom, her gaze locked on something, her expression unsettled.

"What is it?" I whisper.

She briefly holds my hand. "Nothing. I'll wait for you in bed." Leaning in, she plants a quick kiss on my lips.

I watch her walk away, torn between wanting to ask her if something's bothering her and letting her sleep.

A hand lands on my shoulder. "Night, Jack," Huxley says. "Thanks for today."

"Anytime, Lieutenant." With that, he also turns in.

"Well, Quinnie-Bear, it's just you and me now," I whisper.

As I lay on the couch, I willingly become Mattress Jack for him. Nestled between my pecs, the baby rests on his belly, tilting his head to meet my gaze. Our communication flows through gurgles and chuckles, which I interpret as his happiness and perhaps a tale of his recent experiences. I pat his back, encouraging him to share more. Slowly, his head falls, his efforts to stay awake futile against the embrace of sleep.

The room falls silent, interrupted only by the peaceful

sound of Quinton's breathing. When I set out on this journey from Hawaii, I never imagined I would find myself here, holding a baby in my arms, feeling their precious life against my own heart. It's a wonder, a deep connection that can only mean one thing—this paternal instinct has always been in me, waiting for the right moment to awaken.

"I love you too, Quinton. You're a brave boy," I murmur as I carefully get off the couch. I faintly shush him as he stirs, planting a light kiss on his crown, my lips tickled by the touch of his hair.

Passing Elmo, who's asleep next to our bedroom door, I enter and place Quinton in the crib, his tiny body snug and secure.

"Good job," Ava whispers, her voice still alert despite the late hour. Rolling out of bed, she rushes to Quinton's side. She watches him, occasionally giving his belly a gentle touch.

I strip to my boxer shorts. She may disagree, but she needs to rest, or she'll risk passing out. I hold her, whispering, "Come to bed with me."

She slowly lets go of Quinton, then follows the tug of my hand. Together, we slip under the covers.

"Don't tell me you're not sleepy," I tease as she settles herself on my chest. "Quinton has done better than you." I don't think she's had a wink of sleep since the first time I saw her in Helena—and I don't mean when she was unconscious.

Minutes pass, maybe ten. Despite her efforts, she's unable to hide her restlessness.

A growl escapes her parted lips, bouncing off my chest.

"What is it?" I ask.

She hums out her impatience as her fingers glide over my abs.

"That's nice," I moan, absorbing the arousing effect of her caress.

She leans forward, her hand reaching for my lips. Her touch intensifies as it lands precisely on my pulsating, uncontrollably rigid cock.

The discovery excites her. A hunger flickers in her eyes as she moves down.

Fuuuck...

She takes me into the warmth of her mouth. I shuffle the sheet off her, eager to maintain eye contact with her. Her lips, slightly swollen from her passionate ministrations, wrap around my shaft in a greedy move. Her sucking exudes urgency, but I can't help but flinch at the speed.

"Sweetheart, sweetheart, wait." The sensation threatens to push me over the edge too soon, but the brashness of her move bothers me even more. It doesn't feel like her. It's a surprise, but not one that brings a spark of delight.

She looks up at me. "Sorry...you didn't like it?"

At that moment, I see a different Ava.

"I like it," I murmur. Damn, it was sensational for my cock. But this woman means everything to me, and I can't go on without unraveling what's driving her this way.

She continues sucking, but I gently withdraw, nudging her shoulders up so she's face-to-face with me.

"Hey..." I settle her on my chest, feeling the rise and fall of her breath against my skin. "Ava, what is it?"

Her lips quiver, unable to speak. Her expression is coated with guilt.

I cup her chin softly. "This isn't about me not liking what you're doing." I examine her glistening eyes, searching for the truth. I have to ask the question now. "Did he ever hurt you?"

She grimaces. I feel the significance of her burden. Last night, amid her distress, she desperately sought relief from me. Now, she's desperate to please me because of a pain that has just surged from deep within her.

"Ava, talk to me," I whisper as low as I can. With how helpless she is now, lying on me, I swear I'll break her if my voice comes out just a little bit louder.

"I wanted to please you until you come. Don't you want that?"

I brush my fingers against her cheek, "I do, as long as you enjoy it too."

She inhales sharply, lost for words.

I probe further. "Did he force you to do things you didn't want to?"

She lets out a sigh, her eyes closing with regrets. "At first, he used to hit me," she confesses, her voice barely above a whisper. "But then, one day, when he broke my arm, I left him."

A pang of pain surges through me, but I push it aside and focus on her. She shrugs as if questioning whether I want to hear what comes next. I stroke her, urging her to release whatever is tormenting her.

She continues, "He came to me, apologizing. He had gone to therapy to control his anger, and he swore he'd changed. I foolishly took him back." Bitterness laces her voice. "Well, he did change. He didn't hit me that hard anymore, and in bed... as long as I did it his way, he would leave me alone."

"I'm so sorry you had to go through all that." The pain inside me resurfaces, stronger and impossible to ignore. I'll make it my commitment to keep that cockbag away from Ava forever.

"I stayed with him for the sake of Quinton. My pregnancy became complicated, and during my final trimester, I was mostly bedridden, so I needed him. I felt like I owed him for all the care he gave me."

"Ava, Ava." I hold her tightly, almost shaking her. I'm furious about the control Willem exerted over her, and I wish it had been me caring for her. "You don't owe that man anything!"

"I know, I don't. But at the time, I couldn't help feeling that way. Willem became a devoted caregiver when he was in the right state of mind, and it was hard not to feel grateful. But when our wedding became inevitable..." She exhales, full of anger. "I just couldn't do it. I couldn't spend the rest of my life with him."

I draw a breath, making it audible to emphasize her safety with me. "Ava, I am not Willem. I love you, I care about you, and I want nothing in return. Even if you didn't love me, I still love you." I guide her hand to my chest, wrapping it with mine. "Tonight, I want to make love to you in a way that pleases you."

Her finger moves under my palm and strokes my pec delicately. "I want to please you too."

"I know. I know." I rub my palm against the top of her hand. "The truth is, Ava Belle, I haven't been in a long-term relationship. But I'm a man who can't take pleasure in sex unless my woman is happy and content. It's a man's role to satisfy his woman. I don't care what other people say, and I'm not talking about equality and all that stuff. It's what I live by. You before me."

She looks at me with a distant expression as though my words aren't registering. I cup her cheek, bringing her back to the present. To me. My other hand coasts down her chest, passing the curve of her breast. I want her heart to take charge first, and only then can she let out her urges. That's the only way she can embrace her true desires—not Willem's, not her past.

"I love you, Jack," she murmurs, crawling up on me and again planting a kiss on my lips. She presses firmly, her breath steady. "And I love you for what you've just asked me."

"I never want you to hide from me."

"I never will." She shakes her head, feebly but clearly. "Willem did things I wish he hadn't, but over time, I learned to create distance. It was like—I let him in, and he was in the same house as me, but I locked myself inside a room, out of reach. He knocked, he tried to kick the door down, he rammed into it, but it held."

Pride fills me. I'm never wrong about her. "I know you have that strength."

"He's out of my life, but sometimes his knock sounds louder, his kick more powerful. It makes me wonder if the lock will ever give way. Just like tonight," she says arduously. "In Clancy today—reading that contract, seeing his name on it, witnessing his cruel tricks—it was as if his force had made its way back into me. I don't know what possessed me to unleash it on you. I'm sorry, Jack."

"No, there's no need to apologize, Ava." I turn my face to hers, pressing our cheeks together.

"That lock still holds. The door remains shut," she maintains. "No matter what happens, I'm still me, okay? Free, not chained. Yours, not his."

I nod in understanding. "Let him come to you. I know you're not scared of him. And if he happens to overpower you, I'll be there, holding that damn door. I'll be the lock, the security bar that stops him from reaching you."

I hold her chin gently, urging her to meet my gaze. "As long as you let me stay with you."

"I always want you in that room with me, Jack." She puts her hand on her heart.

"And when you hear that knock again, tell him to pack his sorry ass."

A smile graces her beautiful face, matching the curls that frame it. We lay in silence, absorbing each other's presence.

She then raises her head. "He's gone. Now, may I?" she pleads with genuine lust this time.

I let her go, allowing her to slink down my torso. But then she stops, whispering, "I do want you to cum in my mouth."

Excitement builds within me. Feeling her jerking her hips, removing her panties, my cock swells, begging for her touch. Without words, I surrender to her, letting her take control.

Her scorching lips nibble at my shaft, sucking it with a steady up-and-down movement.

I spread my legs wider, hoping to provide her with more comfort, but she surprises me by nudging them back together. Instead, she rests herself upon my legs, teasingly rubbing her tits and pelvis against them while her mouth is still accommodating me. Arousal radiates from her body, spreading through my skin. It's so tantalizing and sexy as fuck.

Her hands firmly grip the sides of my hips, and I instinctively take hold of them, intertwining our fingers. As she slowly crawls toward me, her hair tickles my sensitive skin, heightening my senses. I brush her hair back, revealing her beautiful face, and our lips meet in a passionate kiss. Our tongues twist together like a pair of vines as I follow her body's erotic motion. The surface of her entrance stimulates my length. Goddamn. This woman is putting Venus to shame!

Then she flashes me a dirty grin, biting her lower lip, before returning her focus to my throbbing cock. I jolt as her mouth latches on the slick tip. This is the edge, the ultimate threshold that I'm about to breach.

"I'm gonna cum, baby," I mutter, trying to stop my gasp from forming into a moan that will be too loud for the night.

Ava quickens her pace, her breath coming in ragged gasps as she takes my entire length into her throat. This is a pleasure I've never experienced before. I hold back, just to savor her a moment longer. She has penetrated my heart with her lust, skill, and care, and my own fervor has allowed her to do so deeply. I never desired other women, but with Ava, it's different—she's not just another woman fulfilling a physical need. She's my dedication. She possesses every part of me.

I can no longer contain myself, and with a suppressed cry, I release. Everything becomes light, every nerve in my body tingling with ecstasy. I feel gentle pressure along my pulsing member as Ava swallows. Sitting up, I meet her gaze, pulling her up so she rests against my pecs. I kiss her engorged lips, tasting the mingling flavors of my own and her natural sweetness.

We lie close together, our bodies still warm and our breaths heavy with satedness. Then I murmur, "Just give me a moment, and then it will be my turn."

Bliss fills her eyes as she huffs, "I've already come, baby. You're too hot for my body to resist." Her gaze is dreamy, her irises swirling like a storm. She means what she said.

I bury my face in her hair, inhaling the intoxicating scent of her curls. "If you change your mind, just let me know." If she's willing, I plan to go all the way with her. She's as irresistible as a comforting blanket on a winter day. However, her response comes as a weary sigh, a sign that such a possibility is out of reach tonight. She's one tired mama.

I chuckle. "Tell me, did you think of me when you were alone? I mean, after we parted in Bozeman?"

She shifts, rolling halfway to look into my eyes. "All the time. Your handsome face is impossible to forget."

I venture further, asking, "Have you ever fantasized about me and touched yourself?"

She halts her laughter as I gently wipe the sheen of sweat from her delicate nose. "I thought that's what you were asking in the first place."

Thoughts of our time in Bozeman resurface, recalling the

moment I shared my kidnapping story with her. At that time, I believed she saw me as strong and saw no flaws in me, but I never actually sought her opinion of me.

"Did you ever see me as a broken man?" I ask.

She rises slightly, her hand caressing my face. "You're as gorgeous as sin, Jack. And I have a goddamn weakness for a broken man."

Today has been spectacular, but some things cannot be fixed overnight. Broken— that is what I am. She may not fully comprehend the depth of it. But despite that, I will always seek her, clinging to her for as long as she allows. How long that will be, I cannot say. Perhaps until she glimpses the true extent of my brokenness and is frightened away.

"How about you?" she asks. "Did you think of me when you lay in bed alone?"

"You, Ava, are my moon. And it goes beyond the cliché of mysterious beauty. I'm talking about its force—how it governs the earth's tides from such a distance," I explain. "We were apart, but there was no one else in my thoughts, my imagination, my fantasies, or my longing."

Ava's lips curl into a smile as sleep takes hold of her. With a slow blink, I shut my eyes, silently hoping that Scalpel won't make an appearance.

17

———

AVA

Rays of morning sunlight filter through the slender gaps behind the curtain. I stretch my body languidly, savoring the comfort of the bed, but the absence of Jack's warmth beside me jolts me awake. Anticipating a cuddle and the possibility of continuing where we left off last night, I ponder what he could be doing.

I hear the water running; it's from the bathroom next door. I think my man is in there. I rise from my spot, making my way to check on Quinton in his crib. My baby is still peacefully asleep, a true miracle, considering he only woke up once during the night.

"You have my heart. Do you know that?" I whisper. Despite knowing I might wake him, I can't resist rubbing his chest.

The door creaks open, revealing Jack as he enters the room with careful, tiptoeing steps. Outside, the wooden floor groans under the weight of Huxley's footsteps, muffled but still audible. I can smell the aroma of freshly brewed coffee, evidence of Huxley's attempt at silence.

A smile spreads across my face as I take in Jack's appearance. His body, clad only in boxers, pulls me in like a lure. His hair glistens with dampness, his face fresh as if he has just splashed water all over himself. And oh, those abs, they shimmer in the soft light, rendering me weak. It has only been a few days since his arrival, but the military grooming has given way to a thickening beard. I also notice a trail of hairs leading down to his crotch, an enticing invitation.

He comes closer, his lips meeting mine in a light kiss, a smile directed toward Quinton. "I can't believe how cute he is," Jack whispers.

"I can't either." I follow his gaze, watching the little boy puckering in his sleep. "Every time I look at him, I tell myself I want another one. And you know what? If I have another one, I will say the same thing."

His arm encircles my hip, his hand playfully pinching my ass. Perhaps there is still time for a cuddle and maybe even more in bed. But his breathing reveals a hint of exertion, as if he has been running.

"Hey, don't get all serious about what I just said, okay? I'm not trying to drop hints or anything," I murmur. But he hitches as if trying too hard to steady his breathing. I place a hand on his cheek. "You okay?"

He rubs the small of my back, grumbling, "I'm fine."

Slowly my hand lands on his back. As I prepare to give it a comforting rub, my touch arrives at the bump between his shoulder blades. He jerks his back, his usual reaction. Among other things that happened, I never asked about it. Slanting back, I position myself to get a clearer view. "This is a long scar." I brush a finger along it.

"I don't know how I got it. For sure, I didn't have it before the abduction," he confesses, his face reflecting a mix of contemplation and deliberate avoidance. He then drives my hand away, adding, "Can we not talk about it, please?"

I know it's more than just a scar for him. Last night, in the twilight between sleep and wakefulness, he asked me if I saw him as a broken man. Exhausted and sated, my response was casual—*I'm a sucker for broken men.* Perfect men never attract me. Perfect can mean either dull or pretentious. Jack carries his fair share of baggage, and he may be right in calling himself broken. But it's through those cracks in his armor that I connect with him, and I hope to be the glue that binds his shattered pieces together.

Catching my sidelong glance, he nags, "Stop looking at it, Ava."

Seeing his pleading eyes, I know now is not the right time to unearth what he's been concealing. It's not just from me, but from himself as well. It's not a secret. It's a pain that he's not ready to confront yet.

"How about this?" I point at a brown patch located on his left shoulder. It's no bigger than the 'press here' sticker on a talking teddy you'd see in Target.

Glancing at the spot, he asks with a light tone, "What do you want to know? It's just a birthmark."

"It looks like a rabbit."

He responds with a soft giggle. "That's what other people say. Where's your creativity?"

I scrunch up my nose. "How about a jackrabbit?"

"Smarty pants!" He pinches my nose.

I rub the mark, imagining drawing it. "Actually, I think it looks like Elmo."

He breaks into laughter, his face lighting up. "How?"

"If you stretch his ears up, his silhouette will look like this." I trail my finger, forming a circle around the mark that looks more like a temporary tattoo. A cute one.

Amusement weaves into his expression. "Okay, let's settle with Elmo then."

He grazes the curls at my nape, playfully tickling me. A

deep exhale escapes his lips, producing a seductive sound as if his Adam's apple is aroused—if that's even possible. And seriously, what am I supposed to do with the manly smell coming from that tiny space between his lips?

He's about to turn, probably to get dressed, but I don't give him a chance. Not after that testosterone-ridden breath.

I guide him back onto the soft sheets of the bed, my lips forming a mischievous smirk, my eyes silently conveying—*I want you.* He inches closer, and I steal a kiss from his lips, sucking that intoxicating air off him. My fingers shamelessly trace the contours of his abs, then venture lower.

"What's that look?" Jack asks.

Last night, he saw the whole me—uncurated, unfiltered. And he accepted it as if I were the most amazing person he had ever encountered. He didn't shy away from the parts of me that reminded him of Willem; instead, he embraced them.

Now that Quinton is safely home and Jack is in my bed, satisfying my aching core will be the perfect way to top it off.

"Your woman has a request," I answer. My hand moves lower, resting on the bulge that strains against the satin fabric of his boxers.

Jack's grip tightens on my ass, pulling me closer as our lips meet. The collision of our breaths creates a coarse, grating sound as our bodies rub together. My panties are soaked in my arousal, their discomfort a constant reminder of the mounting need to remove them.

"The Comet is out and about." Jack gestures toward the door. The cozy confines of the house amplify every sound. Huxley's room lies just beyond, while the kitchen is nearby.

"Yeah, I hear him."

Jack hums. "It doesn't feel very private right now."

"Isn't that exciting?" I tease, a giggle escaping my lips.

"Ava!" His eyes widen.

"It's like a milder version of enjoying the thrill of being caught."

Jack playfully smacks my ass and shakes his head. "And I thought you were the sweet type." With mischief in his eyes, he pushes me to bed and throws himself on top of me.

I stifle a laugh as he tickles my sides, quipping, "Don't underestimate a mother in heat."

"I'll be damned," he utters in a sexy, low growl.

"What we should be mindful of is Quinton. We just have to hold our sighs, and our moans, and everything else…" My voice stretches, filled with seduction, almost like a challenge.

"Can you?" He lowers himself.

"I can't promise anything," I reply nonchalantly.

His eyes blaze with verve, leaving me guessing what he has in mind. "Have you always been this naughty?"

"I've been hiding my true self for far too long," I confess.

His head cocks to the side, contemplating.

I'm not one to indulge in kinky sex. What I long for is a connection that allows me to witness a man's genuine masculinity in plain view with no gimmicks, trapping me in his honesty. And I've found the man. With that surety, I seek a little play. The idea of someone possibly hearing us excites me, and I make no apology.

He looks at me with a concerned expression as if he's deciphering the subtle signals I've been sending him. "But you just want the two of us, right? Nothing more?"

I let out a silent laugh.

"Relax, Romeo. Threesomes never make my juices flow. Or…maybe I've never actually thought about it." I want to push his buttons and see how he reacts. Truthfully, no matter where my passion takes me, getting involved with another man is out of the question.

Jack pinches my nose. "Just you and me, okay?"

His face close to mine, I answer with certainty, "I don't want anyone else, Jack."

Hearing it, he ravages my lips, his embrace so tight. I sigh, welcoming his weight against me, his morning wood pressed on my stomach. He slides down, his strong grip tugging me along. The cotton sheet caresses my back as he positions me. My legs dangle over the edge of the bed, naked and restless. Feral desire plagues my body, penetrating deep into my bones.

Kneeling between my thighs, Jack's hands exert a firm pressure as they knead my buttocks. He slides my panties down, fueling vivid fantasies of his tongue lapping at my most sensitive areas. My pussy throbs with need. The lips of my sex swell shamelessly, boldly displaying their arousal.

My thighs push wider apart, granting him full access as he answers my call. He buries his face between my legs, his mouth engulfing my molten clit with a hungry fervor. Waves of pleasure travel from my tits to the tips of my toes. His hands grip my waist, preventing me from bucking. In the absence of my ability to freely writhe, I can't even release the pressure through my voice. It's a test of self-control that I may have to forego.

Enjoying my waning resistance, he slips his fingers between my engorged pussy lips, parting them gently. His fingers take control, relentless in their manipulation of my bud, while his tongue adds another layer of sensation. In a desperate attempt to stifle my impending scream, I grab the hem of the sheet and bite down on it.

Jack gives me a momentary reprieve, allowing himself to savor my surrender to the immense arousal. When he crawls up, I notice he has stripped off his boxers. His hardness brushes against my belly, taunting me.

A satisfied smirk graces Jack's lips as he takes in my plea. "More?"

How do I respond? I want him so damn badly, but sooner or later, my screams will betray me, waking Quinton and announcing to our guest outside that I'm in full sexual mode.

But I'm at the point of no return. I ditch my T-shirt, giving him a sign to move on.

His eyes fixate on my bare breasts. But eager to return to my core, he comes back down, drinking me like a mythical fountain of youth. It's a sensation I had long forgotten, but now it's reignited with an exquisite and considerate touch. His eyes periodically raise to me as if assuring me that he's doing it all to please me.

My orgasm builds, tightening my core with overflowing pleasure. This time, he allows me to buck and jerk however I want.

He then lifts my ass with one hand, allowing his tongue to penetrate me at a new angle. Simultaneously, his finger flicks my bud one last time, and I succumb. It's a silent orgasm, yet its impact reverberates louder than any sound I've ever uttered.

Jack crawls toward me, letting go more of his weight on me as if signaling the intensity of his next moves. His cock and balls graze my belly, leaving a trail of wetness.

"Jack, baby," I sigh. With a single look at his stunning face, I affirm my trust and desire for him. In return, he reciprocates my gesture. We're like two souls fusing as one, neither eclipsing the other.

Willem never truly destroyed me, as I refused to let him, but he did take a piece of me. Being with Jack last night allowed me to reclaim my sense of self fully. This morning, he proves his words were not empty promises—it's me before him.

"Damn, you taste so good," he growls, sliding his wet finger inside my mouth.

I savor it, knowing that what I taste is also how he tastes. He then drives my hand toward his hardened manhood. I wrap my fingers around his shaft, rubbing it, encouraging him. Hooking my armpits, he pushes me up the bed, ensuring that my legs are no longer hanging over the edge. He separates my knees, positioning himself at my entrance.

"Ava, I didn't bring any protection."

"I don't have any either."

He takes a few seconds to contemplate. "I'm going to pull out when I come. Are you okay with that?"

My heart swells with understanding. While I would gladly accommodate him completely, I know there are still ghosts that haunt him. Tempting fate would be foolish. "Yes, I'm okay with that," I answer fervently.

"It's not that I don't want to come inside you. I'm just not ready."

"I understand, Jack. It's fine."

He kisses me, his lips brushing against mine with a gentle touch, filled with gratitude. As he eases into me, the head of his cock pushes past my entrance, stretching me. Thanks to his unhurried pace, any discomfort transforms into a sweet ache.

Then, without warning, he thrusts harder, fully spreading me open. I gasp, my core clenching involuntarily as his movements hit the walls deep inside me. My fingers grip his shoulders, my mouth hanging open in a mix of surprise and pleasure. His erection fills me completely, even overflowing, forcing me to open up wider.

Just as I'm about to cry out, he latches onto my lips. My longing for him burns wildly as his body rhythmically moves up and down, his cock resembling a powerful engine piston firing at full speed. Every fiber of my being is obliterated by his relentless effort to bring me pleasure.

His masculine scent blankets me. Driven by his rubbing, my breasts plump against his firm chest. And then, he penetrates me deeply with one long glide. My throat constricts, my voice vanishes as my orgasm cascades more magnificently, surpassing any previous experience.

After witnessing me coming, Jack's breath quickens into gasps, his thrusts becoming more urgent, his testicles lurching as they press rigidly against my perineum. Our bodies continue to grind together, slick with a mixture of sweat and desire. Then, everything in him tenses, followed by a tremor coursing through his hips and pelvis. He withdraws, his head landing beside my cheek, his face flat on the space within the pillow. A muffled scream trembles next to my ear as he spurts his warm seeds onto my belly.

Collapsing with a roll, he avoids crashing into me. With haste, he kisses me, his breath hitching. "You're incredible," he murmurs, his eyes locked with mine as he fondles my breasts.

Oh shit...

I hurriedly shield my nipples, trying to contain the flow of milk. Some cloudy droplets cling to his skin. So, the slickness between our bodies was more than just sweat and desire. I must have leaked during my climax.

I sigh, "Gosh, I'm sorry..."

His kiss mutes my words and his hands cover my nipples, replacing mine. Carrying on with his fondling, he whispers appreciatively, "The beauty of a lactating mother." And just like that, he erases any trace of my embarrassment.

We lie entwined. The residual heat from our sex hangs in the air, enveloping us as we drift into slumber. I awaken to a sudden chill as Jack stirs beside me. Then I hear faint rustling from within the crib. I make my way over to check on Quinton. The boy wears a serene smile, his eyes still shut tight, lost in his dreams. I gently stroke his cheek before turning back to Jack.

His gaze lingers on my naked body. His hand reaches out, urging me to return to his side.

"You're one sexy mama," he murmurs in my ear, his hand tracing the contour of my waist and hip. He doesn't mind the imperfections, the softness, or the stretchmarks that adorn my belly.

"I can't believe Quinton is still asleep."

"He knows we needed this." He presses me against him.

Oh, how we needed it!

"I'm going to take a shower. Can you keep an eye on Quinton?" I ask.

"Of course. Just make sure you're decent when you step out," he says, his gaze lingering on my nakedness.

I chuckle softly. "I think the cat isn't in the kitchen anymore."

"Wherever he is, please, cover up," he pleads.

"No one will see my body except you," I whisper.

He captures my lips in a passionate kiss. His excitement is palpable as he guides my hand to feel his arousal once again. "You've turned me into an addict, don't you know?" his voice husky, so erotic it sets my body ablaze as if he's back inside me.

I respond with a hum, challenging him softly—*what are you gonna do about it?*

He continues, "I'm going to make love to you every single day."

With that, I abandon my plan to shower and ravage him relentlessly.

18

JACK

I hold the door open for Ava as we enter The Thirsty Fox. It's lunchtime, and the place is bustling, especially with their buy-one-get-one-free offer today. This bar is known as the official watering hole for Red Mark staff. Even though I've only been here once, I can't get over how amazing their cheeseburgers are. They say they're the best in Montana.

Ava pushes the stroller through the door. I let her walk ahead of me, captivated by the way her figure moves. It's the first time I've seen her in a dress, and it's not just any dress. The ivory fabric clings to her body, showing off the curves. The skirt gracefully stops in the middle of her thigh, revealing her lovely legs. If I had to kill to indulge in her, I would.

This afternoon, we're going on a double date with Morgan and Tyler, who just returned from their honeymoon. It's been three weeks since I arrived in Helena. After the showdown in Townsend and Clancy, there haven't been any incidents so far. Willem seems to be going about his usual business as well, according to our intel. He's currently in London. Rumor has it he's meeting with Richard Branson. Nobody knows if it's true or if there's anything more sinister in his agenda.

Cass, Sam's wife and the bar manager, has reserved a table for us. She greets us with her usual warm smile as I pull out a chair for Ava and assist her with Quinton.

"Hello, Quinton," Cass greets the baby, gently caressing his cheek with her fingers. It's been a few weeks since we last visited Cass, but he seems to remember her and smiles. "Oh, you're such a sweet baby!" she exclaims. Then, she turns her attention to Ava. "Now I want another one!" the mother of two jokes.

Or maybe she's not joking. Both Ava and I notice her hand discreetly rubbing her belly while her lips quiver, clearly suppressing a broad grin.

"Cass?" Ava drawls. "You are having another one, aren't you?"

Cass looks torn, perhaps caught between letting out her bubbling emotions and berating herself for spilling the beans. "Sam and I decided not to tell anyone yet. Please... don't react," she whispers, her eyes wandering left and right.

Cass is a familiar face to many in this bar, so we keep the beans to ourselves.

Ava continues, "I want three more!" Then she glances at me.

Cass pats my shoulder. "No pressure."

I chuckle, although Ava's intense gaze makes me believe my girl isn't joking either. I'm open to the idea of having children, but I do hope that she has the patience for me.

Cass compliments Ava, saying, "You look stunning, by the way." She winks at me and adds, "Keep her close if I were you."

"Yes, ma'am," I reply. I take a seat next to Ava, holding her hand. Quinton sits on her other side.

"So, while we're still waiting for Morgan and Ty, I'll give you the menus. You know what I'd recommend, right?"

Ava and I chuckle.

Cass offers, "Would you like to order drinks first?"

"Well, let's wait for Ty and Morgie, thanks," Ava says politely.

"Sure. If you need anything, you know where I am," she says before leaving the table.

I press my lips against Ava's hand, appraising her lightly made-up face. The soft brush of mascara emphasizes her long lashes, making her eyes all the more enticing. And who can resist her lips, alluringly covered in cherry-colored lipstick? They tempt me like we hadn't already made love today.

Tyler and Morgan make their way into the bar, instantly infusing the already vibrant atmosphere with their presence. Walking hand-in-hand with his wife, the former SEAL appears rejuvenated, as if he has just emerged from a day spa. It's no surprise, considering he just returned from the trip of his life.

Ava rushes toward Morgan, the sound of her hurried footsteps traceable among the bustling diners. Their tearful reunion begins with heartfelt embraces even before they reach the table. In their silent interaction, I can sense a bond that goes beyond mere friendship. It's tangible in the way they hold each other, and now their eyes convey reassurance in each other's presence.

"Are you all right? Are you okay?" Morgan stammers, their embrace still tight.

"I'm fine, but I missed you," Ava replies, her voice filled with longing.

Morgan was just a toddler when they first met, and with a five-year age gap, Ava has become a nurturing older sister figure to her. But today, they both stand united as equals, sharing the burden of Ava's ordeal.

"You should have called me!" Morgan exclaims, shaking Ava's shoulders.

"You were on your honeymoon, for heaven's sake!"

"I was in Antarctica, but I would have returned to Helena when I reached Argentina. You really should have called me!" Morgan insists in frustration.

Meanwhile, Tyler and I exchange greetings. It has been over a year since I last saw him. Navigating the aisle of the Thirsty Fox, the newly married man wears a contented smile, hinting that his post-wedding affair went off without a hitch.

As I invite him to take a seat, I overhear Ava telling Morgan, "Everything is under control thanks to Jack and Red Mark." Morgan then glances at me, silently expressing her gratitude. The two women release each other from their embrace, and Morgan swiftly heads toward me, enveloping me in a tight hug. No words are spoken, only a few sobs.

"So, how was your honeymoon?" I query, not wanting to dwell on Quinton's kidnapping.

"It was out of this world. Literally. Antarctica is like a world of its own," Morgan says, rounding me to get to Quinton. "Quinnie-Bear! Hello, baby. Do you remember me?" She takes him out of the stroller. "You've grown already! You're so heavy now." She settles him on her hip with an exaggerated grunt.

"Mo!" He attempts to pinch Morgan's chin.

"Yes, I'm Morgan, but I think you're calling your puppy, aren't you?" Morgan says, kissing Quinton like she can't get enough of him.

Quinton cringes, wriggling hard.

"Quinton, it's Aunty Morgie." Ava tries to calm him, but he insists on getting away.

"Huh... I feel like a boogeyman." Morgan sighs, putting Quinton back in his stroller.

"Give him time. He'll warm up to you," Ava reassures.

Cass takes our order while we talk about the newlyweds' honeymoon—from glamping in South America to joining a few scientists in Antarctica, thanks to Morgan being a biologist.

Morgan then looks at Ava. "My God, what have you been doing? You're like... ripped!" She feels Ava's arm.

"I've been working out with Jack," Ava replies.

"For real?" Morgan exclaims.

"USMC boot camp style?" Tyler quips.

"Kind of. The gentle version," Ava says.

I give Ty a proud trainer's wink. Oh yeah, Ava Belle has been hitting the gym with me. I never pressured her because she's always perfect in my eyes. At first, she was just looking for an energy boost, remembering how exercise helped her recover from endless chemo during her battle with leukemia. But once she started, there was no stopping her. She's a pocket rocket that keeps throwing surprises. She can do ten pull-ups without breaking a sweat, and she's solid in her lifting and squats.

Better still, Quinton, my trusty assistant, is always there during our sessions. I especially enjoy our morning jogs with him, where Ava and I take turns pushing his stroller. Sometimes, Elmo joins us, too, as long as we're not going too fast for his little legs to keep up.

"And this is new!" Morgan exclaims, her eyes narrowing as she scrutinizes her best friend some more. Her fingers weave through Ava's bouncy hair.

In response, Ava lifts her shoulder in a nonchalant gesture, leaving Morgan's imagination to figure out the how and why.

I did notice my girlfriend was spending more time than usual taking care of her hair this morning. She transformed her curls into beautiful waves, making them look more voluminous. She used a wand-like device that she purchased during one of our shopping trips, along with some hair products. Her strands appear thicker, and the blonde hues seem even shinier. And she smells phenomenal.

As the burgers arrive, our eyes are drawn to the sight of perfectly grilled patties sizzling and releasing their mouthwatering aroma. I'm dying to savor the soft sesame seed bun and the succulent ground meat melting in my mouth. Not to mention the Thirsty Fox's secret sauce.

"So, you're a new woman now," Morgan remarks. "Thanks to a certain Marine."

Ava raises her eyes to me, nibbling a lip.

Morgan continues, still intrigued by her best friend's change. "I can't even remember the last time I saw you wearing a dress. And to top it off, it's a sexy dress like that!"

Ava responds calmly, "It's the baby-daddy effect."

Morgan mouths a 'whoa,' then says, "That's bold!" She then turns to me, "Has she told you that?"

I cackle. "Something along that line."

I have to admit, I feel flattered to be considered Quinton's father. Ava has mentioned the idea of having more children in passing, but we haven't had a serious discussion about it yet.

Tyler, who has been quietly enjoying his burger, chimes in, "Bozeman feels like a distant memory now. It's hard to believe that Quinton is already eight months old."

"And I was just two months pregnant then," Ava adds.

Morgan cocks her head, asking me, "So, was it really love at first sight? I distinctly recall seeing you completely smitten, offering Ava your jacket. And she..." Morgan gestures toward Ava, "...she was awe-struck. I mean, you were the biggest lightning strike of the night."

I remember that stormy night. Morgan was hiding under the protection of Red Mark after narrowly escaping an attempt on her life. At the time, I was off duty, and Sam was short on manpower, so I agreed to help. That night, Tyler had to travel. I was assigned to stay with Morgan at Tyler's parents' farmhouse in Bozeman. Little did I know, Tyler returned with Ava in tow.

"Oh, look at you blushing, baby!" Ava steps in after my extended silence.

"Shush! Let the man speak!" Morgan protests.

I look at Ava, reminiscing about her kind, radiant eyes even during the miserable weather. And her curly hair, bouncing and shining, seemed to call out to me. Being a Marine who doesn't indulge in impossible romantic notions, I never believed in love at first sight. But with her, everything was proven possible.

I clear my throat. "Well, I didn't just want her. It was a feeling I had never experienced before. I wish I had kissed her then and asked her out," I admit.

Tyler whistles and addresses me by my rank, as he always has since we first met. "L.T., you've given the perfect answer."

Ava leans in and kisses me, then smiles while she thumbs the lipstick marks she's left behind.

Tyler washes down his lunch with a few gulps of beer—Fallen Angel, Cass' own brew, which has apparently become the bestseller at this bar. He asks, "What's next for you guys?"

I reply, "My leave ends next week, and I need to sort things out back in Hawaii."

Ava looks at me, a thin layer of concern coating her face.

Morgan wipes her sauce-covered hands and asks, "Ave, if you could live anywhere, where would it be?"

"L.A. had been my home. But I've fallen in love with Montana since Bozeman. And in the past few weeks, I've felt it even more. If I were a baby and my mother asked me where I'd love to live—California or Montana—hands down, it's here. There's ample space, I can breathe, and we're surrounded by nature. And you're here, Morgie. What else can you ask for?"

"So, more kids are on the cards?" Morgan teases, to which Ava responds with a wink.

I smile, responding to her spontaneous delight. She genuinely wants to give Quinton siblings, as having children is a blessing for her, especially after her battle with leukemia. It's amazing how the drugs never affected her ability to get pregnant. Any children we have together will be so fortunate to have her as their mother. But will they also be lucky to have me as their father?

Morgan continues. "Hey, I actually know someone who works at a media company here. I could put in a good word for you. You may not be producing courtroom sketches, but you could be a good fit in their design team."

"That'll be great!" Ava exclaims, her eyes sparkling with excitement as if her future suddenly becomes clear.

"You're going to be based here permanently, Jack?" Tyler asks me.

"It's a possibility, yes," I respond tentatively. The only military installation in Montana is an Air Force base near Great Falls, which is about a hundred miles north of here. I don't believe there's any opportunity for me there, but I don't want to bring it up at the moment.

"Or, I could come with you to Hawaii," Ava suggests, possibly picking up my unease.

Shifting my chair closer to her, I put my arm around her shoulder and say, "We'll need to talk about it, sweetheart."

"You know what I'm going to say, right?" Tyler nudges. "Would you consider joining Red Mark?"

I lean back, acknowledging his predictable question. "I won't rule it out."

"Comet has been talking about you."

"Has he?" I say. "He's a great kid."

"He's young, but he's had to deal with a lot of tough shit."

"He told me he helped his mother raise his brother because their dad passed away when Huxley was only twelve," Ava says.

"Yeah, that, and did he tell you about Colombia?" asks Tyler.

"He did."

"That he lost his girlfriend in that operation?"

So the Comet omitted that part when he told me the story. Perhaps he hasn't made peace with that yet, knowing it might interfere with his focus at the time.

I shake my head in disbelief and mutter, "That's messed up."

Away from the ladies who are busy putting on a bib on Quinton, Tyler says, "She was a local, a CIA informant. She was shot a week after the raid, her body left on a bench in front of a church."

"Fuck," I mumble to him.

While Ava and Morgan take turns feeding Quinton, Ty and I order our second burgers. The baby enthusiastically devours his carrot puree and honey tea, specially prepared by the chef.

Desserts arrive, drawing a collective gasp of surprise from everyone at the table. Even the ladies, who initially said 'no' to the huckleberry pie and ice cream, give in to the temptation.

My phone buzzes in my pocket. I glance down and see a message from my captain reminding me about my leave.

Noticing my expression, Ava asks, "You okay?"

Unable to bring myself to discuss it right now, I dismiss the message and stroke my partner's hand, silently telling her we'll talk later.

19

JACK

A sneer creeps onto my face as I gaze at the photo in the newspaper. The image captures Willem Botha, a man who falls into the despicable category of assholes. And there are two types of despicable assholes—the ones who have the audacity to confront you directly, and the ones who cowardly taunt you from a distance.

Willem belongs to the latter group. It baffles me how he can appear saint-like in that picture, considering what he has done to his own son. He stands there, all smiles, alongside a group of esteemed information technology scientists at a prestigious London summit. Richard Branson's absence is notable, but the article emphasizes Willem's respect and recognition in the industry, even labeling him a trailblazer.

Ava wraps her arms around me from behind. "You're still staring at that photo?" she comments, resting her chin on my shoulder. Her apron carries the scent of freshly roasted potatoes and vegetables.

"I'm trying to envision what's going on in his mind."

"Power, money, pride," she scoffs. Then she turns me

around, giving me a casual smile. "By the way, how much sauce would you like?"

Tonight, she's preparing my favorite dish - fillet mignon with mushroom sauce and all the trimmings.

"The more, the better," I respond eagerly, turning my head to give her a quick peck on the cheek.

"I thought you'd be the saucy type," she quips.

As she moves away from me, I reach out and catch her hand, not wanting to let go. "Next time, I'll cook your favorite. By the way, what is it?"

She looks at me, thinking. "Baked halibut with fresh herbs."

"It sounds delicious. I'll make it happen," I assure her. "Helena isn't well known for its seafood, but I won't let that stop me from getting fresh fish."

"Maybe you can cook me it when we're in Hawaii?" Ava winks at me as she walks away.

I know she would go to the ends of the earth for me, but she's happy here. She has her best friend, and there's a promising job opportunity in the city that may restart her career. And I must confess that Montana is a great place to raise children.

I close Willem's article and search for seafood markets in Helena where I can find fresh catches. As I peruse recipes for her favorite meal, I recall my days at St. Leo's monastery. Cooking was a skill I acquired under the guidance of a nurturing nun, though I've never attempted a dish with halibut before.

Shortly after, as half the house starts to smell like a steak restaurant, Ava calls dinner. We take our seats at the table.

"I talked to my captain," I inform her while spreading butter on my bread.

She nervously gazes at me. "And?"

"He's given me an extra week," I reveal.

She lets out a sigh of relief and says, "We can use that time to prepare for our move to Hawaii."

Ava is the type of person who will make sacrifices for her loved ones. Even though she doesn't get along with her parents, I learned from Morgan that Ava decided to give her relationship with Willem another try because of them. I don't know the specifics, and I don't agree with her choice, but it demonstrates her willingness to prioritize others over herself. I won't ask her to do the same for me. 'She before me' applies to more than just our physical relationship. In the face of harm, I'll stand before her. But anywhere else, it's her before me.

After the pause, she adds, "Let Quinton and me come with you, Jack."

I set down my knife to hold her hand. "Deep down, that's not what you want, is it?"

"That's what I want. I want to be with you."

"Look, sweetheart. It's not just about Hawaii. Living a military life means moving from one base to another. We might be in Oahu for the next few months or weeks, and then it could be California, Florida, North Carolina, or even overseas."

"We'll work it out, Jack. How many military families are there? They make it work."

"Some don't."

"Well, we'll make sure we're not one of them."

I admire her belief and optimism. But I've witnessed couples and families deeply in love, who believed they had the strength to endure, only to be torn apart by the harsh realities of logistical challenges and prolonged separation.

Growing up, I never had a male role model, and my understanding of what a childhood should be is as blank as a white sheet of paper. The idea of nurturing a family is already a daunting task, let alone leading a family in the demanding context of the military.

I'm not afraid of Ava leaving me—if she feels it's necessary, I will not stand in her way. What I'm afraid of is that she'll choose to stay with me no matter what, sacrificing her own well-being for my sake—and there would be no stopping her. And, heaven forbid, if something were to happen to me, I don't want to leave her and Quinton to pick up the pieces.

"I would give up the Corps for you, Ava," I assure her. I won't abandon her. If it means leaving the Marine Corps, then so be it.

"Don't let me be the reason for ending your career. You love your job, you're good at it, and you're needed there."

Confusion clouds my mind, making it impossible to decide. "I won't leave you alone. Especially when Willem is still a free man."

"We can't live in his shadow, Jack," Ava says. "We need to uncover the connection between Quinton's abduction and him. Until then, I don't think we can plan our future properly. So for now, I'm okay with taking things one step at a time."

I gently caress her, admiring her practicality. "You're right."

"Until Willem is behind bars, please don't make any rash decisions," she advises.

She is both intelligent and talented, and there are moments when I question how I am deserving of her. But she is undoubtedly the one for me. She loves me for who I am, and I reciprocate that love in a way that no one else can. Because of this, I believe we are deserving of each other.

I clear breadcrumbs off my fingertips, then move on to take my first bite of the steak. I dip it in the thick, creamy sauce. Damn! It's cracking. "This is delicious!" I exclaim, a proud smile forming on her face. I know she has skills in the kitchen, but I also appreciate the love and effort she put into making this meal. I almost clean my plate with my tongue, savoring every last bit.

Ava notices my enthusiasm. "Didn't I make enough?"

"Oh, you made plenty," I praise. "It was just so good."

After we finish eating, I try to stop her from helping me with the dishes, but she insists since Quinton is already in bed. Watching her diligently wipe the plates and glasses, I wonder how much Willem truly appreciated her when they were together.

She catches my expression. "You seem far away."

Her encouraging face gives me the confidence to start, "I've been wondering about you and Willem."

She picks up another plate, drying it with a kitchen towel, and teases, "You want to know if it was love at first sight?"

I chuckle. "Maybe."

"Apart from you, love at first sight had never been part of my history," she quips. "I met Willem while on an assignment in Sacramento. I worked for CBS at the time. You know, court artists aren't actually affiliated with the justice system. The media hire us to cover trials where cameras aren't allowed. W-Bot had just won a contract with California DOJ. We met through my manager at CBS. He and I became friends, but I never felt any romantic connection. He tried, but I kept my distance."

Ava places the stack of dried plates on the shelf, and I decide to abandon the rest of the cleaning. I guide her to the living room, ready to continue our conversation. Sitting beside me on the sofa, she puts her feet up and leans against me.

"Everything changed when I fell ill," she goes on.

"Your leukemia?"

"Yes, the most aggressive kind. It was almost a death sentence, even with the right treatment."

Uncomfortable heat sprawls at my back, hearing the word

'death' associated with her. It reminds me of the two kinds of danger there are in this world—the kind you can protect your loved ones from, and the kind that will win no matter what you do.

I tighten my hold on her. "You're clear now, though, right?"

She smiles, telling me not to worry. "I've been cancer-free for three years now."

I nuzzle at her neck, inhaling her scent. "So Willem helped you?"

Letting out a sigh of frustration, she takes hold of each of my fingers as if using them as a visual aid to help convey her explanation. "He did. And to make matters worse, my father's taxi business went under, leaving us with no way to afford my medical expenses. He made sure I had access to the best doctors and paid for everything without questions. I never asked him to do it. I was grateful for his help, but at the same time, I didn't want it."

I can picture Willem acting that way, barging into her life without considering her opinions. But the truth is, I can't deny that he saved Ava's life.

She continues. "I beat the cancer, but it wasn't easy for me to rebuild my career. I was just an intern, so after being absent for months, I had to start from scratch. Besides, the demand for courtroom sketches had dwindled. Willem, with his connections in high places, managed to help me secure a permanent position as a graphic artist with CBS while still working in court on an assignment basis.

"With a steady income, I could afford to send money regularly to my parents. But my parents... they have no shame! They kept accepting Willem's money to get things they didn't need—it was all for prestige. But I had never seen my parents so happy, and at the same time, I became stronger and got back on my feet, all thanks to Willem. So I gave in."

She sighs deeply, pressing her lips in regret.

"Hey, don't blame yourself," I say, rubbing her shoulder.

"You probably think I'm gutless."

"No, you're not! I would have done the same thing," I assure her.

"No, you wouldn't," she insists.

"I would. I was an orphan after being kidnapped, so I can't understand your situation with your parents. Well, my father is still around, but it's not the same when you met him for the first time as an adult."

Her head nods a little.

I interlock my fingers with hers, saying, "But I know I would have done what I could to make my family happy. And I would have felt indebted to Willem for what he had done. I hate that man. God, I really do! But if it weren't for him, you wouldn't be here. In your shoes, I would have done the same, Ava."

A small smile appears on her face. With newfound confidence, she continues, "After enduring his anger and abuse, I finally ended things with him. But my parents begged me to take him back, especially when my mom got sick. They've done so much for me. Even before the leukemia, I was frequently ill as a kid. So, I got back together with Willem, and I became pregnant."

There is pain in her voice, but I can also see a glimmer of joy on her face, perhaps reminiscing the moment she discovered she was expecting.

I nudge her closer, feeling her tiny waist in my hands. "You wouldn't trade it for anything, would you? Your Quinton?"

"No. Not in this life or the next. He's been my best friend, even when he was still in my belly." Her face beams with happiness. The light above catches her rosy cheeks, adding a soft glow to her features.

For so long, I never felt like I had a family. But when Sam found me and I reconnected with my dad, I finally understood the true value of family. I look at Ava and say, "No family is perfect, but you do whatever it takes to protect your loved ones. And Ava, you're here with me. That shows how resilient and determined you are."

She leans back, meeting my lips with hers. I feel the warmth and softness of her kiss. I think she's made peace with her past, something I haven't been able to achieve yet.

I continue. "We have less than a week to uncover the connection between Willem and Quinton's abduction, or at least with the bearded man. Cora-Lee is back on duty after her surgery. With her help, we'll get there faster."

"Okay."

"And if the week is up and we haven't caught that bastard, I think the only way to keep you and Quinton safe is to bring you both to Hawaii."

Ava flashes a smile, a visible release of tension. "Good plan."

Time is slipping away, and the looming end of my stay in Helena is putting everything in fast-forward. One thing is certain. No matter where I am—in Montana, Hawaii, or anywhere else in the world—I'll have to confront my nightmares if I want to make things work with Ava. She's faced her fair share of adversity, and I can't be the one to add to it. Once our business with Willem is done, I'll do whatever it takes to find Scalpel.

20

AVA

The trip to the local supermarket this afternoon put our endurance to the test. Quinton, overwhelmed by the unusually hot day and perhaps tired from not sleeping well, had a full-blown meltdown that caught everyone's attention. It was every parent's worst nightmare, but for me, it marked the completion of our family outing.

Back at home, after a few hours of swapping Quinton between us, Jack finally succeeds in calming him down. Laughter fills the room as the two boys play a game of 'who's behind the shades,' with Quinton donning the *Paw Patrol* sunglasses and Jack his Ray-Bans. The cheerful soundtrack of the show blares in the background, providing a welcome change from the constant demands of our baby.

I observe the interaction between the imposing Marine and the little one. Jack's hair has grown thick, a delightful change that allows me to have fun with more of him. Just like what Quinton is doing. Meanwhile, Jack's arms swathe the boy from shoulders to toes like a blanket—an experience I can only dream of unless I magically shrink myself.

On top of his luscious hair, Jack has allowed his beard to

grow, though he always has time to keep it tidy. It seems like he's enjoying the more relaxed grooming requirements while he's still off duty.

The mere sight of him stirs my core. I imagine the tingle of his beard against my body and the satisfying grip of his hair as I approach orgasm.

Carefully, Jack rises from his seat.

Oh my goodness! He has managed to lull Quinton to sleep. Jack discreetly signals for me to switch off the television as he passes by the bedroom door. I stay as quiet as possible. The last thing I want to do is undermine Jack's hard work after his marathon effort.

A few moments later, Jack finds me in the kitchen. He walks up behind me, slipping his hand around my waist, leaning on me as if he can't stand up anymore.

"I never thought a twenty-pound person could defeat me," he quips.

"You've come out victorious." I slide my fingers through the strands of his hair, feeling its smoothness against my skin. It hasn't grown too long, but damn! How can a man's hair be so sexually stimulating?

I rub the outside of my shorts pocket, feeling the object that I've been on me since we got home. But I ignore it. "Tea?" I offer, and he nods, placing his hand on my belly.

It's almost dark outside. With the kitchen lamps acting as a backlight, I gaze at our reflection in the window. Despite our fatigue-laden faces, I admire the two of us. No need for cues. We gravitate toward each other, lean into each other. It all happens naturally. It's inherently in us as if we'd been born with the instinct.

Jack seems to notice, flashing a funny face while tickling the side of my neck. I swear, we don't just look good—we look freaking adorable!

Turning to face him, I suggest, "Why don't you wait on the porch? I'll bring the tea."

He releases his hold on me and heads outside.

The spicy aroma wafts under my nose as I steep a few bags in the pot. The scent reminds me of how far I've come from the day I made the life-changing decision to leave Willem's Beverly Hills mansion behind. The frantic drive, Quinton's abduction and rescue—they feel like a distant past.

I join Jack, serving his cup, then settling into an oversized armchair on the back porch. The light is fading, the clouds obscuring the sunset. Nevertheless, this autumn day in Montana is surprisingly warm despite the occasional southerly breeze.

"You're too far away. Come here," Jack beckons me to sit on his lap.

"Isn't your lap getting cramped? Quinton was sitting on you for a few hours." Despite my will to be considerate of him, I can't resist lowering myself onto him.

His finger lands on the tip of my nose. "Quinton might've defeated me, but you'll never do. I mean, I'll always have time and energy for you."

I turn to look him in the eye. "You're amazing with Quinton. Have I ever told you?"

With a face full of pity, he answers, "No," as if I truly hadn't told him.

I sigh as my body melts into the curve of his abs.

"Before Quinton, I had never been around babies," he explains. "Not even Sam's son. But with our Quinnie-Bear... it was like an instant connection."

Our Quinnie-Bear. There's nothing hotter than a man who adores babies. Especially with Jack's physique and what he does, it's scorching.

I shift my position, wrapping my arm around his neck to

get closer. Jack ducks, his gaze fixed on my pocket brushing against his belly. "What's in there?" Sensing the texture of an item behind the fabric, he smirks when he realizes I've been keeping a condom there. "When were you planning to seduce me?"

I blush. I had hoped, but I didn't want to bother him after his efforts to put Quinton to sleep. "I wasn't going to." I tidy his hair and wipe his face. "You deserve to rest."

He runs his hands along the curves of my body, a gesture he enjoys. "I'm tired, but that doesn't mean I'm not up for pleasing you."

I coo, my hand caressing his abs while my eyes remain locked on his. The blue of his eyes has deepened, and the twinkle around his irises seems brighter, like they have their own source of light.

My hand glides upward, grazing the exposed skin where his shirt remains unbuttoned. It's more than just his thick ash-blonde hair and light-brown beard. His chest and abs boast a velvety softness that adds to his irresistible allure. How is it possible for a man to be this sexy? It's a crime!

Jack holds me, motioning me to face him directly. His gaze unravels my soul, drawing out my longing as if unspooling a ball of yarn.

"You know," Jack begins. "I want to have children with you. And you know I'll raise Quinton like he's my own."

My heart swells. "I know, Jack. I never doubt it."

A tender smile curves his lips. "If you really want another baby now, we'll make it happen. I know having children means a lot to you. It's my duty as your man to fulfill your wish. I trust you more than I trust myself, so I will change my life to suit yours. I've lived alone for far too long. I won't let my doubts ruin it for the both of us."

His words resonate deeply, and I admire his unwavering

commitment to my happiness. But I won't let our relationship be a one-sided affair. So I reach out to him, conveying my disagreement. "Jack, happiness is a two-way street."

He traces the outline of the condom. "Are you really willing to wait for me, even without knowing how long it will be?"

"Bringing a person into this world is a monumental decision. We both need to be ready. And honestly, I'm not ready right now either," I reply, my hand finding its place on his shoulder. "And you've got to know this, Jack. Having you in my life brings me more joy than the prospect of having more children."

It's the truth, but I have faith that he won't shatter my dream of having a big family. His past could create some obstacles, but I won't let that affect us. I'm bigger than his past. He'll choose me over it. Sooner rather than later, he will realize that granting my wish is not just about putting me first but also enriching both of us.

Jack's hand shrouds mine, radiating warmth. It could be from the teacup he just puts down, but I believe it's just his nature. Always warm, always comforting.

"You've changed my life, Ava," he confides. "Unexpectedly, at a speed I could never have imagined. You and Quinton have made me a better man, nothing that the military or anyone else can ever do. I want you to know that." His touch is gentle as he caresses my face. "I know you could live without me, but I hope you never do."

I know how to rely on myself when a situation demands it. So, it wouldn't be true to say that I can't live without Jack. I could, but I never want to. I have a man whom I trust completely, and I want to depend on him for everything. And it feels incredible to have such a person in your life.

"Living without you would be like living with a jagged

shard buried in my heart. I'd survive, but I'd slowly drown in my own blood," I respond deliberately as if trying to comprehend how it would feel. "I know pain. But that kind of pain is one that I'd struggle to bear."

He crashes his mouth onto mine. As I get lost in the contact, a strong force pulls me off the chair, and I feel as if I'm floating. I hold onto him tightly, my heart racing as something halts me from sliding, in addition to his hands. His bulge rests underneath my crotch like a rock on a climbing wall.

Jack settles me on the balcony balustrade, getting me to lean on a pillar. He breaks the kiss with reluctance, then murmurs, "I still haven't reconciled with my past. You may need to wait, but I'll make it worth your while."

Still scorching from his previous kiss, I can only sigh my acceptance.

He rewards me with yet another kiss, his lips exploring mine with a hunger that matches my own. I tilt my head, seeking a better angle, and our tongues dance in sync, a delicious tango of desire.

I feel a hand supporting the small of my back while another hand tackles the buttons of my shorts. His touch sends electric currents through my body, igniting a fire deep within me. His finger slips under my panties, teasingly sliding inside my wetness.

"Damn, you've started without me," he comments.

And he's already hard!

Jack's tongue intertwines with mine once again, exploring the depths of my mouth with a fervor that matches his finger's rhythm. He adds another finger, stretching me in the most pleasurable way. Every glide of his skilled digits propels me closer to the edge of ecstasy. The tantalizing build-up weakens me, teasing my senses, heightening my craving for the release that only Jack can fulfill.

I release a grunt.

Jack chuckles. "You know, you're attractive when you're impatient."

With a slow and gentle motion, Jack's fingers sail deeper. I drive my hips forward, hungry for his offering. The sensation of his fingers plunging into me takes me to a place where colors explode like a shower of confetti. It's blinding, it's messy, it's fucking spectacular!

Heat coats my neck, the tremor in my core reverberating like a chain reaction. Lost in the moment, I almost forget that I'm perched on a balustrade, and I'm nowhere near the pillar that once supported me. In a sudden twist, I lose my balance and begin to tumble backward, but Jack is there, catching me effortlessly. "Losing focus, are we?" he teases, his voice filled with playful affection.

Despite the unexpected interruption, my senses remain heightened. "Thanks to you," I reply, shifting the blame to him.

He steadies me. It's pitch-black out here, the only source of light emanating from the kitchen window. But desires have a way of transcending darkness. Their presence is always palpable. I anticipate his next words, but his patience puts me to shame.

"What I said remains true," he asserts. "You're mine, and I'll give you anything you wish for. It's how I find pleasure. So, baby, tell me, what do you want?"

"Why is it always about me?"

"I have a weakness for feeling desired by you. When you moan in my ear, when you try to resist, clenching my cock—that. That's what turns me on."

His admission, the way he describes it, unleashes my fantasy. As surety settles, I let arousal take over. A woman deserves to dream, to make those dreams a reality with the right partner by her side.

I wrap my arms around his broad shoulders, clinging to the nape of his neck. "Carry me." The whisper launches out of my mouth with urgency.

As he lowers his pants, I fumble to unbutton his shirt. With each button released, his chiseled muscles are unveiled, a sight that has become familiar but never fails to entice me. His rigid cock springs forth above his powerful thighs. I have come to know his body intimately. As formidable as he is now, he's just getting started.

I take his throbbing length in my palm, feeling its heat and weight, my fingers instinctively exploring every ridge and contour. The crown glistens with beads of precum.

"Ah, damn!" he exclaims, his sensitivity momentarily overwhelming him.

"You know I love touching you." It's a privilege to touch a man as stunning as him, to explore every inch of his body.

He responds with an intoxicating growl, giving me permission to indulge in his manhood however I please. I pull my T-shirt over my head, letting Jack pepper my breasts with quick kisses while simultaneously reaching into my shorts' pocket, searching for the condom.

Once he sheathes himself, he lifts me effortlessly off the railing, allowing me to remove my shorts completely. As if driven by a silent command, I spread my legs, inviting him in. He hooks his hands under my ass cheeks, pulling me to straddle his waist. I wrap my legs tightly around him, rocking against his length. With one hand holding me, he deftly flicks the door handle down and uses his leg to kick the door open.

We slip inside, barely making a sound, and Jack swiftly turns us around, pressing my back against the door. He maintains control, ensuring it doesn't slam and potentially startle Quinton. With my back pressed firmly against the wooden surface, I watch as passion erases his tiredness. I lay a challenge to him, "No walls."

A smile spreads across his face. "You want me real deep?"

I nod amid the rising heat. We've barely started, and I know my imagination only scratches the surface of how intense it could be.

Jack takes a step back, guiding me away from the door. With his strong arms, he lifts me, my body weightless in his embrace. The tip of his cock brushes against my crotch, seeking entrance. I'm slick everywhere, so I rock myself against his hard-on, guiding him to find the sweet spot.

I cling to him as the position demands. Making love in an upright position, face-to-face—a threesome with gravity—lays bare the unity Jack and I share. This is more than a tango. With the position our bodies have committed to, it truly takes two to keep this union on course. There's no part of me that doesn't touch him. In return, he gives everything he's got to support me, a kind of reciprocity that brings a sense of safety and treasured intimacy.

A moan escapes my lips as he steadily lowers me onto him. I'm fastened to him, allowing me to loosen my grip on his neck, surrendering. The sensation is overwhelming, as if the impalement itself is what keeps me alive.

I moan his name, the sound echoing in the hallway.

"That's what I love to hear, baby." His grunt of approval fuels my desire even more as he rubs me up and down his cock.

With each rocking motion, my walls squeeze with heat. My arms wrap tightly around his neck, and my legs locked around his hips. The pressure prompts him to withdraw, only to thrust back in, a move that drives us both to the edge.

While he manages to hold back his release, I can't contain myself any longer. A climax washes over me, my body convulsing in a frenzy of pleasure. As the balls of fire burst, a wave of intense heat leaves me unable to move.

Jack repositions me, his muscly arms cradling my body as if rescuing me from a faint. As he withdraws his length, a tickling sensation dances along the curve of my pelvis. His confident grin warns me to be careful what I wish for, but I've yearned for this moment for so long. Now, with one of the best Marines at my disposal, the vision of heaven eradicates any lingering need for rest.

I adjust my legs, aligning my body perfectly to his. Arching my back, I fling my arms behind his neck, locking eyes with him to express my gratitude for all he's done for me. His hands firmly support me, providing a solid foundation. Our bodies reconnect, my dripping core embracing the tip of his throbbing manhood once again.

In a bold move, his hand shifts up to encircle my waist, leaving only one hand supporting my ass. "Let go of your left arm, sweetheart," he requests.

I comply, and in the same instant, he propels me further up, effortlessly thrusting his manhood deeper inside me. My inner thigh muscles exert themselves to counter the impact. My head jerks back as my chest opens up. With precise timing, he dips his face into the valley between my breasts, using his arm around my waist to hold me tightly in place. My breasts respond eagerly, rising with a newfound sexual excitement that feels as if he has invented it just for me.

"G-god, Jack!" I scream, my free hand flailing against his chest, the heat of our bodies mingling in the air. My fingers finally find his nipple, hard and erect, mirroring my own. I rub it, pinching it with a desperate fervor. A groan escapes his lips, its sheer sexiness making me confident no one else could replicate it.

As I descend, I grip him with both arms again. He takes

the opportunity to reach my nape. His lips trail a path of generous kisses, even sucking a patch of skin on the side of my neck, nibbling it.

I respond to his move by saying, "I love you, Jack Kelleher." The words flow out in a whisper, but their intensity matches a booming shout.

"I love you, too. More than anything. You know that."

"And I need you." The declaration burns through me like a possession. "Now!" I'm not a pushy type, but in this moment, with a true partner, I allow myself to.

Something unlocks within him. He's ready, oh God, yes, he's ready. His hips shudder with an urgent speed, his length ravaging my canal with an even greater ferocity. Amid the burning pain, he squeezes my buttocks together, creating unbelievable friction. He grunts, surprised by the tightness he has created.

Struggling to hold back his release, he hits my spot, causing me to bury my face against the curve of his shoulder, muffling my scream and nearly biting into his muscular mound. "Jack..." My voice barely a breath, yet filled with a rawness that seems to reverberate through him.

"Let me hear it. Let me hear you call my name," he huffs impatiently.

"Jack..." I respond with a hint of suffering and satedness.

"I'm gonna cum now, sweetheart."

I hum, my head nodding against the side of his neck. His vertical thrusts drive me to another powerful climax. My four limbs strain to maintain my upright position, face-to-face with him. It's not enough for me to simply feel his release; I need to witness it in the depth of his eyes.

Our bodies move together as I observe pleasure consuming him. Even in the dim light, desires can be seen, just as the satisfaction of a man can be felt. His gaze softens, blurred by sheer ecstasy. His mouth opens, exhaling hot breath that brushes against my face like a sea breeze at the height of summer. His smile spreads to my lips.

He guides me through the bedroom doorway, his footsteps whispering on the carpet. A captivating fragrance envelops us, a tantalizing mixture of musk and lust. Even after our wild lovemaking, a display of prowess only few possess, his control remains palpable as he gently lowers me onto the soft sheets.

He lies beside me, cuddling me like he doesn't want to part. His voice, low and filled with satisfaction, caresses my ear as he whispers, "I hope it was as good for you as it was for me."

Doesn't he know what he's done?

"Every time we make love, it's more than just sex." I cup his chin. "It's amazing sex."

21

AVA

My muscles strain, aches overwhelm my every limb. The line between pain and pleasure has never been thinner. Last night was a fantasy fulfilled. I had never stretched my legs so wide and exerted pressure on them simultaneously. All while enduring the relentless thrusts of Jack's formidable length. It was mind-shredding, bordering on torture, but I actually thought about making a pact with the devil so my man and I could keep doing it until we're both old and wrinkled.

"Lift! Good work. Again!" Jack, switching gears from being my lover to being a fitness coach, encourages me as I push through my leg lifts. "Did I tell you this is my favorite exercise?"

I huff and puff, forcing myself through the pain.

"Come on, lift! Ten more." He leers at my ass, then runs his arm along the back of my legs. "God, you're so sexy, baby."

My core pulsates mercilessly, along with my glutes. Pleasing? A little. Helping? Absolutely not. With only six reps to go, my body gives way, and I collapse.

Jack flashes me a cheeky smile and extends his hand. I

grasp it, and he effortlessly pulls me back up. I'm drenched, my face flushed as if I was sunburned.

"Did I break you?" Jack teases.

"Last night or this morning?" I tease him back.

"Both."

"Last night, yes. This morning, not really," I maintain my pride.

He smirks with a shake of his head, but he stops short of forcing me to admit otherwise.

Last night, he certainly broke me, but in the process, he granted me the most intense orgasms I've ever experienced—yes, multiple.

I smear my sweat onto his equally damp tank top as he sensually rubs me through my Lycra pants. "If I may, I'd like exclusive access to your ass," he hums.

"You already have."

I take my medications and then check on our assistant coach, Quinton, who has been quiet all morning. We've been working out at the Red Mark gym. Being considerate of others, we always come at a quiet time. Bringing a baby along means things can be unpredictable. We ensure this kind of disturbance doesn't bother anyone.

Seeing me, Quinton cries in his stroller. I wrinkle my nose and ask Jack, "Can you smell it?"

"I'll take care of him," he replies jovially, taking the baby out of the stroller. "Come on, Q-Bear. Your *Paw Patrol* clown is at your service."

Jack heads to the bathroom to change Quinton, and his cries gradually fade as they leave the gym. Just in time, as a row of gorgeous strangers getting ready for their workouts start coming in. They politely nod and smile as they pass me by. I'm faithful to one man, but the tempting sight of these Red

Mark agents flaunting their toned physiques has caused me to sprout horns and a demon tail.

Bruno Mars' "Runaway Baby" plays in the background. If I had control of the playlist, I would've chosen "It's Raining Men."

Among the beats, I hear my phone ringing inside my bag that's hanging on Quinton's stroller. An unknown number flashes on the screen. Dragging the empty stroller with me, I retreat to a quiet corner.

I press the device against my ear, chills forming at the nape of my neck. My fingertips tingle. My instincts tell me to hang up immediately, but part of me craves to hear what he has to say. And I'm desperate to say my piece.

"So you've been keeping busy," I reply with a controlled tone. "But I guess nothing's new there. How's Mr. Branson?"

"Ava, Ava," Willem says calmly. "When did you suddenly become interested in my business affairs?"

I know that tone all too well. It's the one he adopts when he tries to mask his true emotions. In the past, more often than not, his anger would get the better of him, and he ended up taking it out on me. Thankfully, this time, distance is on my side. Plus, with the people I'm surrounded by, this wretched man wouldn't stand a chance even if he were here.

Neither of us utters another word as if gauging each other's position.

I restart, "What do you want, Willem?"

"Before you unleash whatever is on your mind, I called to tell you that I forgive you."

"Forgive me for what?"

"The betrayal, and for running away." If he were standing in front of me, I would have slapped the audacity right off his face. But he continues, undeterred. "Let's forget about everything. Start fresh. You, me, and Quinton. And our future kids. Didn't you tell me you wanted at least three?"

"Have you no shame?" I retort. "You kidnapped your own son and placed him with strangers just to play your game?"

"I have no idea what you're talking about. If anything, it's you who kidnapped my son," he scoffs. Of course, he wouldn't admit to his own crimes.

"I will never return to you, Willem. And you will never lay eyes on Quinton again."

"Ava, I know I haven't been the best partner, but I'm really trying to change. Doesn't every man deserve a second chance?" he speaks, his tone familiar. It reminds me of when he begged me to take him back after I initially left him.

"Save your breath," I reply coldly.

"No, no. I need you to understand that I'm not a monster. I've proven this to you, haven't I?" He pauses, exhaling into the phone, seemingly trying to convey his emotions intentionally.

I remain silent, giving him the space to continue.

Taking the cue, he goes on. "Do you remember those days? The days when you and your parents received that devastating news about your cancer? I was there for you, by your side, supporting you every step of the way."

"I'm grateful for that, Willem. But I can't repay your kindness with my life."

He releases a disappointed sigh, then continues, "I held your hand during your chemo treatments. I urged you to persevere even though the outcome was bleak. And have I ever asked for anything back when I picked up the hospital bills? I even helped your father with his struggling business. I did everything I could to keep you alive and your family afloat, Ava."

The memory assaults my mind. He did spend countless hours with me, offering support. He went out of the way to help my parents, too. My mother always said, 'Willem was too kind.' He was, perhaps, driven by the fact that he was practically an orphan after his mother left him and his father remarried. That was why his generosity ended up costing me my own freedom and happiness. It was all for himself, whether he realized it or not.

I could give him a lecture about abandonment, but I simply say, "You did it because you wanted me."

"Of course I did. But may I remind you? You were dying, Ava! So, think about what was in it for me. I simply cared about you."

"Willem, you helped me, yes. And I will forever be grateful. But if you genuinely cared about me, let us go."

"I will do whatever it takes to reclaim my family!"

"We're not your family," I counter. I will not fall for his sorry plea this time.

"Quinton is my son." His tone tightens.

"No, he isn't!" My words may come across as harsh, but the fact that someone is a biological father holds no significance for me or Quinton. I refuse to accept that my son should be burdened with being an asshole's prodigy. I will do everything in my power to protect him, and when the time comes, I will tell Quinton the truth.

"Ava, don't resurrect what nearly destroyed you. You are nothing without me."

"I am everything when I'm without you! So look in the mirror, pack your sorry ass, and never call me or try to see us again!"

At this moment, Jack is standing behind me. Quinton is already back in his stroller, and Jack angles it so he's looking away and sheltered from the tension of our conversation.

He snatches the phone from my hand, his voice firm, "If you ever dare to come near her or intimidate her again, I will leisurely chop off your fingers, one by one. Then, I will cut off your ears and scoop out your eyeballs. But I will let your tongue remain intact because I want to hear you curse at me, and I want to relish the moment when your voice fades away."

From the speaker, I hear Willem speaking over him, but Jack doesn't back down. It's more than just a clash of egos—it's a clash of two men seeking to possess me for two different reasons.

Jack then delivers his punchline. "So, like my girlfriend said, pack up your sorry ass!"

He quickly ends the call, almost slamming the phone down, but then realizes that it's mine. He hands it back to me.

I take a moment to compose myself as Jack steps away and begins pacing the room toward the shelf where the dumbbells are. I lift Quinton from the stroller, gently swaying him back and forth. He appears happy in his fresh diaper, expertly put on by Jack. The air around me is filled with the soft scent of baby powder. I can't help but wonder if the tough guys on the opposite side of the gym can also detect the scent.

Soon, Jack comes back to me, asking if I'm okay.

I nod, placing Quinton back in his stroller and leaving him to play with his giraffe teether. Then, under my breath, I mutter, "That man had the nerve to call me like that."

"Did he mention anything about the kidnapping?"

"No. Not surprising, really."

"This has to end!" Jack declares with determination. I embrace him, agreeing with him. But how we'll make it happen remains uncertain.

22

———

JACK

I wake up, startled by a buzzing sound next to my ear. As my eyes adjust to the brightness, I find myself clenching my teeth, my fingernails scraping against the fabric of the sheet.

Fuck!

Saved by the phone as the vibration of a new alert breaks through my rolling nightmare.

My nails tingle with an odd sensation as if I had been scraping against something rough, more than just the cotton sheet. I look toward Ava, her body softly rising and falling under the covers. I huff, grateful that she was spared from witnessing whatever I had been doing.

I slide my legs over the edge of the bed, careful not to make any sudden movements. The sheets hang onto my skin as I rise to a sitting position. Ava stirs slightly but thankfully doesn't wake up.

Just like his mother, Quinton also remains asleep in his crib, his tiny chest barely visible under the blanket. I take a moment to watch him, marveling at his innocence and vowing to protect him from any harm for the rest of my life.

Satisfied that no one noticed my nightmare-induced sleep, I silently slip from the room.

As I head to the bathroom, Elmo trots in behind me. It's unusual for him to follow me so closely, especially with that worried expression on his face. I wish he had been sleeping inside —he would've probably woken me up before my phone did—but having a dog who thinks his humans should wake up at the same time as him is not an option for everyone in the bedroom.

"I'm fine, buddy," I say to the goofy-looking mutt, stooping to pat him.

I splash cool water on my face, feeling the remnants of Scalpel dissipate. I check the alert that woke me up, a notification I had set to alert me whenever the name Willem Botha surfaces online. I head to the kitchen, and the news that floods my screen leaves me stunned.

The bedroom door clicks open, and Elmo excitedly runs over to greet Ava. I take a break from reading the news to observe the two. Elmo has a different way of greeting her compared to me. With me, he appears polite, but with her, he dances around, leaning against her feet and begging for a pat. Ava happily obliges, giggling as she rubs Elmo's belly, then stretches his ears up. "Are you a bunny?" The dog responds with a grin. "Actually, you look like a bat."

Ava showers the dog with more attention, then walks over to me. "You're up early." She kisses me and takes a moment to appraise my appearance. "You look like you've already gone for your run without me."

I pull her close. Having her against my chest, I become aware of my huffing breath and make a conscious effort to steady it. I admit softly, "I just couldn't sleep."

"You have too many things on your mind," Ava comments.

I smile at her, assuring her not to worry. "How's Quinton?"

"He was up for a few minutes, but then he went back to sleep." She gazes out the window and remarks, "It's such a lovely morning."

"Why don't you go sit outside, and I'll bring us some coffee?"

"Sounds good," she says with a sultry smile, her hips swaying as she makes her way to the back porch. I catch her stealing glances in my direction, her eyes filled with a familiar craving.

The air carries her scent, tempting me to give in, but there's something important I need to discuss with her.

I brew the coffee. The aroma boosts my wakefulness despite still feeling slightly groggy from the nightmare. I then make my way to the back porch. She's curled up on the armchair, a blanket draped over her legs.

"Flat white for you." I set a mug on the table.

"Thanks, Jack."

I settle down in the adjacent chair, and we sit in comfortable silence. In the distance, a few jays fly across the field while a breeze rustles through the grass that has grown untouched since we arrived and neglected any gardening.

"I need to show you this." I break the silence, showing an article on my phone.

Her eyes widen as she grabs my phone to read it. "Willem is missing?"

"It was the last night of the summit. He went out with a few attendees, but he never returned to his hotel, and no one has seen him since."

She grumbles. "Sometimes, cow farts can smell like chamomile."

I shake my head, perplexed yet entertained by her words. "What did you say?"

"Never mind," she sighs.

"What about chamomile and cow farts?"

"Willem loved chamomile tea." She exhales her disgust, then concludes, "Well, he tried to fake his death once. This is just another one of his tricks."

Hence the cow fart.

Observing her furious expression as if her ex were present, I hold back a laugh and choose not to dwell on the smelly subject. I continue by summarizing the information from the article. "Apparently, there's been a target on his back. A particular rival who has dealings with the dark web."

"There's always a target on his back, Jack. Being a successful businessman comes with that territory. But he does have a security team to handle that kind of threat. He called me just the other day, and now he's suddenly missing?" She scoffs. "It's too convenient if you ask me!"

I admire her logical thinking. "I agree. It does seem rather convenient because…" I interrupt myself, asking for my phone back and then quickly pulling up another article I had stumbled upon last week. "This journalist has been tracking Willem for years. He suspects Willem's AI chip is based on stolen intellectual property—if there is such a thing on the dark web."

"That wouldn't surprise me," Ava utters, crossing her legs.

"Behind the façade, he might be a wanted man."

"Cora-Lee said she's also investigating W-Bot," she reminds me. "Perhaps it's time we paid her a visit."

We meet Cora-Lee at Red Mark. Alluding to her bandaged nose, the head of tech jokes that the doctor threw in free rhinoplasty during the surgery to remove a sinus polyp. Apart from some slight swelling around her nose and eyes, she seems to have recovered well from her time in the hospital.

As we settle into the meeting room, Huxley offers to babysit Quinton.

"The meeting room is a bad environment for a young child," he says with the baby nestled on his chest. He then whispers, as if not wanting Quinton to hear, "Especially when the conversation revolves around his former dad."

I simply pat his shoulder.

Ava warns, "He's already been fed, so please don't give him any more food."

"Is that right, Quinnie-Bear?" Huxley asks the boy, who responds with a gurgle. "Don't worry, we'll play and burn off all those calories, huh?" Equipped with everything *Paw Patrol*, he takes Quinton downstairs to the lounge.

Cora-Lee watches as her colleague walks in a comical manner, clearly trying to entertain Quinton. "You know, sometimes I feel like Comet isn't as old as he claims to be. I mean, we all have our inner child, but his is disproportionately big. I'd watch out for those toys if I were you," she comments before closing the door.

"I think it's just empathy." I reason, giving Huxley one last glance through the glass wall. Then I turn to Cora-Lee. "So, what do you think of the Willem Botha shenanigan?"

"Mr. Gordon Clark from The Capital Chronicle hit the nail on the head," she responds, referring to the DC-based journalist who has been following Willem for years. "W-Bot's AI chip has been developed based on someone else's intellectual property. Although, at the same time, Mr. Clark has been barking up the wrong tree."

"How?" I ask, leaning forward in my swivel chair.

"Willem's disappearance has got nothing to do with the dark web. He's been stealing ideas from a company called

Rufus-10, a start-up that operates openly in Silicon Valley. The company has created a next-gen computing platform solely for AI. It's built with new algorithms, using both photons and electrons to carry information. Basically, their innovation defies the Dennard Scaling."

We stare at her, totally puzzled.

"Sorry! Sorry!" Cora-Lee realizes her enthusiasm translates like a foreign language for me and Ava. "I haven't had coffee, and it's already midday. Anyways, here's a better version of what I wanted to say."

Ava and I smile at her, encouraging her to continue.

She explains, "Willem has been working on a new type of chip that utilizes similar technology, but not enough to be considered an infringement on intellectual property. In fact, W-Bot's version is significantly more powerful than Rufus-10's innovation. This information has been published in scientific papers, but it was never disclosed that the algorithm used is the same, which is the root of the IP conflict."

"If Rufus-10 is just a start-up, why all the fuss?" Ava asks. "Willem could've easily taken over that company."

"Spot on, Ava!" Cora-Lee looks animated, as if relieved that her last explanation made sense. "Rufus-10 has remained the small guy, even though what they've produced is far from insignificant. This issue is coming to light only now because Rufus-10 has recently been acquired by Bone Intelligence, an entity striving to compete with the incumbents. You know, Microsoft, Google, and Apple."

"Damn," I sigh.

Ava rolls her eyes, saying, "All I can say right now is that I'm glad I'm here."

I'm more than glad. I am overwhelmingly relieved.

Cora-Lee chimes in. "I'm not sure why Willem didn't try to acquire Rufus-10 before Bone Intelligence. Maybe he thought he could get away with his loot and underestimated his competition."

Suddenly, my phone buzzes with another notification. I glance at it and mutter, "Maybe it's because he's broke. W-Bot's shares have plummeted." I keep skimming the news. "Investors are pulling out. Apparently, Willem's research was rigged, and he's been spending money that isn't his."

Ava sighs and remarks, "His Pandora's box has just been opened. I bet it smells like cow farts!"

Cora-Lee and I erupted into fits of laughter.

As we settle, Cora-Lee continues, "I'd hate to be Willem right now. Bone Intelligence has already engaged the Interpol to look for him."

"Hence his disappearance," I remark.

"Exactly," Cora-Lee says. "I really hope they find him soon. To be honest, I'm worried about his ambition. W-Bot's strength lies in its pneumatic microchips, which use pressure instead of electricity to encode data. Willem's plan is to combine his own technology with the one he stole from Rufus-10, creating the biggest and most powerful chip on the planet, supposedly even bigger than the latest version of WSE."

"English, please, Cora-Lee," I interrupt.

She chuckles, apparently intentional in her use of the acronym. "Wafer-Scale Engine, currently the most powerful chip in existence. Anyway, Willem's tests have failed so far."

"Did you say pressure?" Ava asks. "I remember there was an accident at W-Bot not long before I left L.A. An engineer lost his hand."

"Right on again, Ava," Cora-Lee responds. "There was an explosion in one of W-Bot's pressure chambers."

"I wonder what will happen to his other business, the database tech thing," I ponder.

"No doubt the DOJ is after him too," Ava adds.

It's music to my ears that Willem's power is diminishing. But he's not going to give up just like that. He's a wounded tiger. I haven't forgotten his ego. He's losing control of his company and has already lost what he considers his family— Ava and Quinton. He won't let go of both easily. He needs to hold on to something. His invisibility will make him more dangerous. And I detest facing an enemy I can't see.

23

JACK

Craving a change of scenery, today we take advantage of the sunny weather and bring Quinton to a picnic at a downtown park. Little Quinton has become quite the chatterbox. His joyful babbling fills the air as he crawls eagerly across the picnic blanket. Meanwhile, Elmo relaxes at the edge, his contented gaze fixed on Quinton as if guarding his every move.

Willem has disappeared without a trace, while the ticking clock reminds me of our impending move to Hawaii—a decision that has been burdening me.

"We can stop by the store on the way home. I think we might need an extra suitcase, don't you think?" I say to Ava.

"Good idea. We might even need two." With a drink in her hand, she stretches to stop Quinton from climbing into the picnic basket. "Oh shoot!" she suddenly exclaims. She has spilled cranberry juice on herself, causing a large stain on her shirt. "Stay here. I'm just going to quickly wash this off."

As she sprints toward the park's restrooms, my phone vibrates with an incoming call. It's been so long since I relied on my phone like a lifeline.

"Jack Kelleher," the voice says.

A mix of anger, surprise, and hate churns in the pit of my stomach. "Willem Botha. The missing man," I respond. "Are you trying to make friends with me?"

"Don't flatter yourself."

"You're in a lot of trouble."

"I'm never fazed by trouble. You should know that by now."

While still engaged in conversation with the man, I quickly scoop up Quinton and rush toward the restroom. Elmo automatically tags along.

I warn the cockbag, "I'm sure you remember what I said the last time we spoke. If you try to threaten us, I'll chop off your fingers and torture you until you learn how to stay away. So, Willem, hang up and run far."

He dismisses me with a scoff. "I'm calling you because I have a proposal. A peaceful one."

"A man who would try to kidnap his own son is never capable of promoting anything peaceful."

My heightened state of alertness amplifies. It might be unfounded fear, but I have the sense that he's nearby.

"Yet you're still talking to me," Willem mocks.

I am. I want to feed his ego, figure out his next move, and buy some time because if he's here, I need to know where.

He continues, "I'm a businessman, Mr. Kelleher. When two people have wants, there's always a deal to be made."

"I have reservations about entering into a deal with a man whose days are numbered."

"Your wants and my wants are not time-bound. It doesn't matter when or under what circumstances. The two of us will always be on a quest for it." He pauses as if giving me time to ponder over it. "I'm aware of your past. You know I have access to the DOJ database. Well, not for long, though. In that context, you were right. My days are numbered."

"I have no interest in joining your criminal activity," I state, clutching onto the phone like I could squeeze answers out of it without involving the villain who hurt the woman I love.

"How far would you go to find the truth, Mr. Kelleher?"

My mouth clamps shut, contending intentions spinning in my throat like a tornado gathering speed.

He responds on my behalf, "You'd go as far as you need to. Am I right?"

My attention diverges as I hear a toilet flushing behind the wall.

"I have your truth, Jack," Willem's voice sneers through the phone. "And I'm willing to trade it for something in your possession."

My head bows, contemplating the tantalizing prospect of finally unraveling the mystery that has haunted me my whole life. However, I respond resolutely, "Go to hell, Willem!"

His response is surprisingly calm, "Okay, I can't coerce you into doing something you're unwilling to do. This is a peaceful negotiation, after all." I pick up on a faint sound of breathing just before he mentions, "By the way, don't bother searching for me. I'm currently in the middle of the Atlantic Ocean."

He lets out a sinister laugh before ending the call. I immediately raise my voice and call into the restroom, "Ava, are you all right?"

"Yeah. Just give me a minute. I'll be right out," she replies, followed by the sound of running water from the tap.

Suddenly, I feel a tug on my jacket. I pivot, preparing myself to defend against an attacker. To my surprise, it's a young boy holding out an envelope. He looks no older than seven or eight, and there is no sign of any adults who could be his parents nearby.

"Who gave this to you?" I ask the boy.

But he turns around and sprints away.

Caution fills me as I gingerly peel open the envelope, revealing a photo inside. The image shows a room, its dimness making it hard to distinguish any details. However, what catches my attention is the crumbling ventilation on one of the walls, causing my heart to beat faster. Leaning against the restroom's plastered surface, I shut my eyes. Trembling fingers remind me of the scratching sensation from my nightmares, now vivid in the harsh daylight. The basement's damp smell attacks my senses as the image of Scalpel looms in my mind.

I pack the envelope away and hide it in my pocket. Just then, Ava appears.

"Everything okay?" She throws a glance at the abandoned picnic blanket and our belongings. Perhaps trying to find a reason herself, she perplexedly asks, "Was it raining?"

"No. Quinton wanted you," I say.

"What is it, Quinnie-Bear?" Ava takes over carrying him, and Quinton smiles as if assuring his mother everything is as wonderful as the cloudless blue sky despite her picking up some odd behavior from me.

I glance down at Elmo. The dog looks back, seemingly acknowledging that my secret's safe with him.

24

———

AVA

The bed shakes, and for a moment, I mistake it for an earthquake. As my vision adjusts, I catch sight of Jack, his face contorted in agony, his body convulsing violently on the bed. The sound of his labored breathing soars, mingling with the thuds as his massive frame repeatedly crashes against the mattress like a stone slab.

I hover above him, caressing his face. "Jack, baby, wake up."

Despite my touches, his eyes remain shut as he unleashes a roar.

"Jack, it's me!" My voice struggles to match the intensity of his menacing tone. I press both of his cheeks, tapping them repeatedly.

He thrashes, his arms flailing and clawing at an invisible target.

As I grasp his heaving shoulders, his hand swings wildly, his fingernails scraping against the top of my chest. I recoil as three distinct red lines etch themselves onto my skin, breaking open in a few spots, releasing a trickle of blood. I snatch my robe, concealing the scars.

Searching for a way to take him out of his nightmare, I return to him, clasping his wrists as his fingers turn rigid. All this time, his physical strength has become a symbol of his protection and masculinity. Now, for the first time, I taste what it's like to be on the wrong side of Jack Kelleher. The man wrenches himself free as if my grip is paper-thin. In a burst of movement, he sits upright, seizing my arms and unleashing another piercing scream.

"Jack, baby, listen to my voice!"

He opens his eyes. As if confronting a different man, I see fear suffocating him. I don't think he sees me. His expression and pose look as though he's defending himself against a great enemy. Gritting his teeth, he has my left arm in his locked grip like it was a twig.

"Let go." I grimace in pain. "Jack! Let me go!"

His grip loosens as awareness slowly rises in his eyes. At the same time, the sound of Quinton crying echoes in the background. Jack fights for each breath, his back contorting in spasms.

"Let me see it," I whisper, meeting his restless hand hovering the scar between his shoulder blades. It pains me to witness his current state, and I'm questioning if this is merely a glimpse into the depths of his brokenness.

He calms, and I drive his hand away from the scar, afraid he'll scratch it and make it bleed.

"I'm okay," he mumbles, and a familiar touch lands on my hand.

I seize the moment to attend to Quinton.

"Mommy's here. It's all right. It's all right." I hold my baby in my arms, rocking him back and forth, comforting him with gentle strokes on his back, and planting kisses on his tear-streaked cheek. I grab his giraffe teether and dangle it in front of him before gradually offering it to him. He takes it, but he won't stop crying.

Still rocking Quinton, I approach Jack.

He looks at me in anguish and shakes his head in disbelief, murmuring, "Ava, I'm so sorry."

"Hey, it's okay." I lay a hand on his shoulder. "I'm going to take Quinton outside, then I'll come back."

He nods.

I settle down on the couch in the living room to breastfeed Quinton while processing what just happened. So this is why Jack always wakes up before me. It's the first time I've seen the reason behind his morning huffing, like a runner who's out of breath.

After a few minutes, Quinton starts wriggling, his 'I want to play' kind of fussing. So I place him on the mat, surrounded by toys we've accumulated during our time here in Helena. Among the usual suspects of *Paw Patrol* toys, there are also a few of his new favorites—a truck-shaped pillow and a squishy rubber donut. Although, the giraffe teether is still his number one.

I let Elmo do his usual thing, keeping a watchful eye on Quinton.

"Mo!" Quinton babbles, resting his head on the pup's back, dipping his fingers into Elmo's thick fur.

"Yes. Elmo."

Suddenly, Quinton smiles at me. "Mama."

His call resonates with intention, a departure from his usual babbling that often resembles successive 'ma.' I smile back at him. "Quinton? Did you just say 'Mama'?"

He reaches out one arm to me as if wanting to shake hands. "Mama."

"Yes. I'm your mama." I take his tiny hand, trembling with

happiness. I lay down beside him on the mat, embracing the small bundle of love close to my heart, wishing I could hear his call under less tense circumstances.

Right then, Jack emerges from the bedroom. The density of his pain is evident, and it breaks my heart to witness. What he did in bed just now doesn't hinder my admiration for him, nor has it altered who he is to me. The situation has changed, but he has not. His posture is slumped and defeated, but he's still my hero.

I kiss my baby and whisper to him, "You wait here with Elmo, okay? Mama will be back."

Resetting myself, I approach Jack. He welcomes me with a tight, sorrowful hug as if he was mourning a loss.

"You okay?" I look up at him, running my fingers through his hair, knowing he intends to shave it all off before our trip to Hawaii.

"Yeah." He gulps, rapidly blinking as if trying to erase the haunting images of his nightmare. "How's Quinton?"

"He's fine." I steal a quick glance at my baby, who appears content while snuggling up with Elmo. "He just called me 'mama.'"

Jack's glum expression fades away, replaced by a twinkle in his eyes and a gentle touch as he strokes my cheek. His smile stretches wide. "That's fantastic. I wish I heard it."

"It won't be a one-off, for sure. So you will hear it soon," I say. "Should I...teach him to say 'dada?'"

His laugh is hesitant, but his touch is firm as he cups my chin. "Did I scare you just now?"

I purse my lips, torn between wanting to spare him further guilt and the need to address the problem. "Do you want to talk about it?"

Suddenly, his eyes widen and lock onto the front of my

robe, fixated on a small bloodstain. "Did I...?" He gasps, peeling the robe back to sneak a glimpse at my chest. "Did I do that?" he exclaims upon seeing the scratches.

"Jack, you didn't mean it."

"God! Those are nasty, Ava." He shakes his head in disbelief. "What have I done?"

"Sit down, Jack." I guide him to the couch so I can watch Quinton as we talk.

"Ava..." His face transforms into a mask of sheer horror.

My robe has slipped off my shoulder and arm, revealing faint shades of bruises from his grip.

"Ava, did I do that too?"

"Jack..."

"Did I do that?" His face cringes even more, shrinking like the peel of an orange.

"It's nothing."

"Oh, God. I'm so sorry." He trembles, his hand covering his mouth.

"It wasn't your fault. Maybe I spooked you when I tried to wake you up."

"Don't shift the blame to yourself, please," he emphasizes, full of anguish. He rises from his seat and paces restlessly across the room, stopping only to watch Quinton. The baby gazes back at him with a radiant smile, tiny arms outstretched. Overwhelmed by the sight, Jack can't resist the urge. He kneels, engaging in playful interaction with him.

As Quinton becomes absorbed in his rubber donut, Jack's attention returns to me. Worry paints his face as he asks, "What are we gonna do? I scared Quinton too, didn't I?"

Seeking to reassure the guilt-ridden man, I reply, "He was just startled."

However, Jack resumes his agitated pacing, this time leaving the room entirely. Elmo follows him.

I stand in the hallway, caught between the living room and the distant recesses of our home. "Jack," I call out, halting him in his tracks. "Please come back and sit down."

He retraces his steps, sinking into the seat with a heavy sigh. His face cradled in his hands, he confesses, "I do want us to work, Ava, but you and Quinton can't bear the brunt of my mess. Now you see how broken I am."

"Look, I'm not going to sugarcoat it. You did scare me back there. You were not you, and yes, you scratched me and clutched my arm. But it doesn't mean I'm going to give up on you or on us."

"I hurt you, Ava. That's unforgivable."

"You didn't mean to."

"It doesn't matter. I. Hurt. You." He looks me in the eye. But, as if he couldn't bear my stare, he slouches back with a twisted expression. Clearly, in his mind, he's committed an irreversible mistake.

I scoot closer to him, intertwining my fingers with his. "Now that I know about your nightmares, we can work it out together."

"How? Don't tell me to seek professional help. Been there, done that."

"But you didn't have me then."

He looks off into the distance, seemingly contemplating if my presence would've improved the effects of the therapy. Then, he hums as if indicating a negative response. "Maybe I should sleep in a different room."

"Jack, no! That's not a solution. You're my partner. I want you beside me."

He tilts his head to touch his forehead to mine. "Just when you thought you were safe from Willem, I ended up causing you harm."

I withdraw, facing him straight on. "Don't you compare yourself to that monster!"

"Am I not a monster?"

I embrace him, pouring my heart and soul into every touch, hoping to sway him. "No! You're the man I love. And you love me. You're not him!"

"It's not going to get better. I've had this nightmare since I knew what a nightmare was. I was so drugged, and everything was a blur. I couldn't distinguish between reality, visions, dreams, and nightmares. I've had other dark dreams, but they'd come and go. This one has persisted.

"At first, it made no sense at all. I mean, *I* didn't make sense. As far as I knew, I had never been born—I was just placed there in Florida when I was twelve."

He told me this in Bozeman, and my reaction remains consistent. His description translates to murky surroundings between the dark of night and the complete absence of light inside an airtight box. I won't say I understand, but I'm sure my vision is exactly the fear and hopelessness he's sharing with me.

Jack continues, "When I had the nightmare, I used to think what I saw was my parents' basement. Maybe they were the sick type, a pair of child beaters or something. Other times, I thought it was my mind trying to reconstruct itself out of what's left in me. Then, my life flipped once again when Sam found me and explained what had happened."

I expect him to lighten up when he mentions his brother, but the burden seems heavier.

The time is now to unravel the dark place in him, so I ask further, "Did Sam make you remember the bad things after you were taken?"

"Well, things started to make sense, and I could find fragments of reality within that nightmare," he sighs, shaking his head painfully. "Did it make things better? Half-revealed visions only serve to confuse. They make nothing better."

"Did you wish Sam hadn't found you?"

His eyes flare, not believing my question. But he nods, acknowledging that it's worth answering. "Maybe I did. Sometimes, I thought I was better off not knowing at all. But... no, no. My brother has been the best thing that has ever happened to me." He then squeezes my hand. "Before you."

"A life surrounded by family is better than a life alone. And a life knowing where you came from is better than not having a past, no matter how painful it is. You've got to admit it."

He draws my hand and kisses it. So heartfelt, I can feel his vulnerability in each wrinkle of his lips. He then says, "I don't know exactly what I usually do when I wake up from that nightmare, but I swear, this morning felt so much worse."

"What do you think made it worse?"

"I don't know, Ava. I don't know," he mutters. "Maybe I could consider myself lucky that I didn't find out about the abduction until I was an adult—well, a reasonably stable adult. Otherwise, I can't even begin to imagine what I would have turned into!"

I hold his hand. "Don't give up on us."

"I can't keep hurting you." His whisper carries the weight of his remorse. "This will happen again."

"I won't let you hurt me," I assert. "As an immediate solution, when you have your nightmare again, I'll walk away. Then I'll come back to you when you're calm. Then we'll seek help—you and me, together. Don't keep it bottled up. Let's talk about it."

"Oh, Ava..."

"There's always a way, Jack," I assure him, my hand reaching out to touch his shoulder.

He shakes his head, his eyes filled with despair. "Sometimes, I don't know what to do with your optimism."

I pull him closer, wrapping my arms around him.

"Please don't touch me there," Jack mutters as my hand inadvertently settles on his scar.

"Sorry, I didn't mean to."

Suddenly, Quinton exclaims, "Mama!" his joyful voice cutting through the heaviness. I join him, tickling his belly as Elmo wags his tail in excitement. "Yes. Mama. Now, can you say—" I start, but my words are interrupted as I catch a glimpse of Jack rising.

He stands tall, towering over me. The sound of his uneven breathing reaches my ears as he declares, "Staying with me means you will wait a lifetime to have the children you desperately want. I can never be a real father."

He turns around, marching like he's in the barracks.

The room feels suffocating, as if the walls are closing in on me, squeezing the air out. I dismissed his brokenness before, treating it as if it were a passing rain shower rather than a destructive storm. I will still choose to stay with him even though that means Quinton won't have a sibling. But I can't lie. His revelation crushes me.

I follow him. "Am I wrong about you, Jack?"

"I don't know what you think of me right now. But this is who I am, and I'm a danger to you."

"What has changed? Tell me!'

He moves even further away from me. "I'm gonna get dressed and then take Elmo for a walk. Please, don't follow me," he requests. "Keep your phone close. If there's anything, anything at all, call me. I won't be far."

I'm not wrong about him. I'm wrong about *me*. I had this belief that I would be the reason for him to keep fighting and overcome his past. I now realize that it was merely my assumption. I never bothered to ask or really listen to him.

I respect his need for space. But as he walks out the door, I feel a pang of emptiness. He's just out walking the dog, but my mind races with questions. Can I truly live without him? The answer is terrifying.

25

AVA

The news of our canceled trip to Hawaii comes as a shock. Jack dropped a bombshell on me this morning—he had actually managed to get three extra days off work as unpaid leave, but he kept it for himself until the last minute. Apparently, he had a conversation with his captain about his intention to leave the Corps. It comes as no surprise that the captain denied his request and opted to give him additional time to be with me.

The man himself has hardly said a word to me. My frustration has built up to the ceiling. Every time I open my mouth, I feel like snapping at him. I call Morgan and confide in her about my need for a temporary escape. The last thing I want is to push Jack away with something I don't mean to do or say.

My bestie has been working in Yellowstone, shooting a documentary about the behavior of wolves as they get ready for winter—which apparently has changed this year thanks to the warming weather. I'm meeting her as she takes a break just outside the park.

Jack insists on coming with me, which defeats the purpose

of me trying to get away from him. I say, "I thought you wanted some space."

He simply shrugs, his eyes fixed on the road as he drives my SUV. "I'm not going to leave you alone."

I should be glad, but somehow his statement annoys me. Does he have an issue with me hanging out with my best friend? "Well, you've been walking Elmo by yourself."

"Do *you* want space? I'll give you space," and he brakes the car. "I'll ask Huxley to come with you instead. Would you prefer that?"

"Don't pass me off like I'm some kind of job."

"Yes or no, Ava."

I let out a soft grunt. "No. I want you."

"That's settled, then." He resumes driving.

I glance at him as the road stretches out in front of us. His cold expression doesn't give away much, but about halfway there, he asks, "Did you tell Morgan about my nightmares?"

I shake my head. "I just told her I needed to get out of the house."

"And you're not gonna tell her now?"

"No."

"Good. Apart from that, you can pretend that I'm not there."

"I won't tell her, Jack."

His rigid stance softens. "Thanks."

The second half of the trip passes quickly, and we reach our destination in West Yellowstone.

"Is this it?" Jack asks, his eyes reading the sign: *Grizzly and Wolf Discovery Center.*

"Yeah," I affirm.

As I get ready for the visit, Jack lends me a hand. Anticipating some tight spaces inside, I'm opting for a carrier instead of a stroller. This way, Quinton can sit on the front harness and watch everything while I have both hands free. Jack patiently guides me as he secures the carrier, adjusting it for optimal comfort. With Quinton snugly settled, he plants a kiss on my forehead.

"You go ahead, take your time," he says. "You won't even know I'm around."

My heart crumbles as I observe him standing still. It doesn't feel right, but I resist the urge to console him, knowing deep down it's not what he's searching for at this stage. Perhaps, in some way, it's not what I need either. We both crave a sense of space and distance.

Inside, Morgie awaits by the ticket booth. She gives Quinton and me a hug, then calls out, "Quinnie-Bear! Who's my superstar?"

Quinton seems to share her emotions. He coos and babbles as if Morgan is his best friend already.

"Gee, I feel so special," Morgan says, giving me a visitor pass. "What did you feed him this morning?"

"Told ya he'll warm up to you."

"Please, let me carry him. Please...." Morgan begs.

After taking Quinton out, I detach the carrier and help Morgan fit the harness on herself. It takes her some time, but she eventually gets it right. I make sure everything is secure and then pass Quinton over to her. She's rocking it with him, but I know having her own isn't on her to-do list right now.

"Where's Jack?" she asks as we walk toward the wolf's area.

"He's somewhere," I reply, scanning the surroundings but unable to locate him. "He's more like a bodyguard than a boyfriend these days."

"Well, he's both. But I understand what you mean. So, this outing isn't just about getting away from the house?"

"He's grumpy."

"Hmm… guys have PMS, too. Haven't you noticed?" she chuckles.

I scoff at the notion. "Willem never had PMS. Or maybe he had it every day, so I didn't know any different. Anyway, I don't think that's what Jack is having."

"A man, just like any male adult mammal, can experience withdrawal symptoms if his testosterone levels drop."

I laugh at the seriousness in her tone. "I'm sure my man's testosterone is on an optimal level."

Morgan's mouth twists to the side as if implying that I lack understanding of biology. "Every hormone has its up and down, whether it's in Batman's body or our men's bodies. Especially sex hormones."

"That's interesting," I ponder, associating the phenomenon with something else. Could Jack's nightmares get more violent because of a hormonal change? I doubt it.

"Ty has it. Just so you know, his testosterone is fine, but sometimes he gets moody for no reason. His PMS, or IMS—Irritable Male Syndrome—as it's known in men, syncs up with mine. Conveniently. When this happens, I can never find the right words to talk to him in a way that he doesn't misinterpret them. But we handle it."

"I think Jack is overwhelmed with my situation and his own," I explain. "Mine—well, Willem. And his—he can't seem to accept that I genuinely want to live with him in Hawaii. I don't want him to choose between his career and me."

Amid the interaction of the wolves, Quinton adds to the commotion with his excited calls, waving his arms up and down and bouncing in the carrier. "Emmo!"

"Everything is Elmo to him," Morgan giggles. "How wonderful. If there's a tech that can take you back to your childhood happiness, just for a moment, I'm all for it."

"Where would you go back to?"

She ponders. "Maybe when my parents decided I could adopt a puppy. Remember, you and I went together to the shelter and picked Shadow? That border collie cross?"

"Ah... Shadow. Yes. That hyperactive dog! But he was so much fun. I'd go back to that moment, too. Maybe I'll tell Willem about the idea."

"He would probably invent something that would trap you in your most terrifying childhood nightmare, like being carried by a clown." She trembles in disgust.

"Oh, one of your birthdays. When your parents organized a bouncy castle, magicians, and all that?"

"Yeah, scary stuff!" she sneers. "How about your scary moment?"

"Um... the first time I was taken to the hospital. My mother said I had a really bad fever. The room smelled like an over-cleaned toilet—well, that was what I thought then, anyway. The doctor was tall. His medical coat almost blended into the white wall, making his head look like it was floating. The needle in his hand looked massive. I remember bawling in fear."

"When was that? You never told me."

"Before we met. When I was five. But the doctor saved my life. It was meningitis, and I recovered fully because of the early intervention."

"Scary, Ave. You and your hyperthymesia."

"I do not have hyperthymesia."

"You should get a test, seriously. And I bet your results would be positive. You told me you remember your second birthday! How many people do that?"

"It was the pony. My dad put me on a white one, holding me steady like I was riding a unicorn. It was magic."

"That was a much better idea of a birthday party!"

I can imagine my animal-lover bestie choosing a pony ride over a clown ride.

I throw my gaze at the playful wolves, regretting my strained relationship with my parents, all just because of a man. I wonder what they'll think about Jack, not that they'll ever make me change my mind if they disapprove.

We stay behind the open viewing area, allowing Quinton to immerse himself in his own world as he points at the different wolves.

Morgan continues. "Jack is a complicated man. You should know that."

"Isn't every man complicated?" I comment, putting on a front to conceal the real reason I'm here. I've never kept a secret from my bestie before, and it's killing me! But I promised Jack I wouldn't tell Morgan about his nightmares, and I won't break that promise.

"Ave, you're lame," she tells me. "The man was abducted when he was seven. You know his complication extends well beyond that of every man."

"Look, I've seen his trauma manifest itself, but I've vowed to support him no matter what. Please... please... don't ask for details."

"Ava, did he hurt you?"

"No!"

"Promise me you're telling the truth."

"I am!"

Morgan exhales, asking, "Remember that incredible sketch you did? Jack Kelleher with his penetrating eyes?"

Of course I do. "What about it?"

"When you showed it to me for the first time, I thought, I've never seen a sketch of a man with so much pain in his eyes."

Her revelation surprises me. "You never mentioned that."

"You weren't aware of it?"

Her question makes me recall the sensation of being entranced as I sketched him. Pencil against paper, his image materialized, vivid and uncomplicated. It was just Jack.

"Not really. Perhaps my admiration blinded me, or perhaps it was that pain that drew me to him, so I didn't perceive it as pain."

Morgan puts a hand on my shoulder, and a sudden surge of emotion wells up within me, reminiscent of what I felt when I first laid eyes on the completed sketch. "Actually, I did see that pain. I did."

She pulls me close, offering me comfort. "But you weren't fazed by it."

"I saw the pain as his need, and in my imagination, I could fulfill that need. He's been telling me he's broken. And I have to admit, I've been drawn to his brokenness as if it's what keeps me connected to him."

"And you never considered freeing yourself from that attachment?"

"No way. I love him, Morgie."

"Mama!" The sudden call brings instant smiles to both of our faces. Quinton squirms in Morgan's arms, calling me again.

My best friend says in disbelief, "Did he...did he just say 'mama'?"

"He calls me 'mama' now," I say proudly. Seeing the little one restless, I take over carrying him.

Morgan leads the way as we meander along the complex, entering the bear's area.

"Look, Quinton. Bears." I point at the two large, brown creatures rolling in the water.

"Baaaa."

"They're bears," I insist.

"Has he learned to say 'dada'?" Morgan asks.

"Not yet."

"Maybe you should. Impress your man."

I twist my lips. "It'll make him sad."

Morgan cocks her head, her eyes asking questions. She then whispers, "Did he break your heart?" Her face shows that she's ready to fight if I say yes.

"No. But do you remember what you said in Bozeman? When you urged me to give it a go with Jack and not worry about whether it was going to work out?"

"Vaguely."

"I told you I couldn't pursue Jack because I was getting back together with Willem."

"That part, I remember."

"Then you asked if I'd rather be heartbroken by that woman-beater or by an honorable man."

"So Jack did break your heart!"

"The truth is, Morgie, I feel that he's slipping away, but I don't feel brokenhearted. If he had cheated on me, yes, I would've. Or if, one day, we did part ways, and I found out he was moving on with another woman, then yeah."

"If he ever did that to you, I'd make sure to kick him in the balls myself. You know I could!"

I shake my head, chuckling. "Somehow, I can't see that happening. I may be getting ahead of myself, but he's never had a serious relationship before me. And his attachment is so strong. Whatever you call it—dedication, devotion."

"How about you? Are you as attached to him?"

"He's the only one, Morgie. I won't give up on us."

Morgan's smile reveals that she already knows the answer. She pulls me into our signature besties-forever embrace and gives me a peck on my temple. Her belief in me strengthens my resolve as I prepare to claim my Jack back.

26

JACK

I gaze at the array of packed and unpacked bags strewn across the room. Most of them belong to Quinton, but they serve as a constant reminder of my own failure. I never intended to make things difficult for Ava. I just didn't want us to be isolated in Hawaii, even though it meant being apart from Willem. I can feel that evil nearby. I want to confront him, but I also know that I can't handle everything on my own, especially if I want to take a chance on what Willem referred to as 'the truth.' Being close to Red Mark played a significant role in my decision to remain in Helena.

Ava has been quiet ever since we returned from our trip to Yellowstone. Perhaps I've been the one avoiding talking to her. Yes, she did try to start a conversation, but there must've been something in my body language that made her stop.

As Quinton snoozes in his crib, Ava busies herself with laundry. She's been spending time in there, watching the washing machine.

Despite the distant look in her eyes, I approach her. "Why don't you wait for me in the living room? I'll prepare some tea for both of us."

She lets out a grumble, tossing a T-shirt into a basket. It's mine. With an irritated voice, she exclaims, "It's taken you this long to make the effort?"

"I'm sorry. I know you wanted to talk to me, but I wasn't ready. Please, give me a chance?" I plead, my arms encircling her waist. In a moment of surrender, she exhales, releasing the clothes she held—yet another of my T-shirts.

She makes her way to the living room while I head to the kitchen to brew our tea.

Joining her moments later, I settle myself right beside her.

My lungs are in overdrive, expelling air rapidly while struggling to replenish it. Confession is never an easy thing. I'm not merely disclosing a secret to her. I'm about to destroy what we've built together.

"Ava," I start, reaching over to her. I struggle to recall if my voice ever trembled like this when I said her name.

The gentle touch of her hand calms me, but her eyes betray her unease about what news awaits her. Inhaling deeply, I muster the courage to continue. "Willem has made me an offer."

Ava straightens, her expression caught off guard as the news clearly surpasses her worst fears.

"He called me during our picnic," I continue, my words falling out in a rush. "And someone handed me a photo of a basement."

"Don't. Please don't even think about it!"

"There's no way he could've known that basement unless he had legit information about my abduction."

Her reaction is immediate, her face contorting with worry. "He's going to trap you," she warns. "The DOJ has withdrawn their contract from W-Bot. If you go near that system, you'll be committing a crime."

"I've been trying to piece my life together for two decades. A year or two in prison for that would mean nothing!"

She cringes. "What about us?"

"I love you with all my heart, Ava." My voice wavers. "And Quinton. But we may need to rethink our future."

"Jack!" Her voice, usually soothing, thunders with emotion. A harsh reminder of the gravity of my words.

"I don't deserve you. I'm not just broken. I'm damaged beyond repair."

"That's bullshit!"

"I learned to speak again when I was twelve, Ava. I was drugged, beaten, brainwashed. And my scar..." My hands tremble as I reach down, gripping the fabric of my T-shirt. With a desperate motion, I pull up the hem, revealing the scar between my shoulder blades. "I got this from running away from my kidnapper. I can't remember it, but the police found my bloodied clothes. It's easy to connect the dots."

She brings a hand to her mouth as if trying to hold back the emotions threatening to spill out. "Jack, I'm here for you. I don't care if you're in pieces. I don't care if you've become dust in the wind. I will gather you, keep you. Please, don't ever seek help from Willem."

"The past has been haunting me like hunger. It won't stop until I give in to it. Everyone has their demons, but I've nurtured mine. I've fed it all my life. I've cared for it, loved it. It's gotten so big that the demon itself becomes me. I can't kill it unless I cease to exist." Sweat escapes my pores as if the demon is about to manifest itself.

Ava reaches out, her hand connecting with mine. "Everyone is broken in some ways." Her compassion shines through as she utters the words. "But you have an endless amount of love to give me and Quinton instead of your demon. Your past has ruined you. Don't let it ruin us."

I struggle to find the strength to respond, but she ought to know where I stand. "Quinton deserves a father who can offer him love, not someone damaged by their past." Rage blazes inside me, cursing the day it happened. But I curb my emotions. "Look at where we are, Ava. We're in a temporary home arranged by my brother. I don't even have a place to call my own—to offer you. The only home I've known is a monastery or military bases."

"And you think that matters to me? Where we live or how many bedrooms our house has?"

She pauses, anticipating a realization from me. But I stay silent even after her eyes encourage me to say something.

Inhaling, she goes on. "Jack, Quinton, and I will come with you to Hawaii. You don't have to choose between me and your career. I'll be happy there because you're there. Why don't you believe me?"

I take a shaky breath, the gravity of my decision sinking my organs. "I believe you, Ava. But it's not just that. I need to find closure. And if it's through Willem, so be it. That's why I decided to stay in Helena."

She slumps back. "Have you forgotten what he did to Quinton?"

I lower my head as she continues, her words filled with caution. "Even if he grants your wishes, what comes after? What if you don't find what you're searching for? What if that time is spent behind bars?"

"I will track down my kidnapper, or I will have no peace."

"Without me and Quinton?"

"My leave ends in two days, but I won't return to Hawaii. I will face the consequences and resign from the Corps. I will be penniless, living like a wanderer, maybe even a madman. I can't be the man you deserve. I am not just broken, Ava. I am not even dust in the wind. I'm a pile of shattered glass. Who knows what harm I might cause you—it could be more than just a scratch or a bruise."

She stands up and walks away. I find her leaning against the chilly surface of the kitchen counter. Oh, how I despise myself! How could I ever bring that woman to tears?

I approach her, the floor creaking under my weight. "Ava," I whisper. "If I could erase the path that led me to that disaster, I would. I would set fire to the fair in Syracuse so that fateful night would never happen. Or if it was destiny for me to be kidnapped, I would have hunted down those policemen who neglected their duty and abandoned me!"

The room falls silent until she whispers, "It's too late though now, Jack. Isn't it?"

A dull ache settles in my chest. "I could've denied my need to find closure. Because of you, because of Quinton. But I would've lied. I would've kept having nightmares. I need to know the man responsible for ruining me. Where I'm going next is Florida—I'm sure that's where the basement is. Then, who knows what I'll find? What if I have to go to Mexico? Or one of those dangerous countries where child kidnapping is rife? You may be able to support me, but we can't drag Quinton into this."

"Don't use him as an excuse."

"I'll never use a child as an excuse. He is your guide, Ava. Whatever you do, you need to do it for him."

"Jack, have faith in me."

"I have faith in you, Ava," I say, my voice softening. "And I know you'll see why I'm doing this. I can't let it go. I've tried for years. It's still haunting me."

She looks at me. "I'm not talking about letting go. I'm talking about letting me in."

"Here," I say, pointing at my heart, "is a dangerous place. And I have to protect you from it."

"Jack…"

I retreat slowly, tiptoeing down the hallway. The faint scent of baby powder lingers in the air as I reach the bedroom. Moonlight spills through the half-open curtains. Gently, I lean over the crib to kiss sleeping Quinton.

He stirs, his drowsy eyes fluttering open for a fleeting moment.

I quickly press my hand against my mouth, muffling the cry that threatens to escape. My body relentlessly trembles as if I were trapped inside a vigorously shaken snow globe. Through the haze of tears, the room becomes a blur, distorted and distorted.

"I'm going to take Elmo for a walk," I use my standard excuse. It may be lame, but I desperately need it.

She ignores me. But I locate her phone and place it in her hand, giving her the same instructions.

"This is your answer?" she grumbles, clutching the phone as if about to crush it. "Why am I feeling that I'm the only one who's fighting for us?"

"We're not heroes, Ava."

"No. I was clearly mistaken about us."

"It's impossible to fight for me."

"Then what have I been doing all this time?" She looks at me straight, laying a challenge.

I wish she wasn't so darn stubborn. "You think you're fighting for me, for us, whatever. I'm sorry to be blunt, but you're only fighting for yourself."

Suppressing her gasp, as if unwilling to reveal her agitation, she asserts, "If you have any intention to leave me, leave me now. I'm sure Huxley will be more than happy to keep me and Quinton safe."

I growl, but I walk away before I allow myself to speak.

With the flashlight guiding my way and Elmo's leash in my

other hand, I navigate the perimeter of the front yard. Truthfully, my lone walk with Elmo never takes me further than a few steps from the front door.

The frigid wind pierces through my body, infiltrating my bones as I deliberately abandon my jacket. I need the numbness. I need the icy chill to freeze my heart. I need to make this decision with my head.

After what feels like mere minutes, I return to Ava, who immediately wraps me in a warm blanket. Tears drip along my cheeks, watching sweetness fill her gaze. Yes, *sweet*— leaving me wondering why she wears such an expression. Didn't we just discuss my intention to leave her? And that she'd be happy to have Comet guarding her and Quinton?

"I'm sorry, Jack. I said things I didn't mean just now."

I take her hand, which feels unbelievably warm on my skin. "I'm sorry, too. I was harsh on you."

"I didn't want Huxley. I want you," she states. "But you were an ass for saying that I was only fighting for myself."

I let out half a chuckle. "I was. I'm sorry."

"I clearly haven't listened to you. I mean, *really* listened to you. When you said you were broken, I assumed I knew what you needed. I thought I was the answer, but I hadn't taken the time to ask what's really in here." She places her hand on my heart.

"You are my answer, Ava. I just got lost along the way."

She then softly asks, "Willem's offer. Was it why your nightmare was violent that morning?"

I close my eyes, considering the possibility. "I don't know."

"Since the day we met, your past has remained unchanged. Tell me, have your nightmares ever been that violent before?"

"Not when I was around someone. Or at least no one had ever told me." And I can't recall if they were when I was alone.

She continues, "You're putting too much pressure on your-self because you want to shield me from your past. Let me say this gently, Jack. Quinton and I need your protection in the present. You may not get what you want, and I'm not promising to erase your nightmares. But I'll be there to cushion the pain."

With both head and heart, I had already made my decision before coming back just now. Nonetheless, her words strike me deeply, and my heart aches for the right reasons.

Ava holds my shoulders and declares, "I will protect you from your past, not by burying it, but by being your support. Please let me in, not Willem. Whatever he said to you, don't heed his words. Don't do it, Jack."

For the first time since Willem's attempt to poison me, I feel clarity. Love isn't measured by the tears shed when you're gone but by the determination of that person to keep you on the right path. This woman never gives up on me, and I will return her faith.

Unable to hold back any longer, I confess, "I'm not gonna do it."

Ava collapses against me, the heft of our emotions over-whelming us both. It's painful to let go of the past, but the thought of losing my future hurts even more.

27

AVA

It finally happens—we're flying to Hawaii today. The anticipation has been escalating, given the short time we've had. As we pack the last of our belongings, I can't shake the sense of déjà vu. But this time, it feels like we're packing for a well-deserved break, like a stepping stone toward our future together.

We're aware that we'll always have unfinished business as long as Willem remains at large. But today, we feel a renewed sense of resolve, as if we're riding the clear skies after a storm. Morgan has arranged a chartered flight for us, courtesy of her connection to a company that sometimes flies Red Mark personnel and their clients. Flying on a private jet will make things easier for newbies Quinton and Elmo, and we won't have to worry about being seen.

Taking a break from packing, I prepare some blueberry oatmeal for Quinton.

Jack joins me, wrapping me from behind like a cape. I slant my face, admiring his look after visiting the barber. I will miss running my fingers through his thick hair, but something about his military-crop look and smooth, clean-shaven face stirs my core—a 'Lieutenant Kelleher, make love to me please' kind of yearning.

"You're all right?" I check in on him. We woke up at the same time before dawn, just as he gripped the bed sheet and was about to scream. I don't think he had a deep sleep, but we agreed not to discuss it and simply hug each other instead. Sometimes, silence is all you need.

"I'm still nervous about the trip, but I think we've made the right decision," he says, planting a light kiss on my cheek before grabbing the oatmeal for Quinton, who is already seated in his high chair, happily tapping on the plastic table.

"I can't believe we're really leaving." I look around the kitchen, reminiscing the moments we've shared during our stay—the meals, the coffees, the teas, the baby formulas. Lost in my thoughts, I gaze out of the window.

"We'll create new memories, sweetheart," he assures me.

"For sure," I respond. However, my eyes remain fixed on the porch through the window, specifically on the railing. New memories or not, it will be hard to top the incredible night we had. Carry me—not many men could have pulled it off.

"Ava Belle, do you know if Elmo will need to fly in his cage?" asks Jack, interrupting my thoughts about that spectacular night.

I notice him keeping watch on Elmo while feeding a spoonful to Quinton. The mutt has been inspecting every nook and cranny of the house all morning, and now he's scratching at the back door.

"I don't think so," I answer, pulling Elmo away from the door. "What is it, Elm?" Elmo raises his eyes to me as if revealing a sad premonition. "Oh, don't look at me like that. You can be a passenger like your humans. But you'll have to go into quarantine when we reach Honolulu."

As soon as I let go, Elmo dashes to the door again. I look

out the window. One of the bushes moves, and I'm sure that's what my dog is concerned about rather than his flight. A black-and-white creature runs across the yard.

"Everything okay back there?" Jack asks.

"Yeah. It's just a skunk."

Elmo whimpers and then continues pacing around the house.

As I wipe the kitchen bench, I bring up the topic we haven't had a chance to discuss amid all the rush. "So, will we be living on the base?" I ask, trusting my man to have made all the necessary arrangements for our arrival.

"My current on-base accommodation is more of a bachelor pad, definitely not suitable for a baby."

Pausing in my cleaning, I turn to him. "Why? You have posters of topless women?"

"Ava!" he exclaims.

"It's okay if you do," I deadpan. "I just need to warn you that Quinton might think it's mealtime all the time."

"Ava!" Jack exclaims even louder, trying to stifle his laughter. "I do not have posters of naked women. It's just that the space is small and the ventilation isn't great. That's all."

"I'm just teasing," I say as I scrub away a stubborn dried oatmeal stain on the stone bench. "So, we'll have accommodation outside the base?"

"Yes. It's only twenty minutes away."

Becoming a military partner never entered my mind. But this unexpected turn is nothing less than a blessing and a miracle—even though I only know a little about the USMC lifestyle and island living.

I approach Jack, who is making engine sounds while he feeds Quinton a spoonful. I ask, "Is there a group or something where I can meet others?"

Jack wipes a bit of food from Quinton's mouth. "I'll introduce you to my friends. They all have partners or families, so you won't be alone there. Just so you know, being a single man, I'm bucking the trend in our community. When I left, that is." He smiles.

I return his smile, feeling reassured. With Jack by my side, I'm open to anything—learning, adapting, pivoting. "So, you'll be with us in that off-base accommodation, right? Not in your bachelor pad?"

Jack puts the oatmeal bowl down and hooks his arm around my waist, pulling me closer. "Ava, we're family. I'll take care of you and Quinton, and we'll always be together, no matter where we are. I promise."

I chuckle and reply, "Well, I do have a long shopping list for when we arrive."

Jack raises an eyebrow and teases, "Oh, really? Like what?"

I lean into him as he presses against me, feeling his warmth. "Well, for starters, I need a bikini. And maybe some lingerie."

He smirks and playfully rubs against me. "Damn... of course, you can shop to your heart's content. Just promise me you'll let me help choose the important items."

While I'm busy packing the large bag of trash, Jack takes the time to refill Quinton's mug with drinking water. When he returns, we discover that the bowl has toppled over, leaving Quinton covered in oatmeal.

"Oh, Quinton!" Jack exclaims in dismay.

"Oh dear," I sigh, regretting my choice of using fruit that stains easily in the meal.

My hands are full of trash, so Jack offers to help. He picks up Quinton from his highchair. Carrying the baby as if he were flying, he mimics the actions of a captain. "To the changing station!"

I chuckle as I drag the trash bag out. As I pass the front

door, I notice that Elmo has peed in the corner of the living room. "Oh, Elmo!" I sigh, but the mischievous mutt is nowhere to be found.

"Elmo! Come here, boy," I call out, but there's no response.

I check outside to see if he is trying to chase those neighborhood skunks. With no sign of him at the front and on the street, I circle around the rear of the house, tracing the path of dog tracks that lead me to some damaged shrubs.

"Elm, come on, come to me."

As I scurry, it's as if the bush has sprung to life, with two arms emerging from it to grab my neck and silence my cry for help. The man is soldier-like, wearing a ski mask. I desperately want to call Jack, but all I can do is watch helplessly as I'm pulled behind the bushes and out of the backyard. The lack of any visible getaway vehicle only adds to my confusion. How did this captor manage to ambush me so effectively?

Finally, I spot Elmo in the distance. With menace, he sprints toward us, his short legs moving surprisingly fast. I've never seen my dog like this before. He fearlessly tries to defend me, his loyal nature shining through as he sinks his teeth into the man's foot. But his brave efforts are quickly thwarted as the man heartlessly kicks him away.

No...

Elmo's body sprawls across the ground. My cheeks are drenched with tears, yet a suffocating grip clamps my mouth shut, stifling any cries. The pain of losing my loyal companion shatters my heart. I didn't even have a chance to say 'good dog' or even call his name. Meanwhile, the man mercilessly drags me farther away from the house.

I gyrate, desperately trying to break free from my captor's grip. But my attempts are futile. In a desperate act of self-defense, I start hitting his neck with all the strength I can muster, hoping to weaken his hold on me. Just as I feel a glimmer of hope, another man appears out of nowhere. He moves swiftly, overpowering me and pinning me down.

"Where the fuck have you been!" the first man complains in a voice I don't recognize.

"Chill out!" the other man replies, his voice calm and collected. He shouldn't have bothered wearing a mask. I know he's the bearded man.

Before I can even process my next move, a sudden, sharp prick pierces my arm. In a matter of moments, everything around me turns blindingly white. The world becomes a void, a blank canvas, as if all the colors have been erased.

In this empty space, I can only think about Quinton. As long as Jack is with him, I know he'll be safe. And as long as I breathe, I will fight for my survival.

28

JACK

I wipe Quinton with a warm washcloth. We sing along to the music pulsing through my phone, its volume turned up. Ava often compliments me on my swift baby-changing skills. Little does she know, my secret lies in my choice of playlist. Without fail, the rhythm and beats captivate Quinton, coaxing him to cooperate effortlessly.

"Mama."

"She's just outside, buddy. But don't tell her about the music, okay? It's our little secret."

After changing him into fresh clothes, I gather the dirty pile and stuff it into a plastic bag.

"Okay. You're ready for the real flight, Captain Q-Bear." I kiss his belly, taking in the delicate fragrance of white lilies and jasmine from his baby powder. "Who am I, Quinton?"

"Emmo..."

"No. Come on, say 'dada.'"

The cheeky little one simply laughs. I believe he's aware of how amusing it is to everyone when he refers to everything as Elmo.

"You're not gonna say it, are you?" I give him a funny face, and he continues giggling. "All right. How about 'aloha?'"

"Oaaa."

With a chuckle, I praise him as I stop the music and pack up Quinton's diaper bag.

How my life has changed. A good day used to mean successfully pushing my Marines to their absolute limits. Now, simple things like singing a duet with a baby are enough to fill me with satisfaction.

I lift Quinton into my arms and carry him out of the room. The air is still. The house is quiet, as if I'd just stepped into a museum.

"Ava?" I meander from room to room. "Elmo..."

I search both the front and back porches, but there's no sign of them anywhere. All I come across is an abandoned trash bag by the door.

Desperation creeps in.

I put Quinton in his baby carrier, strapping him securely on my front, facing me. For the first time, I feel a real threat while Quinton is with me—on me. I carefully don my ballistic vest. It's got to be in an unconventional way because, somehow, I have to adequately cover both Quinton and me.

With Quinton fully protected, I reach for my SIG.

I cautiously step out of the front yard and onto the street. When I hold a weapon, my brain instinctively switches to military mode. I'm currently adjusting to the combination of this mindset while feeling the presence of Quinton hanging on my chest and wearing a vest that fits like a rice sack.

The baby moans, reaching up to me. He's probably feeling a little warm, thanks to the Kevlar around him. "Easy, baby. Stay quiet," I whisper, hoping the baby will understand. While keeping myself concealed behind the trees and bushes of the front yard, I yell, "Ava!"

The stillness is deafening, but suddenly, a faint whimpering reaches my ears, coming from the rear of the house. Without a second thought, I sprint toward the back, my heart pounding in my chest. And there, in a heartbreaking sight, I find Elmo, his body contorted in pain, dragging himself with a broken front leg.

My God... what has just happened?

I kneel as Elmo collapses at my feet.

"Emmo!" Quinton squirms in his carrier, eager to catch a glimpse, but his view is obstructed by the ballistic vest. Maybe it's for the best that he can't see, given the condition the dog is in.

The longer I stay here, the more I expose Quinton to danger. But there's no way I'm going to give up on that loyal creature. In battles, I stand by the notion of 'no Marine left behind.' In life, I will never leave a friend behind—human or animal.

I run back to the house, grab a sheet along with Quinton's bag which I'd forgotten, then come back. I wrap the sheet around the dog to create a makeshift sling. With great care, I lift him up and place him gently into the cargo area of Ava's SUV. My senses heighten as if there's evil behind every tree surrounding me. Keeping my gun within reach, I secure Quinton in his baby seat.

Free from the tenting ballistic vest, he looks around, searching. "Mama..."

"Everything will be okay, baby. Don't cry, please don't cry." I caress his cheek. "I'll find Mommy. But first, we've got to get out of here."

Although I'm eager to locate Ava, my gut feeling warns me that I'm deep within a dangerous territory. I scream north to Helena as fast as I can with a baby and an injured canine on board.

I call my brother. "Ava's gone!" I pant. "It's that mother-fucker, Sam!"

"Don't fuck with me, Jack!" Sam growls in anger. "Where are you? Where's Quinton?"

"Quinton is with me, and I'm on my way to Red Mark. Are you there?"

"Yeah."

"Can you arrange for a vet? Elmo is badly injured," I request.

"I'll get a vet. Don't worry about that. Just get your butt over here."

The stretch of road ahead is desolate, with only a few scattered cars passing by. The surrounding landscape is dominated by dense clusters of trees and bushes, creating countless potential hiding spots. Eventually, I arrive at Red Mark without any complications.

Sam is already there, accompanied by Huxley and a lady I assume is the vet. As I prepare to carry Quinton, Huxley and the vet take Elmo inside.

"Are you both okay?" Sam inspects me and Quinton.

I huff out a 'yes' as Sam hands me a bottle of water.

"Let's go inside," he says.

In the lobby, Elmo lies motionless on the floor as the vet examines him. His eyes remain open and occasionally blink weakly.

I lower myself and gently stroke the top of his head. "How is he, doc?" I ask.

She replies, "He has a broken leg, which could be complicated by his skeletal dysplasia. I will need to take him to the hospital for emergency surgery. My team and I will do everything we can, I promise."

I whisper, "Good dog, Elmo. Hang in there," while Quinton stretches himself to pet his loyal friend.

Sam leads me to one of the dayrooms upstairs. These rooms are regularly used by Red Mark agents when they have to stay overnight. I realize it's the same room Ava was taken to the first afternoon she was here after Quinton was taken from her.

We sit together in silence. In the past, dealing with a fucked-up situation like this, I would have hit the gym and vented my emotions on a punching bag. But I'm a different man now. Just like I advised Ava that evening, I'm now following the same principle and using Quinton as my guide in any decision I make. I cannot allow my emotions to over-power me.

Soon, Huxley enters the room, holding Quinton's filled bottle. "Sweet tea for you, baby bear," he offers Quinton and then suggests, "I can take care of him. You two can talk outside. We don't want to stress out Quinton. He can sense it."

We agree, knowing that Quinton will be in good hands with his 'Uncle Comet.' Sam leads me into his office.

"Willem has information about my abduction," I admit, rousing uneasiness in Sam. "You know, during your search, you never discovered the location of that man's base in Florida."

"No, I never did. Once I found you, it became irrelevant," he responds, narrowing his suspicious gaze. "Why are you trusting him?"

"Willem sent me a photo of a basement," I explain.

My brother shakes his head. "It could be any basement, right?"

"Not this one. The photo looked exactly like the space that appears in my nightmares." I rub my face in frustration, growling to myself. "He offered it to me, but I told him to go to hell. He didn't specify what he wanted in return, but we both know who he's after."

Sam nods, his concern evident, but he's showing no trace of blame on his face. "Now he has one of them."

I feel the burden pressing down, but his calm demeanor soothes my frayed nerves. I tell him, "I was changing Quinton with the music playing. I didn't hear anything from outside. She was gone, just like that. I didn't have the luxury of exploring. I couldn't risk Quinton's safety. But from just scanning around, it was clean, as if there was nothing."

Sam nods understandingly. "My guess is that Willem gained access to information about you from the DOJ database his company was responsible for managing."

"His access won't last for long. It might already be too late. I don't know. I don't care. I need to get to Ava!"

I rise from my seat, my thoughts converging in my head with Ava at the center. Willem wants her, but he won't hesitate to hurt her. To what scale—I don't even want to know. But one thing is sure. I will end him. Today.

"He wants you in his lair, Jack."

I decide, "I've got no choice but to meet that cockbag there."

Sam sighs, "The question is, where's his lair?"

29

AVA

When I open my eyes, the blinding white light has vanished, replaced by a darkness that hovers between a cave and a closet. Disoriented and disconcerted, I try to ascertain my surroundings. I'm inside a cargo space of a car, likely a van, lying on the floor with a blanket covering me from head to toe. I detect a slight vibration indicating a steady speed on a smooth road, likely a highway. I don't know how long I was unconscious, but chances are, I'm now far away from Helena.

Overwhelmed by weakness, my feeble senses barely register the existence of my own body. The knowledge of my arms being tightly bound behind my back is the only tangible sensation I perceive.

With a rough, jarring maneuver to the right, the car halts. The door swings open. I feign slumber as one of my captors peeks under the blanket. The abrupt change from darkness to light made my eyelids twitch, but he doesn't seem to pay any attention as he places the cover back over me and closes the door.

"Where're you going?" That's the bearded man's voice.

"Taking a piss."

"Be quick. We're already running late!"

Then I hear the bearded man speaking on the phone. He mentions that he's on his way, and the cargo is prepared for delivery. It's clear that he's talking to Willem, and unfortunately, the cargo he's referring to is me.

Realizing that the other doors are open and the two men are outside, I hope the car uses a central lock, which would mean the door to the cargo space is unlocked as well. With a bit of effort, I manage to use my teeth to flick the cargo door open. Cautiously, I press my feet against it to push it, making sure to control my movements. It opens wide enough for me to slip out unnoticed by the men.

I press myself against the back of the van, scanning my surroundings. My heart deflates, sinking like a punctured tire. There's no sign of life, and worse still, there's nothing around to provide cover even if I manage to escape. Around me are fields as flat as the White House lawn.

I nudge the door using my shoulder, enough for it to click shut. The soft ground beneath me helps dampen any noise as I lie down and slowly crawl under the van. One by one, the men climb back onto their seats. I hold my breath, a mix of hope and fear.

To my surprise, the van drives away without me. I stay in my spot until it's completely out of sight. Then, without wasting any time, I sprint toward one of the fields. Although I have no idea where I am, I know that any path will lead me somewhere, and that's better than staying trapped.

After running for a few minutes with my hands still tied behind my back, I hear an approaching car. A glimmer of hope flickers within me—perhaps my day will finally take a turn for the better.

As the harsh sound reaches my ears, my gut instinctively clenches. It's as if the vehicle is pushing itself beyond its limits, straining to move faster than its engine allows. My heart sinks once again as I recognize the all-too-familiar van.

I sprint, desperately trying to put as much distance as possible between myself and the road. The drugs coursing through my veins make it feel like I'm moving in slow motion, unable to gather any real speed.

Suddenly, the van swerves off the road, careening onto the open field directly in front of me. I quickly change direction, hoping to outmaneuver my pursuer. But the open space only allows my enemy to close the gap, as if they're driving into a monster truck arena. Before the van even comes to a complete stop, the bearded man jumps out and swiftly apprehends me.

"No!" I scream, putting all my strength into escaping from him

"You always choose the hard way, don't you?" he gripes, his arms tightening around me with a mix of force and anger, as if he could crush every bone in my body.

"Let me go. You know you're not going to get anywhere with Willem. It's only a matter of time before he meets his downfall, if not already. What did he promise you?"

He remains silent as his partner joins the scene to drag me back into the van.

I persist. "Release me, and I promise I'll never speak a word about what happened in Clancy and Townsend."

The soldier-like man, who no longer disguises himself, looks at his apparent boss, seeking an explanation for my statement. The bearded man grabs me by the neck, growling in my ear, "Shut the fuck up before I slice your tongue!"

"Look, I admire your loyalty. But where is Willem? Sitting on his throne? He doesn't even dare to come and get me," I challenge. "And you believe he's going to give you what he promised?"

The bearded man releases his grip on me, and I'm thrust

back into the van. I crash onto its unforgiving floor, sending sharp pain into my skull while my spine throbs with aches.

But I force myself to recover, looking at the soldier-like man. "You probably didn't know what you've gotten yourself into. Get out while you can."

The bearded man flips my body over so I'm facing the floor, his entire weight pressing down on me. Gasping for air, I struggle to take even the smallest breath as his hand reaches my trembling wrist. The sharp prick of the needle penetrates my skin, a familiar sensation coursing through my veins. This time, my breath escapes me completely, leaving only the sound of the man's voice echoing in my ears. "Have a nice..." His words fade away as I succumb to unconsciousness.

When I eventually open my eyes, I find myself jolted inside a raucous vehicle. The metallic surroundings trap the stale air, adding to the sense of confinement. I hate to accept defeat, but my chances of escaping have dwindled to nothing.

This is no car ride. I'm on a fucking plane!

30

JACK

I pace the length of Sam's office, my eyes darting toward the dayroom where Quinton is. Hours have passed, and the weight of responsibility swamps me as I consider the boy, who is still without his mother.

"He could be anywhere," Sam sighs. He stands right next to me, and I can see the worry lines on his face deepening.

"It's got to be somewhere sentimental to him. He's the kind of man who enjoys playing games to make a point," I explain, racking my brain to uncover what that 'play' and 'point' could be this time. "When he devised that twisted plan to ransom Quinton, manipulating Ava into giving up custody, it may have seemed like a game, but it wasn't. I genuinely think he wanted Quinton for himself, not to fulfill his role as a father. He didn't care about his own flesh and blood!"

"So he's just worried about his succession plan?"

"Maybe. But I bet he has a different motive this time. When Willem was just six years old, his mother abandoned him. Now that Ava has also left him, it appears to be the perfect chance for him to seek his revenge—not only against Ava but also, symbolically, against his lost mother."

Sam frowns. "It's the worst kind of revenge, with deep roots from a time when you can barely tell right from wrong."

This makes the battlefield even more treacherous. But before anything can begin, I have to know where it's going to take place.

"Do you know where Willem and Ava met?" Sam asks.

"Sacramento, the DOJ headquarters. So it's unlikely he's taking her there."

"How about his house?"

"Maybe," I hum, tinkering with the idea.

My brother turns around and sits behind his desk, resting his chin on his hand. "Too predictable, you reckon?" he guesses.

"Everything revolved around him, from his company logo to every possession he owned. His Beverly Hills mansion was not a home. Everything felt staged. He had this giant exhibition of his inventions, those chips, which all looked the same to me. There were also numerous awards and memorabilia, even his pictures with Ava and Quinton, which were the size of paintings in an art gallery. It all felt so symbolic—or maybe just artificial, like the AI business. The only thing that felt human in there was Quinton's room. I'm sure Ava decorated it."

"Anywhere in Montana is symbolic for him?" Sam asks.

I shake my head, uncertainty gnawing at me. "When he called me at the park, he arranged for a random kid to deliver the picture of the basement. He made a joke about being out in the Atlantic Ocean. But I knew he was nearby."

As I say it out loud, I think about the appearance of the boy, making me involuntarily scoff. Sam's gaze becomes sharp, his eyes honing in on my every expression as if he can read the story of my abduction etched on my face. "What are you thinking, Jack?"

"That boy who gave me the photo. He was about my age when I was taken. Skinny, pale, and he didn't say anything."

"It's a sick kind of symbolism," Sam sneers.

"I believed Willem was in Helena then, but I can't think of any place that would particularly appeal to his ego. Well, Ava said it was more than ego. Perhaps it's just his way of life—nothing matters except himself."

I join my brother at his desk, sitting opposite him, recalling the event at the safe house this morning. Elmo was acting weird. Quinton spilled oatmeal all over himself, I changed him, then Ava disappeared into thin air.

Was it Willem who took her? Would that symbolize that nowhere is safe for her?

Maybe.

But why didn't he try to take Quinton, too?

Why did he offer me information about my kidnapper in the first place?

I believe Quinton is no longer his main concern. He will eventually attempt to take the boy away, but for now, his primary objective is to make Ava suffer an immediate consequence. What could be more magnificent than causing her to lose me in the very location that represents his triumph?

An urgent knock on the door interrupts my train of thought.

"Jack, Sam," Cora-Lee says quickly. "I just heard from Gerrard, the pilot of our private jet."

"He knew we weren't flying, didn't he?" I ask.

"Yes, he's fully aware of the situation, and he's been helping us. A plane took off from a private airstrip in Wolf Creek. There was nothing extraordinary there, but apparently, the owner of the plane was initially concerned about one of the passengers—a woman who looked heavily drugged. The two guys with her kept insisting the flight was for a medical emergency that only her specialist could handle, so he let his pilot fly them."

"Let me guess. Her so-called specialist is in L.A.?" I say.

Sam's head snaps toward me in surprise while Cora-Lee responds to me, "Uh-huh. And the plane was last seen near Van Nuys, twenty miles from L.A. There's no sign of the pilot."

I lock eyes with Sam, clenching a fist on his desk. "I know where Willem's lair is."

Sam instructs Cora-Lee, "Tell Gerrard to be on standby."

"Righto, boss," she answers and leaves the office.

"Do you think Quinton can stay at your house tonight?" I ask Sam.

"Of course," he answers. "I'll get Comet and Ben to drive the kiddo to my place. Cass will only be too happy to have him."

Then my brother puts on his holster.

"Where are you going?" I nod at his gear.

"I'm coming with you."

"No, you're not."

"The hell I am!"

While I wish he was coming with me, I won't let him take part in this rescue. He's about to become a father again, and I cannot jeopardize anything for him or his family. "I know about it, Sam."

He sighs, knowing what I'm referring to. "So Cass told you?"

"This isn't your battle."

"You're my brother. Your battle is my battle. I won't let you—"

"I'm not planning to go alone," I anticipate what he's going to say. Then I request, "Give me Tyler."

Sam reluctantly puts his holster away. "All right. He'll meet you at the airport."

"We've got this. I'll keep you posted."

He pats my shoulder, then pulls me into a hug. "Bring her back."

I nod firmly. She's a mother held captive by a deranged man. Whatever it takes, I'll bring her home.

31

AVA

My head hangs low, lazily swaying back and forth. A thin stream of saliva trickles down my mouth as I part my lips. Exhaustion weighs on my eyelids, making them feel like they have been closed for an eternity. I try hard to lift my head, but then I'm hit with an intense pain in my neck and a queasy sensation. Without warning, the contents of my stomach erupt, spilling onto the floor.

"I apologize, darling. It seems you cannot handle the double dose of sedatives," the unmistakable voice of Willem Botha assaults my ears, his amused tone unsettling. "To be fair, it's your own fault."

A hand grips my chin, forcing me to drink. Not even my lips are under my control, but thankfully, it's water.

As I blink away the haze, my surroundings come into focus. I find myself in a room filled with sleek glass cupboards, their surfaces gleaming under the sterile lights. The atmosphere is both high-tech and clinical, giving the impression of a futuristic experiment lab. I told Morgan the terrifying moment I was aware of being taken to a hospital for the first time in my life. This almost feels like it, only I'm in the company of Dr. Willem and his bearded nurse.

"I've never had the opportunity to bring you here," Willem says, his hands gesturing to showcase the room.

My senses sharpen, allowing me to take in more details. The glass cases that line the room hold an array of machines, some fully assembled while others reveal exposed wires and half-finished equipment. It's clear that this place is a work in progress, but it doesn't stop me from wondering what Willem is planning to do to me.

Nervously, I search for any means of escape. My heart quickens as I realize there doesn't seem to be a door anywhere. Perhaps that's why Willem has allowed me to sit in the chair without any restraints.

I clear my throat and mockingly say, "Why don't you take me on a tour?" The drug still has me feeling sluggish. I don't know how I'll do it if he offers.

Willem laughs in response. "I won't, but I still welcome you to my prototyping lab—The Atrium. And I can assure you, you won't be comfortable here."

"You were never a good host. I used to be the one holding your parties together. Why would I expect any different here?"

He takes his time, gently caressing my left fingers. "Where's your ring?"

"It's gone. We're over," I reply.

"Oh, we're not!" His lips curl into a smile. He separates my ring finger from the others and signals the bearded man to approach. The man comes forward, holding a knife like a butcher.

"No! Get away from me!" I try to escape, relying on my days at the gym, but my muscles feel like jelly.

Willem pushes me back into the chair while the bearded man holds my arm steady, positioning the knife at the base of my ring finger. I close my eyes, bracing myself for the sound of my bone crunching under the blade. But instead, all I hear is laughter.

"I still want you pretty and whole for our wedding," Willem says. "That's how much I believe in us. You don't just throw away a relationship like you did. You're wonderful, Ava, but you need to understand loyalty."

"You threw away that relationship the moment you laid a hand on me after begging for me to take you back."

Willem gently lifts my chin, tilting it upwards. "Well, darling, I meant what I said to you on the phone. I've forgiven you. Now, whether you like it or not, you, me, and Quinton will be a family again."

"I'm not yours, Willem, and neither is Quinton," I retort.

"It's hard for me to admit, but you did fool me," he confesses. "I had known about your connection with Red Mark all along because of your bitch friend, Morgan. But Jack?" He repeatedly clucks his tongue and then adds, "I didn't know you had an affair with him until he showed up in Townsend."

"I never had an affair. I left you first."

"Whatever, Saint Ava," he deadpans. "And it wasn't just you that opened my eyes to the reality. That stupid Marine," he sighs deeply, "he surprised me too."

A contented smile spreads across my face. In his world, he couldn't fathom that the true qualities of a good man do not encompass power and selfishness. Despite a challenging upbringing, I believe he had ample opportunities to learn about humility, trust, and kindness—but he never tried.

"You know, darling. Lifelong bachelors like Jack don't usually settle with women like you. I mean, women who are burdened with another man's children."

Burdened?

Quinton is a blessing!

Laughing, Willem continues, "So you got lucky. He's not the kind of alpha who—you know, like a lion who eats his rival's offspring. So I must give it to him. He defied my expectations."

I raise my eyes to him with a flicker of defiance.

He remains calm and continues to speak his wisdom. "Acknowledging a mistake is an accomplishment of a great man. Therefore, I must acknowledge it—I was mistaken," he says. "But what truly distinguishes a remarkable man is his ability to correct his errors. And that is precisely what I am going to do. Starting now."

"What do you want, Willem?"

"Fuck family! It's nothing but a letdown," he carps. "I will not give you a choice. Here is what you must do: call Jack and tell him to bring Quinton to me. In return, I will set you free and give him what is stored in that computer over there. The solution to his life's mystery."

"You'd already tested him, and you failed!" I sneer.

"Let's see if he can maintain his righteousness when faced with such temptations."

"He sees Quinton as his own son and will never give him up!"

"Lies! Quinton is my son!" Willem exclaims, angrily striking the table with his fist, his eyes filled with rage. "I will do whatever it takes to reclaim him. I will love him and ensure he grows up knowing that his mother abandoned him when he was just a baby!"

So this is his revenge—he has found a way to hurt me, not only by taking away my son but also by accusing me of abandonment.

"You will never succeed, even if you kill me," I counter.

"Leave the logistics to me, my dear. I can assure you, I

always get what I want. I've learned this not because I was privileged but because I started from nothing. A loss makes a man stronger, but a betrayal can turn one into an invincible being."

"Quinton will forever remember Jack as his father!"

Willem gives a nod to the bearded man, and he slaps me.

I scoff. "You don't wanna get your hands dirty now? You're an even bigger coward!"

Willem observes his own hands. "Hitting you doesn't give me the same thrill as it used to."

"So reality has finally caught up with you, darling," I mock. "Now you know what defines a man. You realize you're not as great as you believe yourself to be." I don't even need to mention Jack's name for him to understand the implication.

"Do not idolize Jack Kelleher! Yes, he's strong. His past made him so—as I said, loss makes a man stronger. But he's not invincible. You will see. In a battle between brain and brawn, brain always wins." He then forcefully grabs hold of my hand, his grip tightening around my ring finger.

He then declares with malice, "That Marine threatened to chop my fingers if I ever came near you again."

"Willem, no!" I exert all my strength to remove my finger, but his grasp is as strong as an eagle's talon.

"Let him suffer the repercussions of his own threat. Since I'm not going to marry you, no one will ever put a ring on this finger."

In one swift motion, the bearded man swings his knife. The metallic glint of the blade catches my eye just before my vision blurs into a sea of crimson.

32

JACK

Willem took Ava not because he wanted her back but because he wanted me to witness his power. Then he'll destroy me, and perhaps her too. He'd failed to lure me with the information about my kidnapper, and now he's taken the only woman that matters to me. I will end him today.

I haven't heard from him. I'm sure his invitation will come, and I won't give him any more time to prepare. I want to arrive on my terms.

The arrogant man wasn't joking when he had lunch with Los Angeles' lieutenant governor and told him that W-Bot's new headquarters would be fitted with technology so advanced that hacking the AT&T network would be child's play. He was planning something big in that building. It's his pride, and it's where he wants to show me his might and his control over Ava for one last time. Besides, the unfinished nature of the premises will help his cause, providing him with many hiding places.

Tyler and I arrive at the complex just before sunset. It's quiet, a stark contrast with how it was when I first surveyed it. Ava told me construction used to be going on nonstop. Now, there isn't even lighting in here. The cranes and heavy machinery are gone, leaving only scaffolding with messy netting and mud on the ground.

Tyler scans the width of the site, commenting, "Some office!"

"It would've been thirty stories tall if it had been finished." I gaze up. Currently, it has barely reached four or five floors.

Wearing ballistic vests and carrying light packs, we navigate our way over the construction fencing and pick a spot right by one of the mounted cameras.

Tyler takes out a can of spray paint from his pack and covers the camera with it, then we wait.

The complex has been seized, and I'm unsure how much of its security features are still working or if they're being monitored 24/7. If someone notices one of the cameras has gone black, movement should start soon. But for now, it stays quiet.

We run across the field to reach a chained gate into the building, which I break with a bolt cutter to enter.

"Sam, we're in," I alert my brother. "If you don't hear from us in two hours, bring in the LAPD."

Tyler lifts his gaze, remarking, "There's not much to see up there."

He's right. Above ground, the building is nothing but a shell. However, Ava had told me how important the basement was.

"We go down," I say.

There's a lift, but we both agree to take the fire escape to descend.

We enter a space resembling a secret military installation —or what's left of it. The temporary lighting casts feeble shadows, barely illuminating the surroundings.

"Which one?" Tyler asks, gesturing towards the two entrances that stand opposite each other.

Ava could be anywhere within this building, and time is of the essence. "We should split up," I suggest.

Tyler nods in agreement, and we each venture into a different door.

I turn on my flashlight, shining on the bare concrete floor as I scan the area.

"The only way is down from here," Tyler relays on the radio.

I trace the walls encircling me, searching for any sign of irregularity, but I find nothing. "Same here," I respond, making my way down the stairs.

As I traverse each level and continue descending, I can't shake the feeling that there are people lurking in this place.

"Ty, where are you?" I call out.

"Basement three."

"Anything?"

"It's just empty rooms with partially built benches and shelves," he describes.

"There's nothing on this side, only concrete," I explain. "Do you think these two sides could be connected?"

"I'm not sure, L.T. So far, I don't see a way to get to where you are." He pauses, seemingly looking around. "Well, unless you consider the air duct."

"All right. I'm heading to basement four."

"Roger that."

After advancing past an unfinished doorway, my eyes catch sight of a man in the distance, positioned as a guard for another entryway. Obviously, Willem's financial struggles have left him with an inexperienced skeleton crew. That guard bears the hallmarks of an amateur mercenary with his pristine camouflage attire and casual grip of his Ruger rifle as if he's hoisting a flagpole.

"Someone's here," I whisper.

"Should I go over there? I still need to check out one more floor. The layout seems different, and there are rooms here."

"Keep looking. Ava may be hidden in one of those rooms," I command, keeping my focus on the guard.

Stepping into the light, I take down the lone man before he can react. Crossing the threshold of the doorway, I'm transported into a chamber that seems to bridge the gap between reality and imagination.

"I'm inside some kind of lab," I inform Ty. This futuristic laboratory serves as a testament to the millions Willem invested.

"I've scanned all floors. I didn't find anything, not even in these rooms on the lowest basement."

"Come meet me. Once you reach this side of the building, go straight down. You'll see a dead soldier in front of a door-way. Go past it, and you'll find me."

Suddenly, a thud resonates through the air, its origin difficult to discern amid the echoing acoustics. But the impact is unmistakable. The doorway slams shut behind me, trapping me within.

Shit!

"Ty?"

No answer.

"Ty!"

The radio is dead. I think this room is completely isolated.

As I pivot, my gaze meets the figure of Willem himself. If it wasn't for his arms raising in surrender, his whole frame would only reach my chest. He appears in a flawless suit, resembling his pre-fugitive style.

It's clear that my arrival ahead of his invitation is getting to him. But he masks the flash of annoyance with a smile. His eyes turn hopeful, much like those ambitious businesspeople who are eager to befriend you.

"You've read my mind," he says. "Although not entirely. If you had brought Quinton with you, I might have let you go."

I point the gun at him. "Where's Ava?"

Trying to salvage his pride, Willem responds, "You've made it too easy, Mr. Kelleher. You can't do anything about her. But, I must remind you, on the other side of the room, there's a machine that holds the answers to all your life's questions."

Ignoring his words, I repeat, "Where's Ava?"

Willem scoffs, "You'd rather choose her? She's just an emotional crutch for you. Once you uncover your past, you'll feel fulfilled and move on to a bigger and better thing. How does Colonel Jack Kelleher sound? Or even General?" He pauses to appraise me. "Or maybe you'll find another woman instead of stealing someone else's wife!"

I retort fiercely, "She's not your wife! She never was and never will be."

"You're right. She's not, and she won't ever be. Sometimes, I forget that." Willem straightens himself. "But she won't be yours either, Mr. Kelleher. So you might as well take the only offer on the table. I'm giving you the key to the mystery behind your lingering pain, and in return, you let Quinton go. It's a fair deal."

My patience is wearing thin. I press the gun against his forehead. "Your end of the bargain is at the end of this barrel."

Willem laughs. "Go ahead and shoot me. And you'll get out of here empty-handed, or worse still, empty-chested."

With that, the room plunges into darkness. I aim my gun, but it's pointed at nothing but hollow air. Willem has vanished.

"Fuck! Willem!" I shout, but all I hear is the echo of my own voice.

I turn on my flashlight, scanning the room for any sign of him. Then, a light flickers on behind one of the walls, which has transformed into a wide window. Through the glass, I see Ava sitting helplessly in a room filled with computers. Her pale face and the dark circles under her eyes tell a tale of immense pain and hardship.

"Ava!" I yell, pounding at the thick glass.

She rises from her seat, revealing a bandage wrapped around her left hand, blood seeping through. My jaw tightens, and an unquenchable rage soars behind my ribcage. No one can empty my chest until Willem Botha is eradicated!

Ava's voice comes through a speaker as she cries out. She tries to conceal her injured hand, pressing herself against the glass with her right palm, the one unmarred. "Jack... can you see me? Can you hear me?"

"Back away! Back away, Ava!" I shout, hoping she can hear me. She runs back, seeking cover behind a desk on the other side of the room.

I release a few shots at the glass, but to my dismay, I realize it's bulletproof. How the fuck am I going to get to her?

Just then, Willem appears behind Ava, pulling her back, taking her into his arms, and laughing triumphantly.

This room is an illusion, constantly changing its appearance. I search every side, desperate to reach Ava. Finally, my eyes lock onto a lever, discreetly tucked at the end of a shallow hole in the wall, right next to the wide, bulletproof window. My grip on the gun tightens in my right hand as I mentally prepare myself for any potential threats, whether from the other side or lurking behind me.

I extend my left hand into the hole, my fingers finding the lever. With caution, I press it.

Fuck!

A powerful suction pulls my arm in, and I'm helpless to fight it. At the same time, a ring constricts just above my elbow, immobilizing it. The only possible escape is to cut my forearm.

Just like the other deceptive elements in this sinister space, nothing is as it seems, and I have fallen into its trap. My arm is stuck inside a narrow steel tube, the unrelenting air pressure mercilessly tormenting my flesh and bones. It feels as if an enormous weight is crushing my forearm while pliers squeeze my fingers with excruciating force.

Willem's mocking voice emerges from the same speaker as Ava's. "A pressure chamber to a microchip is like fire to a sword."

Ava desperately pleads for him to let me go, but Willem remains unaffected. Behind the glass, he puts on a show, kissing her lips and fondling her breasts.

"Willem you fucking cockbag!" I yell.

He continues his taunting. "It's like a moth to a flame. Like the mighty Jack Kelleher drawn to my trap." He steps close to the window, reveling in my agony in close-up. "This is a proto-type, repurposed just for you," he boasts. "It seems to be working perfectly, wouldn't you agree, Mr. Kelleher?"

Willem then turns to Ava, emphasizing his victory. "What did I say, darling? The brain always wins!"

Ava's pleas grow more desperate as the pressure on my arm intensifies, threatening to crush it entirely.

"Please, stop!" she cries.

"It's a shame that she's such a whore." Willem takes her injured arm, putting it on display. "We would've had the most spectacular wedding, one that you could only dream of giving her. Well, I would've had to reconstruct her ring finger, but hey!"

He cut her finger off?

He fucking cut her finger off?

Rage burns me, intensifying my determination to escape. Tremors course through my body, causing even Willem himself to cast concerned glances at my strength. But the trap is unyielding. I unleash a roar, cursing, "Willem Botha! You won't leave this place alive!"

He touches the bandage on Ava's finger, causing her to grimace in pain. Then, he forcefully pushes her against the glass, making her face him as he closely studies her expression. "Bring me Quinton, or she and you will be another wasted Romeo and Juliet story."

My teeth grind together. The pain from witnessing this scene and the agony in my arm exceed my limits. My skin is about to tear, and everything beneath it feels like it's about to explode, much like flesh in zombie movies.

I have to do something. Perhaps it's time to cut my arm...

Amid Ava's cries and my own screams, the pressure suddenly stops, giving me momentary respite. But my arm remains trapped inside the unforgiving tube.

A man approaches my dangling arm from the other side—the bearded man, Willem's last line of defense. He yanks at my wrist, making me shake in agony. Then, he injects something into my vein.

Pain, tingling, and numbness surge through my body. But I know this is just the beginning. Tyler had better find us before Willem unleashes his worst!

33

AVA

I watch helplessly as the bearded man yanks Jack's limp body by the arms like a hyena on a fresh kill. My heart wrenches in sync with every pull. Jack's left forearm, a grotesque canvas of deep red and hints of purple, serves as a snarky reminder of the unspeakable torment he had endured.

By this time, I've stopped feeling my own pain, unsure about the fate of my hand. I passed out after the amputation, then I woke up smelling burned flesh. I think the men tried to stop the bleeding.

Even in his unconscious state, Jack is somehow fighting. With each laborious step, the bearded man struggles to maneuver him, as if the Marine has become too burdensome. After a few impatient grunts from his boss, he manages to settle Jack onto a chair.

They remove his jacket and bulletproof vest. Jack's biceps strain against his T-shirt sleeves as his arms are tightly bound to the armrests, and the sound of duct tape being pulled tightly fills the air.

Sadism projects from Willem's eyes as he rubs Jack's arm.

"I should've used that vacuum tube on his balls," he sneers

like a juvenile. "Imagine them bursting like a pair of balloons!"

The two bad actors share a twisted laugh, overriding the soft whirs coming from the computer fans around us. Then Willem takes something out of a shelf. He hands me a tablet and a stylus pen.

"I know you prefer pencil and paper. But you're not against technology, are you?" he says. "I'd say your digital work was even better."

"What do you want me to draw, Willem?" My anxiety shoots up as malice oozes out of his stare.

"Draw him," he orders, pointing at Jack, who's starting to wake up.

"What?"

"Draw him!"

The bearded man yanks Jack's head, forcing me to see his bruised and battered face. He then points his gun at Jack's temple.

"Every bruise must be accounted for!" Willem warns. "Or I keep adding it on him. He's got a lot of space for me to do it. I guess, the downside of being a big man."

My bandaged hand trembles, pinning the tablet against my thigh while the other grips the stylus pen. Carefully, I execute each stroke. Lines form randomly, thick and thin, alternating without control.

In my career as an artist, I've put on paper every spectrum of human emotion imaginable. This time, the subject of my art is the man I love, and the result is a haunting portrayal of a helpless face resigned to its impending demise.

I refuse to acknowledge that it's Jack for fear that it will consume me. I must press on, driven by my fear of Willem's insanity. His sick wish must be fulfilled, or I risk testing his already dwindling patience tonight.

Jack lets out a moan, calling my name.

In a display of brutality, Willem delivers a savage punch to Jack's mouth.

I jolt, causing the pen to slip from my fingers.

"You're going to capture this too, aren't you?" Willem revels at his new creation, a grin stretching across his face. He hurls the pen back at me, commanding me to continue drawing.

"She'll never be yours," Jack's words emerge muffled from his split lip, his voice strained and weak.

Willem's fury grows, and he crushes Jack's injured arm. The sickening crunch of the rigid tape wrapping Jack's flesh terminates my breath as if giving me a taste of what death will be like.

Despite the agony, Jack grits his teeth, refusing to give Willem the satisfaction of hearing him cry out.

Willem scoffs at the show of resilience. "So it's true. Marines take pain well. But I know I've broken you."

He snatches the tablet from me, thrusting the sketch in front of Jack's face. "Look at yourself!" he taunts, his voice sparked with delight. "Sunk. Hopeless." Contentment spreads across his features as he tucks away the tablet.

Speaking feels like an uphill battle, but I have to try. "You know how important children are to me, Willem. It's not gonna happen between me and him." My words feel foreign and feeble as they escape my lips. My voice is drowned out by the magnitude of Jack's suffering, but the thorns of my own lie quell me.

In a display of intrigue, Willem averts his gaze from Jack.

With my hope evaporating, I force myself to declare, "Let's try again. We can go back to how we were. It's not too late, you know that. You want that."

He grips my neck, then caresses my hair with an eerie vibe. "See, once trust is broken, it takes more than words to fix it. I don't know if I have enough time or patience to let you prove your loyalty."

"We'll disappear together, and no one will find us. There will be no need for time or patience, as I will only have you to lean on. You *will* have my loyalty."

He pushes me into a corner, the furthest one from where Jack is. The cold, sterile wall presses against my back.

Unexpectedly, he lets me go and takes a few steps backward. The physical separation only amplifies my worry. Something in him is about to erupt.

"Take off your shirt," he commands. His eyes fixated on me like an eager spectator awaiting a thrilling show.

I glance at Jack, his tear-streaked face begging me not to comply. Silently, I communicate to him that everything I do from this point on is for his safety before diverting my gaze completely. The weight of my dignity presses on my conscience as I contemplate its worth in this desperate situation.

"Not here," I decide.

"A shy whore. You're disappointing me, darling." Willem's eyes narrow, and a sinister leer crosses his face as he glances at his right-hand man.

The bearded man exchanges his gun for a knife. Dread claws at my skin. Almost as if in response to the sight of the gleaming blade, my left hand throbs with pain. That man has already taken one from me. What's the extent of harm he will inflict on Jack?

"Take it off. Strip yourself!" Willem roars.

The fear in my veins pulsates, but I refuse to let him break me completely. "Not here, Willem!" I keep protesting. I have a plan, but right now, I'm trying to figure out how to spare Jack from the next round of torture.

But I'm too late. The bearded man stabs Jack's biceps, and

blood gushes from the wound. Jack stifles a scream, his face drenched in sweat, the redness evincing the pain he can no longer contain.

"Please, stop!" I scream and remove my shirt, exposing myself to Willem's prying eyes. "I'm sorry, Jack."

Jack shakes his head, his lips trembling with unspoken words. Willem mocks me as if repulsed by my shirtless body. "You could have been more graceful, seducing me like you once did." But the instant his gaze falls upon my exposed cleavage, his self-restraint wavers.

He pins me against the wall, grinding his pelvis against mine while his lips explore the sensitive skin at the top of my breasts. Impatience infiltrates his breath as he unzips my pants, his hand slipping in behind the fabric.

I writhe, drawing from the contact, only to be reminded of Willem's control. The touch of his fingers abrades my skin like sandpaper. His voice grates on my nerves, and the scent that surrounds him is a nauseating blend of stale meat and pungent sweat. I had hoped to forget this smell, just like the aroma of the chamomile tea he used to sip.

I've promised Jack no one else would see my body. But I take it all with grace because I have something in store for this barbaric assailant.

34

JACK

My vision remains distorted by the effects of the drug. The room spins and blurs, but my instincts kick in. I discern Willem gradually distancing himself from Ava, strategically choosing his position. His voice cuts through the fog as he commands, "Take off your bra."

Rough air swirls in my throat as I try to scream. Rage swells behind my face until it feels like my eyeballs might burst from their sockets. I don't know if I still have a functioning arm under the tight taping, but the agony is nothing compared to the horror unfolding before me.

I tremble in my seat, desperately trying to free my bound arms. The bearded man stands behind me. I should feel the cold blade pressed against my throat, poised to slice through my flesh, but his attention is fixated on Ava. He eagerly watches as she moves her healthy arm behind her back, loosening the only garment covering her torso.

My eyes shut tightly, unable to witness her humiliation, while my body remains paralyzed.

But suddenly, everything stops. Ava stops, refusing to strip herself.

"Do it!" Willem snaps, his annoyance evident.

These precious seconds of resistance give me an opportunity to shift my position unnoticed. Summoning every ounce of strength, I raise my buttocks off the ground, making the metal chair lift. The armrests remain affixed to my body, causing the weight to bear heavily on my arms. The excruciating pain threatens to knock me back down, but the stakes are higher than anything I have ever faced. I've endured peril in battles at remote outposts, where death was more certain than staying alive, but the fight in my hand is for Ava. My move could be my downfall or my last chance to see her, but I must try.

Ava remains still, her rigid posture leaving Willem unsure of how to react.

Suddenly, she swings her arm toward his face. A soft, crushing sound travels to my ear, like a fork piercing a ripe tomato. Then all I can hear is Willem crying out in pain, his body recoiling. In that split second, I glimpse blood oozing from his eye. My God! Ava has just stabbed him with the stylus pen she used to sketch me.

Seizing the opportunity, I rotate myself, relying only on my two feet as my other limbs are restrained. The chair is already off the ground, so it takes less than a second to find its target. I knock the bearded man off his feet as he rushes to assist his master. He tumbles to the ground, and I swiftly drop the chair's steel base over him, crashing onto his torso. He struggles, but he's going nowhere.

Meanwhile, I hear Willem pleading in the corner, "Ava..." His demeanor has completely transformed from just a minute ago. "Let me go, and I will give you the password to that machine. You know what's in there," he says, pointing at the smallest computer.

My attention shifts back to the bearded man who's trapped

under my chair. He discards his knife and reaches for his gun. I grind the steel against his shoulder and neck again and again. Finally, his grip on the weapon weakens, and he becomes limp.

A whimper stretches from the corner where Willem is lying, but it's not his own. I swivel to see where Ava is. Willem's treatment of her makes me feel like I'm on a gibbet, stopping me from breathing. His right eye resembles a grotesque lump of blood, but it doesn't stop his murderous intent. He deprives Ava of air by wrapping his arm around her neck while they are both stretched out on the floor.

"Let her go!" I boom, gyrating. There's no way I can free myself, but I have to snag the bearded man's gun. Somehow.

Shifting my body weight to one side, I exerted pressure on the chair, causing it to tip over to my right, my good side. I maneuvered myself to create space for my taped arm to reach the abandoned gun. Pain lashes my upper body as I strained against the binds, but I persevere, stretching my fingers until they found purchase on the firearm.

My hand takes aim despite the restriction on my wrist. The only hurdle I face is Ava, who is practically lying on Willem like a fire blanket. She must expose him, or the bullet will hit her.

"Ava! Lift your legs!" I order desperately. "Lift them!"

Despite the suffocating grip around her throat, she summons a surge of strength and releases a determined scream. Her legs lift in the air like a gymnast, and her abdomen and buttocks contract with an intense force.

I pull the trigger.

Time slows down as her body descends, allowing me to witness the bullet's impact on Willem's stomach. Given its trajectory, I'm confident it will ultimately reach his chest.

Barely conscious, Ava crawls toward me while I'm still anchored to the chair, lying on one side.

But she stops and screams, "Jack!"

Maimed and perhaps half dead, the bearded man stands over me, holding a knife. He's approaching from the opposite direction of where my gun is aimed, making it impossible for me to get him. He lunges towards me, intent on completing his task.

But his assault is abruptly stopped by a gunshot to his neck. I have no clue where the shot came from, but it was of sniper caliber. As the bearded man falls onto me, his hand releases the knife, and his life slips away.

"Jack! Jack!" Ava rolls the corpse aside and then collapses next to my shoulder.

A voice suddenly calls out from somewhere hidden in the ceiling. I could've mistaken it as God, but it's former SEAL sniper Tyler Hunt—the Red Mark head of ops, my rescue partner. "Jack! Ava!"

"Ty!" I yell back, spotting a hand waving from a small opening.

He says, "Stay there, I'll come and get you."

I hear him crawling away from the shaft, leaving just Ava and me.

"You okay, sweetheart?" I murmur. Her breathing is rough, as if it belongs to someone else.

"Yeah," she rasps, exhaustion plasters her from head to toe.

"Let me see your hand."

"It's fine, Jack."

"Ava, let me see it!"

She holds up her bandaged hand, and I lift my head to examine it. The dressing appears to be secure and neatly applied without any indication of recent bleeding. As I take a whiff, I detect a combination of a burned scent and the smell of antiseptic.

How could those motherfuckers do this to her?

"You feel anything?" I query.

"It's numb at the moment. I don't know what's going on under the dressing, but I think they cauterized the wound. They certainly didn't want me to bleed to death. Don't worry, I'll live."

With broken sobs, I kiss her wrist. "I'm sorry I wasn't there to stop him." I choke out, my saliva tasting like acid. My guilt intensifies as I gaze at her vulnerable form. "And I couldn't stop him from touching you."

"Shh... baby, we're here. Nothing else matters," she warbles. "Remember that room I built to keep him out?" She points at her heart. "The door holds, baby. It holds. He never reached me."

"Come here," I invite her, desperate to feel her presence.

She's aware of my injuries, and she hesitates to embrace me.

But no matter how great the agony, only she has the power to soothe me. "Ava, I need you here." I nod at my chest.

Gradually, she moves closer, maneuvering around the toppled chair to reach me. It feels incredible to have her in my arms, or rather, to be in her arms.

"Quinton?" she whispers.

"He's safe. He's with Cass and Ben."

She lets out a serene huff.

I brush my cheek against her curls. I can't wait for them to smell like baby powder again. Although at this moment, as I inhale the fragrance of her natural scent, it serves as a poignant reminder of her resilience and the battles she has fought.

Her eyes linger on my face as she takes in every cut and bruise as if trying to absorb the pain herself.

"Do I really look like your sketch just now?" I ask.

She chuckles. "No. That was my most terrible creation ever."

I toss her an agreeing smile. If only I could break free from this damn chair and hold her tight.

Her gaze inevitably falls upon the stab wound on my biceps. And even though my vacuum-sucked forearm is still covered under the silver duct tape, she doesn't have to imagine.

I nudge my face against hers, deliberately diverting her attention from my mangled limb. I stretch my neck, trying to kiss her. She flinches slightly, her awareness drawn to my split lip as if she's hurting me.

"Please. I need this," I beg.

She opens her lips, leaning in to meet me. She savors the contact, even though mine are covered with cracks and no doubt tasting like blood. The tingling sensation sends a flow of comforting warmth, telling me we've made it.

We're still nose to nose, our lips hovering over each other, and I murmur, "About what you said to Willem. About having more children—"

"I only wanted to make him stop," she quivers.

"I know. But can I say this, Ava. I will make it happen. Because I love you, and I want to be a dad—again." I kiss her, a smile blossoming beneath my lips. I reluctantly end the kiss simply because I yearn to witness that smile.

Finally, we hear Tyler's voice coming from outside the bulletproof window.

"Ty, in here!" I yell back as loudly as I can. Then I remember. "Whatever you do, don't touch that yellow lever! Do not touch the yellow lever!"

I look around, trying to figure out how to let him in. I turn to Ava and ask, "How did they bring me here, sweetheart?"

Laboriously, she rises from her position and makes her way across the room, kneeling next to Willem's lifeless body. She rummages into his pockets, then takes out a set of keys, separating one that looks like a small, stainless-steel stick.

I grin. "Good girl!"

She comes to a section of the wall that doesn't appear to be a door, but she knows better. As she inserts the stick into a small hole, a hidden section slides open. "Ty, this way!" she calls out.

Noticing that her shirt is stuck under Willem, saturated with his blood, she grabs my jacket that the bearded man had tossed aside. She puts it on, stuttering as she slips her left arm into the sleeve. My heart is heavy, wishing I could be there for her.

Ty emerges, observing Ava's bandaged hand. "Are you okay, Ava?"

"I'm fine. Help my man off that chair. He looks terrible there." Ava gestures toward me.

Tyler straightens the chair and starts cutting the tape on my healthy arm, peeling it off. I immediately hook my free arm around Ava's waist, drawing her to me.

I feel her close, but something isn't right. Her face slumps onto me, as pale as if all her blood had been drained.

"Ava?" I call out.

It's clear that her body has reached its breaking point. She slips from my grasp, but I hang on to her. My other arm strains as Tyler prepares to remove the tape from it.

"Ava, can you hear me?" I shake her gently, hoping to awaken her. But there's only labored breaths coming out of her mouth. "Ty!" I stop my partner. "Take her to the hospital now!"

Feeling herself separated from me, Ava writhes. "Jack...I'm not leaving you!" Her eyes are full of determination, but her voice comes out as a series of huffs.

"Sweetheart, go with Tyler. I won't be far behind," I beg, and she relents.

With her last bit of strength, she kisses me before allowing Tyler to lift her.

Tyler flinches at his unfinished work—my left arm remains stuck to the chair. He says to me, "The LAPD and paramedics shouldn't be far away. I'll call Sam as soon as I get a signal outside."

"Go! I'll be fine!" I assure him, then raise my hand in salute to the man who has saved my life tonight.

He simply nods before he carries Ava outside.

I gingerly continue what Tyler has started, peeling the tape around my injured arm. But I don't get much further.

Mother of hell!

I exhale silently. Even with those two dead jerks around, I'm determined to keep my agony unheard.

Just then, someone arrives, and I can't believe my eyes.

"What the hell are you doing here, Sam?" I grind my teeth in irritation. "Where's the LAPD?"

"They're on their way, the paramedics too. Damn politics got in the way. Everybody wanted jurisdiction over Willem Botha. I came here as fast as I could," he explains.

I wriggle my bound arm, assessing the number of loops I still need to unravel.

"Hold up!" Sam stops me from handling the pesky tape. "You're making it worse. Let me deal with that. But first..." He winces at my stab wound.

"Just a scratch."

"Thought you were going to say that!" He opens his IFAK,

or individual first aid kit, then wraps a bandage around the open flesh.

The surprise keeps coming as Cora-Lee enters the room.

"Sam?" I frown.

My brother signals Cora-Lee to proceed with her task. Inspecting several computers in the room, she checks out what's loading on each one. Eventually, she decides to operate the smallest machine—the one that Willem had pointed out before his demise.

With my stab wound securely bandaged, Sam begins to free my arm. The adhesive clings to my black and purple skin like heavy-duty duct tape on a pipe. My brother's hands move with caution, but—

Fuck... fuck... fuck...

I can't remember experiencing pain that bad since I broke my collarbone at training in Camp Lejeune while I was still a rookie. But if I can still sense pain, that's got to be a good thing.

"Fuck, Jack!" Sam cringes as he carefully lifts my mangled arm, now dark and swollen.

"Just a bad case of cupping," I quip.

"Jesus Christ!" he exclaims. "Compared to that, your stab wound does look like a scratch!"

I ignore him as I wonder how he got here. "You were in the air when I called you, weren't you?"

He shrugs as he carefully spreads ointment all over my bruises. "Our accountant may question my extravagant expenditure on chartering two private jets in a single day. But hey, there's nothing I won't do for my brother."

"You shouldn't be here..." I sigh.

He smiles sideways. "Well, Jack, what can I say? I was as close to the heart of the beast as you were. I *had* to be here."

Cora-Lee remains silent and focused. I have no idea how

she managed to bypass the password, but she's renowned for her resourcefulness, as Sam would say. What's loading and flickering on the screen baffles me, but I'm certain she's well-informed about her search objectives. Suddenly, she shuts down the laptop, rises from her seat, and passes something to Sam just as the distant sound of sirens grows louder.

"Go!" says Sam to Cora-Lee, who quickly disappears.

Sam shows me a small drive. Despite advocating for me to leave my past behind, tonight, he's giving me a choice. "I'll give this to you when you're ready. You can do whatever you want with it."

I pat him on the shoulder. "Thank you for everything, brother." He has moved mountains and dug through the earth to find me, not just tonight but during the two decades of search following my disappearance. Most of my childhood is like a blank sheet of paper. Yet, somehow, the image of him is imprinted on it, albeit faint, like a watermark. Our bond has always been there. Otherwise, I wouldn't have believed him when he suddenly turned up in Kabul, claiming to be my brother.

"Don't get sentimental now!" Sam warns, hiding his glistening eyes.

While he secures the device that may reveal the answers to my life's enigma, my mind wanders to Ava. With Willem no longer posing a threat and both of us standing strong together, maybe, just maybe, I will pursue those answers. But it will be a decision made by both of us—me and my incredible other half.

35

AVA

The news of Willem's death sent shockwaves not only through the tech community but also throughout a significant portion of the corporate network in the country and internationally.

Following his demise, several arrests took place, revealing the extent of Willem's illicit activities. Many conspiracy theories arose, claiming that the man behind W-Bot was alive, but most investors knew their chances of getting retribution were non-existent.

The bearded man, as it turned out, was Willem's childhood friend. His true identity had remained a mystery until authorities discovered a connection to a deportation case. According to reports, when they were both seventeen, Willem rescued him during a climbing accident. This incident could have been the reason for the bearded man's loyalty, or maybe Willem had made promises to aid him with his deportation case. There is good in everyone, but unfortunately, Willem crossed the point of no return.

As with any headline, Willem eventually became old news after a few weeks.

Meanwhile, Jack and I have recovered from our injuries.

His stab wound and torn tendons have healed fully, although he's still undergoing physiotherapy to regain full strength in his left arm.

As for me, I have been equipped with a 3D-printed prosthetic. It's made from custom resin specifically designed to construct artificial bones. The bearded man sliced it just below the bottom knuckle, allowing the prosthetic to attach to my real finger, functioning as an extension. The bionic mechanism takes some getting used to. Sometimes, it reduces me to tears. But Jack never fails to uplift and motivate me. Now, I'm getting the hang of it.

It's the first day of winter, and we've decided to return to the safe house until we figure out our next move. I'm busy in the kitchen while Jack watches Quinton play. Elmo circles around me and eventually settles at my feet. Thanks to the expert team of vets, his broken leg only caused him a slight limp. These days, the pup hardly leaves my side, even if it means being away from Quinton. Maybe he senses that Jack is taking care of the baby, or maybe he's still affected by my abduction.

I crouch down to pat him. "It's okay, Elm. You can go play." But he doesn't move. "All right, you can stay there."

I place a tray of freshly baked vanilla cookies on the counter. Elmo's ears perk up, and his eyes beg for a taste.

"Here." I give him half of a cookie.

While Elmo enjoys his snack, I make coffee and test my grip in the process. I've been practicing for weeks, and I can't help but squeal in excitement when I finally get it right on my first try.

"You okay back there?" Jack asks from the living room.

I bring the mugs to him, with Elmo following closely behind. "Jack, look!" I show off my elegant grip.

Jack comes over, showering me with kisses. "Well done,

sweetheart." His dark blue eyes turn brilliant as if passing me a star. He doesn't have to say much. I know he's proud of me.

I pass him a mug. "Yours."

He takes it and smells my hair. "Vanilla, huh? Where are those delicious goodies?" He slips into the kitchen and returns with a plate full of cookies.

"Do you like them?" I ask as he munches away.

"They're absolutely delicious," he replies, sitting on the couch, alternating between devouring the cookies and sipping his coffee.

I smile, then play with Quinton for a while. I can't believe he's still crazy about his giraffe. "You'll have a full set of teeth soon, Quinnie-Bear." I gently fix his hair. "What will you do then?"

Quinton simply laughs.

"Hey, come sit here," Jack invites me to join him on the couch.

Elmo looks at us, appearing content that I'm in good company, and then he turns around and sits with Quinton.

"He's the most amazing dog," Jack remarks.

"He is. When I brought him home from the shelter, he was this little puppy with droopy eyes and ears that looked bigger than his face." I cackle. "People had given up on him, but not me. Just look at him now."

"That's the power of love. It can make any living being thrive," Jack says. "Hey, check this out." He wraps his arm around my shoulder, showing me a photo app on his phone. "I made this for you. A snapshot of what I remember about myself."

I move closer to him, leaning against his side. The first photos are from his childhood.

"This was us at our house in upstate New York," he says, swiping through the pictures.

"You really look like your mother," I comment.

"Everyone says that, and I never dispute it," he says. "Sam said she was a nurse at a military hospital. That was how she met my father."

"Your father was in the military, too?"

"Air Force," he replies, studying the photo. "It's a shame I never knew her. Or that my memory of her has never returned."

"I know it's painful. And it might be something you'll never resolve until the end of your days."

He brushes his fingers against my forehead, fixing a few curls on my fringe. "I've survived with that thought all these years, so I think I'll be okay."

I continue swiping through the album. "Oh, look at you and Sam." The image of them with their arms around each other warms my heart. Jack must have been only three or four years old.

He laughs. "Look how small I was compared to him back then. I bet he never thought I'd surpass him."

My man is tall, the whole six-foot-six of him!

The following photo in the queue takes me back. It's a blurry, black-and-white image of a boy squatting on a sidewalk in front of a butcher shop. He's thin, his eyes barely open. I hesitate, "Was this... you?"

"For years, he was known as 'the sidewalk boy.' Sam discovered it, and it led him to St. Leo. Here's another picture."

"Oh, my..." I sigh, perusing the photo of a nun hugging Jack. She had a tender smile, and Jack looked a lot brighter here. I recall Morgan mentioning her name. "Sister Laura?"

"Yes. I'm glad Sam had a chance to meet the woman who raised me," he replies with fondness in his eyes. "You know, she told Sam my birthmark looked like a rabbit."

I chuckle, remembering the brown spot on his shoulder that we all agreed looks like Elmo with his ears up.

Chuckling too, Jack adds, "After all the questions that my brother asked her, the bunny was the final proof that I'm Jack Kelleher."

"We should stick with rabbit, then?"

He shakes his head lightly, taking a glimpse at our dog, who seems content watching Quinton. "Elmo is better."

"Where were you when Sam met with Sister Laura?"

"I was in Kabul, frantically arranging outbound flights for my men. While everyone was fleeing that doomed place, Sam was running in. Just to find me."

Awe fills me. That wasn't ordinary courage, not the kind you casually throw around, like a risky business move or stepping out of your comfort zone. I have never witnessed a stronger bond between two men than the one between the Kelleher brothers, and I consider myself fortunate to be a part of their family.

The end of the album comprises photos from their reunion. The two forces of nature—Sam and Jack—pose with their dad, along with Sam's family: Cass, Grace, and their three-legged German Shepherd, Maximus.

"I presume Sam's son hadn't been born yet in this photo."

"No, only Grace," he replies, smiling. "Last one." He swipes.

"Holy smokes!" I exclaim. It's a picture of us in Bozeman, sitting on the front porch, laughing at each other. Morgan must have taken it while we were unaware. Even then, I could see our gazes were filled with affection.

"So that was my story in a nutshell, Ava Belle," Jack concludes.

I lean in, planting a soft kiss on his cheek. "I'll make sure we keep adding to it with ones like this." I point at our photo.

Jack nods, inhaling deeply, the sound of his breath filling the space between us as he steers the conversation to the topic we've been postponing. "About the information from Willem's computer. What do you think?" His words hang in the air.

The USB drive has been locked inside a drawer since Sam handed it to us, its presence a constant reminder of the secrets it holds.

"What if we destroyed it?" I pose a question instead of answering.

"I guess I'd always be wondering about it, I can't lie." His words betray his inner conflict. "But I trust in what we decide. I'm okay with letting it go."

"And if we opened it?"

He bites his lip, then says, "I'd meet that man face-to-face. You know, I had plans to kill him." He pauses, his hand rubbing the top of mine, an ambivalent gesture amid the darkness of our conversation. "Maybe it was to stop him from hurting other children. But the truth is, Ava, I wanted to do it for revenge. For myself."

This revelation, though unsettling, is not entirely unexpected.

"But," he adds. "I've grown since then. I've been blessed with so many things that I never saw coming." This time, his words resonate with a sense of gratitude and determination. "In my nightmares, I could only speculate what he looked like, how his voice sounded. He scared me to death, but perhaps by seeing him in the flesh, I can erase my fear of him. Because I hope, in reality, he's merely a monster without teeth."

I nod with an approving smile. "In that case, open it, Jack. I'm right here with you."

"What if I end up wanting more than that?"

"I'll stop you," I reassure him. "Love has the power to keep things alive, but it can also kill."

Jack's eyes flare in confusion.

I explain, "We'll use our love to kill your demons. Let's open the files, Jack."

He remains hesitant. "I can't drag you into this."

"No. I'm dragging myself into it."

He pulls me close, breathing out a relief moan.

We plug in the USB drive and start with the README file prepared by Cora-Lee—another gem of a person from the Red Mark family. It reveals that just before W-Bot went out of business, Willem had managed to copy parts of the US Department of Justice database. They included a master list of law enforcement personnel, which was consolidated to establish a national standard and centralized account-ability.

The copy that Cora-Lee downloaded is unformatted. Most of the content is without line breaks, with some missing spaces. But it's clear there is a convicted child kidnapper who lived in the Tampa Bay area.

"Goddamn. This is why..." Jack sighs.

The kidnapper made the list in the database because he was a police detective!

Jack was kidnapped more than two decades ago, but the case that brought the perpetrator to justice concluded only a year ago. He was clearly a prolific criminal with a long history.

"49 Amethyst Avenue..." he mutters cautiously while opening a folder. "Fuck!" He releases the mouse, drawing a deep breath as photos of the property appear on the screen.

"You recognize this place?"

"I don't remember the house, but this..." He points at the third photo, his finger trembling. It depicts a dark space, surrounded by crudely painted walls, with only one ventila-tion. "Ava... that's my nightmare," he says with a heavy sigh. "That's my nightmare."

I feel his cold, sweaty hand quivering in mine. "Jack, maybe we should take a break," I suggest.

He shakes his head, frowning. "How did Willem know this?" he murmurs. "What tied this detective to me that he knew?"

"Maybe we should see what's in the next folder."

Jack follows my suggestion and opens it. "Detective John Cooper. He started his career in New York City, then moved to Syracuse. He left the Syracuse PD to take up employment in Georgia," he reads aloud, paying attention to the dates. "Hmm... that was around the time I was abducted."

"Did he handle your case in Syracuse?" I ask.

"No, he didn't. Never heard of his name before. But that doesn't necessarily mean he couldn't have meddled with it."

I read on, summarizing the last few lines, "He eventually moved to Florida, worked with the Tampa Police, and left the force twenty-one years ago."

"The same year Sister Laura found me. And not long after, the Syracuse PD found my bloodied clothes," Jack explains. "So Cooper went back to Syracuse and staged it all, making sure everyone thought the case was local."

I mentally draw the chain of events in my head. "So Willem deduced all of this based on the timeline and locations that could have aligned with yours?"

He ponders, and his breath passes through his steepled hands. "It wouldn't have been hard for Willem to piece everything together. Red Mark has been involved in a few high-profile cases; it's public knowledge that Sam founded the company partly because of my abduction. He's determined to spare other families from experiencing the same ordeal. When Sam finally found me, a magazine featured our story—Syracuse, St. Leo, it was all there."

Willem must have meticulously compiled this data,

undoubtedly with the intention of manipulating Jack into giving up on me. However, considering the substantial nature of the information, I can't help but wonder if he felt some sympathy toward Jack for being an orphan. I will never know for sure, and ultimately, it doesn't matter. But something worries me, and I caution Jack, "There is still a chance that this detective may not be your kidnapper."

"You're right. But I'm ready to roll the dice on it," he states, his finger hovering over the mouse. Finally, he clicks open the folder labeled 'IMG.'

Mug shots begin to load on the screen, and he fidgets in his seat, leaning forward and reaching toward the spot between his shoulder blades. Suddenly, he stands up, gasping for air as if his lungs have failed him. He keeps mumbling a name, something like Scalp.

"Jack, baby," I say, rushing to his side and holding him. Sweat forms on his face. It hurts to see the strong man reduced to such a state of terror. But I know he needs this. He needs this pain to combat the greater pain within him. "So he's the one?" I murmur.

Jack closes his eyes, nodding as if he's being slowly sliced apart. "Scalpel. So, his real name is John Cooper. I hate to say it, but I'm a trembling mess when I think about him."

After a full minute of huffing and cursing, Jack moves back toward the laptop, indicating that he's all right now. He stares at the front-on photo of the man he's been hunting for years.

He scoffs. "He was a plain-clothes detective. I guess he was allowed to keep long hair, although I'm curious why. It was more than just his style. He was concealing something on his neck."

"I suppose being part of the police force helped him cover his tracks," I remark.

"His operation never had a fixed base, always moving around to avoid getting caught. And he was damn good at it."

"But I guess everybody has a weakness."

Jack's eyes narrow as if mocking Cooper. "He just couldn't resist. Maybe Amethyst Avenue held some significance to him. For whatever reason, he returned. That son of a bitch returned." His voice trembles with anger.

"You need a break?" I check in, hoping to give Jack a moment to collect himself.

"No. Let's finish this. There's got to be more to it." He sits back down, determined.

He clicks on another document that summarizes the income Cooper received from selling his kidnap victims to various underworld mobs, spanning from New York to Mexico. If Cooper kidnapped his victims to sell them, I can't imagine the chances that Jack escaped, thrived, and ended up with me.

Nothing on the page seems to catch Jack's interest, so he moves on to another document, which appears slightly different. Although it still lacks proper formatting, there are headings. It provides information about Cooper's arrest and trial.

Jack smiles victoriously.

This time, a nine-year-old boy had bested the crooked cop. The boy was from Cuba, abducted at a shopping mall in Orlando. The boy fled from Amethyst Avenue and positively identified his kidnapper in a lineup. That was the end of Cooper and his reign of terror.

"Take that, you despicable slime!" Jack exclaims.

Then both our eyes land on the same section of the document, stating that Cooper is currently serving time in Florida State Prison.

His face pleads with me, but he lacks the courage to say it.

"Tell me what you want, Jack."

He takes my hand in his. "Ava. Sweetheart. If I'm honest, I don't want to face him alone. But asking you to come with me to a prison and confront a criminal you should never meet would be too much."

His honesty validates that we have come to a point in our relationship where we can communicate without any reservations.

"Nothing is above me, Jack. I'll go with you to Florida."

A smile spreads across his lips. Nothing and no one can prevent me from supporting the man I love.

36

JACK

Dread and anticipation lace my heartbeats as I prepare to confront Scalpel—John Cooper, the man who ruined my childhood. Thankfully, I have Ava by my side, my rock and pillar of strength.

We arrived in Tampa last night. The flight from Helena gave me ample time to feel anxious, but I had someone else taking care of that for me—baby Quinton. Well, to be precise, it was Quinton and his entourage, Morgan and Tyler. The journey was easier than I anticipated.

We just finished our breakfast at the hotel.

"I owe you guys," I say to Morgan and Tyler.

"Hey, don't worry about it," Morgan says. "It's like a second honeymoon for us. Only with a baby."

Ava smiles at her best friend. "Consider it practice, Mrs. Hunt!"

Morgan looks at her husband for support, and Tyler seems to be on Ava's side. "Well, she's not wrong, baby," he tells his wife.

"Babe, I love kids," Morgan admits, her hand tickling Quinton's belly, sending the baby to giggle and bounce in his chair. "But it's nice to be able to hand them over to their mother when you've had enough."

"I won't pressure you, Wolf Girl, you know that," Tyler affirms, calling Morgan's nickname. The couple shares a kiss until Tyler reminds himself, "We have a lot on our plates. In fact, I'm actually on the clock here."

Red Mark, or rather, my brother Sam, insisted that Tyler come with us to be Quinton's official bodyguard while Ava and I visit the prison.

"Can we go now, Ava Belle?" I whisper.

Her eyebrows burrow. "Our visitation isn't until this afternoon."

"I want to show you something."

She agrees, and after settling Quinton with Morgan and Tyler, we head north. Her hands are on the steering wheel, but she never forgets to reach out to me every now and then. Sitting next to her, I admire her fearless nature, having gone a step further than just knocking gloves with her once formidable fiancé. I'm certain that Quinton will grow up to be just like her.

"Here," I say, pointing to the St. Leo monastery.

Ava slows down, taking in the view of the 1930s complex. "You grew up here? It's almost unbelievable."

"Sister Laura found me wandering around there." I point at the west corner of the abbey. "I was drunk and completely drugged. But I remember... I remember her holding my hand and leading me into a kitchen. My God, the warmth and the smell of fresh pumpkin soup. Yeah... as far as I know, my life started then."

Ava wraps a hand over mine. "Bless Sister Laura. I wish I'd met her."

I nod, thinking that it would have been wonderful. When Ava and I met in Bozeman, I was on bereavement leave from the

Marine Corps after Sister Laura's passing. It dawns on me, the sentimental tie that exists between the woman I saw as my mother and the woman I fell in love with when we first crossed paths.

I say, "I owe it to Sister Laura. For a while, I couldn't talk. I couldn't even walk properly. I was called 'Snowflake' then because I was so pale."

"So, where was that butcher shop? You know, that black and white photo of you."

"Oh, that sidewalk? It was about thirty miles from here."

"So you roamed around."

"I have no recollection of it, but I guess a picture paints a thousand words. Yet I came back here." I gaze at the corner where Sister Laura found me. "Amethyst Avenue is about a block away from here. Whatever I was thinking, escaping that place, only to circle back?"

"It saved you."

"I guess," I sigh. "Like I said, Scalpel never had a permanent base. He abducted me in Syracuse. And then we must've moved from place to place until we ended up here. But he had a pattern. He chose a place near a church to hide his victims. That was his signature. As if asking for forgiveness from God while committing his despicable act."

"Perhaps he was making fun of the Big Man, doing the sin right under his nose," Ava argues.

I scoff as I motion to her to drive on, getting closer to Amethyst Avenue without her realizing. By now, I should've been an emotional mess, surrounded by the air that belongs to my nightmare. But I'm not.

"Where to now?" Ava asks innocently.

I make a bold request. "Drive me there, please?"

"Jack... I don't think it's such a good idea."

"Please."

She reluctantly agrees. Following my instructions, we make our way to the sinister house—Scalpel's one-time fortress.

"I don't remember this building, yet I hate it." I take in the details of the house as I step out of the car. The paint on the walls is peeling, and the roof is weathered. "I learned from Sam that our mother died of a broken heart. It's all because of the man who used to haunt this place."

The door to the basement is broken, neglected by whoever resides there now. I pass it by. I never even contemplated going back into that repulsive prison cell. Instead, I explore the gardens, looking for the ventilation that keeps appearing in my nightmares.

I find myself on the eastern side of the house. Approximately five paces from the front, I squat, using my bare hands to dig the soil against a wall.

Damn.

There it is.

I don't have a detailed memory of this place, but the darkness and putridness stay with me. Along with the presence of Scalpel.

"Jack... Jack... baby!" Ava's voice sounds far away, but as she keeps calling, it gradually comes to me.

My hands freeze, being held by Ava. I don't realize they're trembling, my fingers bent, desperately scraping at the paint surrounding the ventilation.

"I'm sorry." I expel air rapidly. "This is me, Ava. This is what I meant by being broken beyond repair. I have nightmares about this place almost every time I close my eyes. I never meant to hurt you in my sleep."

"You never hurt me, Jack. And you're not broken." Her grip on my hands turns gentle, her eyes understanding. "We're working on it. I keep a safe distance when it happens, and it hasn't been as violent as that one morning."

"How am I meant to confront him?"

"With me," she determines, then engulfs me in her arms.

It's moments like these that remind you why fighting alone is the way of the doomed. Partners may come and go, affiliations form and break. Nothing in life is permanent, nothing is faultless. I'm aware a man can never be perfect. But I know I'm whole because this amazing woman is by my side.

Ava pulls herself away so she can appraise me. "Meeting Scalpel won't cure your nightmares, but those demons will know they're dealing with both of us now."

I take her left hand, breathing into her soft knuckles. She has left her prosthetic at the hotel to avoid any complications during entry into the prison. The authorities have strict visit regulations. Even bras with underwire can result in lengthy searches.

If Ava can get over her nightmare of losing her finger, I should be strong enough to handle Scalpel.

Ava stands in front of me, her stature below my shoulder. I can still see the house behind her, unobstructed. Despite this, her aura is larger than her physical presence as she speaks. "Your nightmares and heartbreak will always be a part of you, but perhaps they won't cripple you as much as they do now."

Pausing, Ava tilts her head in thought and then adds, "Actually, I take that back. You were never crippled. You've been fighting your nightmares for me and for yourself—and I believe you've risen above them."

"How do you know?"

"Because you're here. You could've walked away from me, dealing with your nightmares as you always knew how—in private. But you didn't. You've chosen to face them with me."

Those words fill me with a newfound sense of liberation. I

won't let John Cooper break me ever again. I'm not my night-mares. I'm fighting them. She said it. I swear on God's name, she's the only one I'll ever believe in.

Checking her watch, Ava glances at me and says, "It's time."

WE ENTER the Florida State Prison with Ava acting like my bodyguard. She leads the way as if making sure I never step onto unfamiliar territory. After going through several check-points and getting searched, we enter the visiting room, where an officer ushers us to a table.

I turn to Ava, appreciating her effort to be my guardian angel today. "I'm okay now," I tell her.

As we wait, inmates begin to emerge. Finally, the last man walks out and takes a seat at the table next to us.

"We've been stood up," I complain to Ava in a whisper. It seems the coward couldn't bring himself to face me.

Ava asks the guards for information, but their responses leave us empty-handed.

Just as we're about to lose hope, a silhouette emerges. The stocky figure moves with a noticeable limp. Nothing about him strikes a chord of recognition except for his long, dark hair. Its thin strands possess a slight wave, tangled in places.

Clad in his prison garb, John Cooper appears puffed up with edema. There are no distinctive features on his face—so ordinary that he could pass for anyone walking by on the street. As I had hoped, the monster is toothless.

Prepared as I am for this moment, being in the same room as the haunting monster rekindles my primal urge. My fingers tingle, itching to wrap around his neck and delight in the crunch as his throat snaps.

Ava's touch on my hand dissolves the thought, guiding me back to my safe place.

"John Cooper." I greet him in a dull manner, stripping away any sense of significance he might have.

The sixty-year-old man scoffs, rolling his eyes with disinterest. But he has no choice; he has to face me. I observe the creases on his face as he forces a smile, perhaps thinking this meeting was a joke. For so long, I could only imagine what he looked like based on slivers of clues from my nightmares. In my mind, he remained forever in his thirties. Now, seeing him as an ancient warlock, years of torture felt like a mere second.

Cooper leans forward. "What's your name again? It's completely escaped me. No offense, I just have too many to remember," he dribbles, moving his mouth as if gritting a toothpick.

I stay silent, keeping things to myself.

His attention shifts. "But this lovely lady? Now, that is a face to remember." He leers at Ava. "What's your name, honey?"

Ava stares at Cooper with venom in her eyes, showing her amputated finger as a warning. Damn, the man looked away. I bet he has never encountered someone like Ava West before.

"She's my girlfriend," I declare firmly, wrapping my arm around her waist, keeping her close.

Cooper twists his mouth as if he were spitting out the invisible toothpick. The scumbag knows I'm no longer his victim. He's alone, paying for his crimes, while I stand on the other side, a free man.

"Touching," he jeers. "But I still can't remember your name. Don't get me wrong, I'm sure you were one of my cargos back in the day. Otherwise, you wouldn't be here."

"My name isn't important. I just want to know what you did to me."

"How could I do that when I can't even remember your name?"

"Kidnapping is a game of faces, Mr. Cooper, and you do remember me. Because I was the one who got away. Just like the boy who sent you here."

The prisoner grunts.

"Come on, Cooper," I taunt him. "You're in here for life. I'm sure you won't mind sharing how you broke me once upon a time."

"I destroyed you! You're done for!" His face contorts with bitterness. "But that fucking Castro mini-me? Gotta hand it to that boy." He waves his index finger repeatedly, probably regretting the day he got caught. His eyes scan left and right as if considering a confession. Suddenly, he turns around, making me instinctively shield Ava. A guard approaches, but Cooper's actions aren't meant to harm us. Instead, he lifts his hair, revealing something hidden.

It all clicks into place in my memory. The tattoo on the back of his neck. That's why he always keeps his hair long. I recall seeing it once before when his hair was inadvertently brushed aside during the chaotic moments of him chasing me or me desperately trying to escape from him.

I mockingly ask, "So that boy recognized you because of your tattoo?" Taking my time, I burst into laughter. "Did he ever say it resembled the shape of a poop emoji?" I wait for Cooper to process my comment, but he remains indifferent. I challenge him, "So what did you do to me?"

"Like I said. There are too many to remember. But let me tell you, you all had one thing in common. Your wails, the smell of your fear and hopelessness—you were all the same!"

The way he describes it triggers something in my head, like damaged film clips flickering on a massive screen. "You tried to kill me, but your knife only inflicted a surface wound.

I was bleeding, but I still got away," I grit. "By then, I was already addicted to the drugs you constantly loaded me with. You staged my bloodied clothes, convincing everyone I was dead so the investigation would cease. But guess what? I got away right before your eyes."

He hangs his head in defeat, knowing that he won't be able to forget that.

I continue taunting him. Why not kick him while he's down? I say, "And here's the best part. I ran far, but you know, I came back. I was found by a nun only a block away from your sin house. You could've gotten me, but I guess God has a funny sense of humor. I slipped...right. Under. Your. Nose."

"Fuck you! You're nothing but trouble!" His voice bears no substance, as if uttered by a playground wimp.

Satisfaction sings in my heart like a choir. The man has just admitted that he remembers me. I lean in, lowering my voice. "Nobody will remember your name, only the man with a tattoo resembling a pile of shit."

Cooper scratches the back of his neck. Perhaps no one had ever told him that.

I rise to my feet and take Ava's hand. "Come on." I help her up, then we head toward the exit.

But something halts me—Cooper's distinct call, which my brain suddenly recognizes, the reason why I got the knife wound on my back.

I turn around as the prisoner is about to be escorted inside. I declare proudly, "Actually, my name is Jack Kelleher—*the troublesome one*." My voice echoes, momentarily pausing the mutters and chit-chat in the room. "And you'll remember that for the rest of your life."

With my head high, I walk away, firmly gripping Ava's hand. There are still five minutes left in the visitation, but that man doesn't deserve even an extra second from us. He may still haunt my nightmares, but as Ava said, we'll face it together. And with my mind filled with her love, thoughts of Quinton, and dreams of our future children, he will be nothing more than a speck of dust.

As soon as we reach our car, I kiss Ava.

"Thank you." There's nothing more I can say to her. The rest is in my eyes, on my lips, and in my shivers.

"You did it, Jack."

Tears choke my voice as a wave of numbness washes over me, transforming into comforting relief. Ava pulls me into her arms—an irreplaceable source of calm after relinquishing a lifetime of fear.

"*We* did it, Ava Belle," my voice breaks at the end of my sob. "You have no idea how much I needed you in there."

"I'm always here for you. But don't forget, I need you too—I always will. There's no safe place quite like you." She rubs my chest as if feeling its strength.

"Let's go home."

"Where's home for you, Jack?"

It's the easiest question I've had to answer. "Montana. My family is there."

"And your demons?"

I lift her chin. "They've met their match." Hell yeah! This woman is stronger than any demons I've faced, and I'm humbled that she still seeks my protection.

"Let's go home then." Ava grins, holding on to me.

"Actually, can we make a detour?"

She cocks her head. I bet she has no idea what surprises await her.

I whisper close to her ear, "Just you and me, and Quinton."

37

JACK

We bask in the sunshine while the tranquil shore fills our senses with peace. Thanks to my stint at the Marine Corps Base in the Kaneohe Bay community, I have discovered some hidden treasures known only to the locals. One of these gems is a little island that is only accessible by boat from a remote jetty. Today, it has become our own private paradise.

"It's beautiful here, Jack," Ava's voice merges with the afternoon breeze. The palm trees that dot the pristine shoreline sway in unison as if disturbed by the same breeze.

"Not a bad detour, is it?" I remark.

With Quinton cradled in my arms, we both marvel at the colors of the coral reefs beneath the crystal-clear water. Occasionally, I take him down to let his tiny feet glide through the calm ocean.

As the afternoon progresses, we find a seat on an old tree log, awaiting the sunset.

"Could you see yourself living here?" I ask.

She rubs her arm. "Maybe. If we do move here, I'll need to work on my tan."

"Uh-uh. Your tan is perfect." I kiss the spot she just

rubbed. Her skin is fair and smooth, dotted with soft freckles that make it flawless. My lips linger on her arm as my eyes trace the curves of her bikini-clad body. She looks hot and stunning!

"I think I still prefer Montana," she affirms.

"So, maybe a Montanan wedding and a Hawaiian honeymoon?" I hint.

"That's an idea!" she responds with a grin as Quinton squirms on my lap, reaching out for her.

"All right. You want Mommy." I give in and let the munchkin go.

Ava coos, taking him in her arms and showering him with kisses, delicately removing tiny leaves that have found their way into his hair. "So, what did your captain say?" she asks, sluggishly kicking the white sand with her feet.

I smirk. "He gave me the usual farewell speech. He said my legacy would live on through the next generation of Marines I had led. Well, actually, he said 'shredded to pieces.'"

"You were that tough, huh?"

"Those guys will surpass me," I reply confidently.

"I don't know about that, Jack."

"It's all part of the Corps' evolution. The captain was disappointed, understandably. Especially that he wouldn't see me in the next USMC marathon. Apparently, he's been training hard. And oh, he also blamed you," I confess.

She laughs. "It was his loss, I'm sure. But it was time for the Corps to let you go. Quinton and I need you more." She plants a tender kiss on Quinton's rosy cheek. "Isn't that right, Quinnie-Bear?"

I pull them both into my embrace, still in awe that these two incredible beings are a part of my life.

"Jack..." She trails off, contemplating. "I want you to meet my parents."

"Okay," I tentatively respond.

"They had sided with Willem, as you know. But it wasn't entirely their fault," she explains slowly. "Willem was just too manipulative for them to see through. I think it's time I made peace with them. After all, they're my mom and dad."

I flash a smile at her, my fingers playing with the tip of her chin. "I don't know how it works with in-laws, but I would love to meet your parents."

She steals a kiss, full of joy. "Although I prefer to introduce you as 'my Marine boyfriend' rather than 'my former Marine boyfriend.'"

I shake my head, giving her a teasing glare. "Well, Ava Belle, there's no such thing as a former Marine. Once a Marine, always a Marine."

In the fading light of the sun, I witness her figure standing before me. Her whispered voice says, "I feel honored."

"Well, I'd feel honored if you would call me your Marine fiancé." Without giving her a chance to react, I drop down on one knee, my palm cradling her left hand.

She's in disbelief while Quinton laughs, witnessing a pose he's never seen before.

"Ava West. They say love takes time. But there's a love that defies the ordinary. It's so powerful that it cannot wait. That's what we have. Because I've loved you since the first time I saw your eyes—ardent and kind—and your magnificent curls framing your face."

I gulp, composing myself while caressing her ring finger. It's more than just flesh and bone, with a part of it made of synthetic material. But there's nothing artificial about what it represents. It's her strength and tenderness in one.

Ava caresses my cheek, and her smile penetrates me.

Continuing, I say, "Back then, I offered you my jacket. But tonight..." As I hold out a ring, I declare, "I offer you everything I am. I will always be yours, Ava. Will you be mine and marry this man?"

Quinton squeals in excitement as if understanding this moment. Ava, overwhelmed with emotion, fails to hold back her tears. "I will, Jack. I will."

I slip the ring onto her finger. She wasn't born with that prosthetic, but it has become a part of her. It's perfect. She's perfect.

This is a defining moment in any man's life, one that I had only hoped for from a distance for a long time. Now, I'm living it, and I have an amazing woman to spend the rest of my life with.

Ava wipes away my tears, then quickly takes my hand to help me stand up. She slings her arms over my shoulders, then gradually, her hands make their way down my arms, passing the scar on my left bicep, caressing the forearm that was once covered in bruises. Her lips quiver as she finally rests her palms on my bare chest. We share a kiss, and this time, we both let our tears flow freely—there's no distinction between hers and mine. They all cascade down our cheeks.

We chuckle when we break our kiss. She looks at Quinton and says, "For once, it's the adults who are crying."

"Your mom and I are going to get married," I tell the little man.

"Mama!" he babbles. "Dada!"

I nod, filled with pride. It all started with him calling me 'Po po po,' then he briefly learned to say 'Jack,' which sounds like 'check' as he clicks his tongue. Recently, Ava has been teaching him to call me 'dada,' the best one he's mastered. We have planned for his adoption, and obviously, Ava thought the preparation for her baby to embrace me as his father couldn't come soon enough. One thing remains. Regardless of what

Quinton calls me, he always laughs every time he sees me in my Ray-Bans.

Ava admires the ring on her finger, its ruby glowing brilliantly in the sun. "It's stunning. When did you get it?"

"It's my mother's." My voice breaks a little, remembering the woman I long to recall. But I smile, full of joy.

"It means a lot, Jack."

"Only you can wear it. And I can't wait to see you in a wedding dress."

We take a leisurely stroll before darkness falls. The gentle lapping of warm water against our feet brings back memories of evenings I spent alone at K-Bay. I throw my gaze at the horizon. The sun is at its most beautiful when it sets, but its beauty pales in comparison to Ava's radiance.

My phone rings. However, it's an interruption that doesn't bother us. It's my brother, Sam. I put him on speaker.

"How did it go?" he asks.

"Well, the captain accepted my resignation," I reply.

"Of course he did, but I wasn't asking about your early retirement. I meant your proposal."

"Of course she said yes!" I deadpan, which Ava laughs at.

"Congratulations, you two. I can't wait for the invitation," Sam says, then takes his time to clear his throat.

Ava cocks her head, mouthing, 'Is he crying?'

I smirk. "Sam, Ava is asking if you're crying."

She pinches my arm, eyeballing me.

I laugh while my brother seems unable to respond.

After a moment, Sam restarts, "Now you know, I can get sentimental sometimes. I...um... I'm happy for you both."

"Thanks, Sam," Ava says.

I try hard not to get tangled in his emotions, thinking about what he has done for me. After years of solitude, I finally have a family again in Sam and my father, all thanks to that man. And now, because of him, I have a chance to have a family of my own.

Once more, Sam clears his throat. "Well, actually, Jack. Since you're now officially unemployed, have you thought about my offer?"

Despite his provocation, I play it cool. "Maybe."

"Comet says hi, by the way."

That young man is something. I'll be thrilled to work alongside him, learning from each other—whether it's about rescue strategies or life.

"Let me talk to Ava about it," I reply nonchalantly. I won't hesitate to join Red Mark. I just want to make my brother wait.

"Should you decide to join, which I'm sure you will, you'll have to get used to dressing up. Can you handle it?"

"Oh, I know how to dress up. I'm a Marine."

"Excellent," Sam says. "I'll leave you to it. Semper fi, Jack."

As soon as I hang up, Ava greets me with a smile. "So, you're going to start wearing suits?" She runs a hand over the neckline of my T-shirt.

"It's an unwritten rule of Red Mark I've got to follow. But I've known how to dress up since my first ball," I explain.

"Aha. Speaking of which, are you allowed to wear your dress blues at our wedding?"

"What did I say, Ava Belle?"

"Once a Marine, always a Marine," she replies with confidence.

She hooks an arm over mine, and I take the opportunity to caress Quinton. I hint, "So, didn't you say you wanted a sibling for him?"

She hums with a seductive tone. "Siblings," she emphasizes the 's.'

I murmur in her ear, nibbling her lobe. "What do you say?

We go back to our room, put Quinton to sleep, and we can start?"

She grunts, a signature sound that indicates she can't wait to tear our clothes off and ravage each other. Without wasting another moment, she ransacks my lips, gluing her breasts against my pecs. Her soft belly grinds against my abs erotically as if the bed were just inches away. "How about we do it there?" She gestures at a nearby shed.

"Ava..." I understand if she wants that thrill of getting caught, but not tonight.

She giggles, telling me she'll let me get away with it this time.

We leave the beach in a hurry, hoping Quinton is tired enough that he'll fall asleep easily. The fading rays of the sunset play with her hair as I imagine life in beautiful chaos, overrun by children and pets.

"I love you, Ava West," I murmur.

"Jack Kelleher, I've loved you since the first night I met you."

My fingertip glides along her lower lip. She has captured the very words I should have expressed first. I have loved her since that moment, too, but at the time, I believed in the power of my demons instead of in her, drowning my true feelings. But our reunion has proven how solid we are.

Faith is the life force of love, and Ava is the love that fills every fiber of my being. My body will tirelessly protect her, and my heart will stay faithful to her until its last beat.

THANK you for reading *Her Faithful Protector*.

The adventure continues in **Her Redeemed Protector**. Dive

into Huxley 'Comet' Cometti's tumultuous quest for peace and his pursuit of a hard-won happy ending.

If you haven't yet, explore the gripping story of Jack's abduction and his emotional reunion with his brother in *Her Unbreakable Protector*, as narrated by Sam. This tale will keep you on the edge of your seat.

For Tyler and Morgan's story, be sure to pick up *Her Steadfast Protector*. Find out how they navigate danger together, proving that true protection comes from the heart.

More thrilling escapades and heartfelt stories await in each book of the series!

ALSO BY ALESSA KELLY

Her Remarkable Protector (Chase's story)

Coming soon

Download the FREE prequel to the series, STAYING FOR YOU.

Burning for You: From Enemies to Fearless Lovers

He's a simple farm boy at heart. She's a big-city girl. Thrown together by revenge, will their explosive chemistry endure a hostile takeover?

Fighting for You: From Strangers to Fearless Lovers

She's ready for a soulmate. He's sealed away his heart. When attempted murder brings them together, can they survive long enough to find love?

Longing for You: From Secret to Fearless Lovers

He's a notorious mercenary boss, she's a no-nonsense oil tycoon. When legal entanglements take them on a collision course, will they rise to beat unsurmountable odds?

Hold Me Forever

She's a traumatized survivor. He's a closed-off veteran. Can two lost souls find safe harbor together?

Cherish Me Forever

Two wounded hearts. When unexpected love comes within their grasp, can they learn to trust before it's ripped away?

Protecting Her

He's a disgraced ex-cop. She's on a mad quest for justice. When they're trapped in a deadly game, can they escape into each other's arms?

Join my newsletter for release updates, free books, and more ➜ alessakelly.com.

Her Faithful Protector: A Rescue & Protect Romance Suspense Novel (Red Mark Rescue & Protect Book 4)

www.alessakelly.com

© 2024 Alessa Kelly

ISBN

ePub: 978-1-922363-33-6

Paperback: 978-1-922363-34-3

THE MEANING BEHIND THE RED MARK LOGO

Red Mark is named after its two founders, Samuel Redley Kelleher (nicknamed Red) and Mark Connor. The fox is their mascot; it's a resilient and resourceful animal with sharp tracking instinct, and one of the most protective in the canine family.

For my family

VISIT ALESSAKELLY.COM

Alessa Kelly

GRITTY HEROINES, PROTECTIVE HEROES